BY THE SORCERER'S HAND...

Windbourne appeared in the doorway to the tunnel.

Rondasu had Eleva down, her back pressed to the overturned chair, his blade almost at her neck. Windbourne jumped onto the dais, reached down, and seized Rondasu's neck.

There weren't any flashes, any noises. But Eleva gave a gasp...and Rondasu let the knife slip from his fingers, looked down at his hand, uttered a shrill scream, and slumped forward.

Within a few heartbeats, his hair had gone white and he had shriveled like a raisin.

Berkley Books by Phyllis Ann Karr

FROSTFLOWER AND THORN
FROSTFLOWER AND WINDBOURNE

PHYLLIS ANN KARR

FROST FLOWER AND WINDBOURNE

BERKLEY BOOKS, NEW YORK

FROSTFLOWER AND WINDBOURNE

A Berkley Book / published by arrangement with
the author

PRINTING HISTORY
Berkley edition / October 1982

ISBN: 0-425-05591-4

Chapter 1

"Hellbog," Thorn said, "all we know is that a priest died tonight screaming about green wasps flying down at him. We don't even know we have the right sorceron. You haven't had time to search the whole stinking town."

"Why search?" said Third Master Clearthinking. His speeches rarely matched his name. "We won't find many of them outside their dens in the middle of winter. Not this deep in the midlands."

"All right," said Thorn, "let's say you were the only sorceron in the area. Would you sit down in a town the size of Five Roads Crossing, with a barracks of ninety warriors, while you sent out a spell to kill a priest?"

Clearthinking flattened his palm on the table. "It is impossible to think as the sorceri think! No decent creature should attempt it."

"At least credit them with a little survival instinct," said Thorn.

Master Youngwise, who had grown out of the first part of his name forty years ago, smiled tolerantly. "All this is interesting, but irrelevant. Obviously, we cannot learn the truth until after we've power-stripped him."

"What difference does it make?" asked Strongneck, who had

not earned her post of Second Wallkeeper by virtue of intelligence. "Better off to kill 'em all, stinking sorceri."

"Is that all His Reverence's death means to you?" said Thorn. "A bloody excuse to kill a sorceron, whether you've got the right one or not?" Thorn glanced at First Wallkeeper Eaglesight, her one potential ally. But Eaglesight's sense of justice had been worn down over the years to fit everyday expedience, and she only mirrored Youngwise's smile and shook her head slightly at her Third Keeper. (Warriors' God! thought Thorn, don't let living ever do that to *me!*) Aloud, she said, "Strip a sorcerer and you ruin him for life—not to mention the poor bitch of a warrior who does the work. If this one's innocent, you'll have wasted two people for nothing."

"No such creature as an innocent sorceron," said Strongneck. "You call 'em people?"

Eaglesight slapped her palm against the table. "Skin you, Thorn! You're nothing but a stopgap wallkeeper, and we gave you the post because you were lucky enough to clean that bloody nest of outlaws out of the Westmarsh Wastes last summer, not because we wanted your opinions on sorceri."

"Eat stones, Eaglesight," said Thorn. "I'm only trying to save you one of your women."

Youngwise smiled again, squinted at Thorn through the age puckers around his eyes, and rose to his feet. "We waste time. Even now the sorcerer may be gathering his power for a spell against us. The problem is not whether he should be stripped, but whom we will choose for the task."

"Yes!" said Smoothermore. "A sorcerer who can throw his spells from Five Roads Crossing to the hearth of Deveron's own farm—Gods!" he added, making the circle gesture for protection. "He'll shrivel the woman who touches him like a dry leaf in the fire!"

Thorn snorted. "The women who brought him in are still safe, aren't they? If he's so damned powerful, why hasn't he blasted us already?"

"Likely he spellcast His Reverence four days ago when Their Reverences came to town to give the Midwinter Ceremonies," suggested Clearthinking, "and the spell only burst open tonight, after smouldering inside His Reverence all this time."

Smoothermore made the circle gesture again. Strongneck muttered, "Kill 'em all!" Eaglesight rubbed her cheek and began, "That newest one of ours—Bumprick—she calls herself a good milker."

"Keep Bumprick," said Youngwise, looking at Thorn with an expression as near a grin as he could stretch from his withered lips. "Who better for the work of power-stripping this deadly sorcerer than the woman who singlehandedly defeated Dentblade and her entire outlaw pack?"

"Yes!" said Smoothermore. "The very woman—oh, Thorn can drain him if anyone can."

Demons gut you, Smoothermore, you should know, thought Thorn. Gods, once was enough with *you!*

If Thorn had not tried, like a bogbitten idiot, to help the sorcerer, it would have been natural for her to protest. But she had trapped herself with her own mouth. Inwardly cursing them all, herself included—it gave her thoughts something besides fear to work on—she rose, turned her back on the Council, and strode to the door. Flinging it open with a crash that sounded of splinters, she crossed the drafty hall to the prisoner's room, guarded by a copper-cased oakwood bolt and two nervous spearwomen, Clampen and Sharp, wearing copper headbands, heartdisks, belts, and wristguards. One of them even had a copper disk sewn near the hem of her tunic.

My last act as Third Wallkeeper of this stinking town, thought Thorn, noisily thrusting back the bolt. After a glance around to be sure the other wallkeepers and townmasters were watching her through the open Council Chamber door, she went into the prisoner's room. Slamming the door shut behind her, she slid the inner bolt into place.

"Wallkeeper!" exclaimed Clampen, "if you bolt yourself in—"

"Dice with Smardon!" Thorn shouted back. "If I can't even slide a bloody bolt when I'm through, you can let us both rot in here!"

She leaned against the door a moment, forcing herself to breathe softly, listening for any noises that might tell her how closely those outside were pressing their ears to the wood and how much sound might carry through. Then she turned and had her first look at the sorcerer.

He lay on the bed naked and spread-eagled, his arms and legs held down by copper clamps, his face turned toward her. He was aroused, and shivering desperately. Maybe it was the cold—the fire had burned to white embers, the winterboard and fur drape over the window did not keep out all the draft, and the two candles and one oil lamp added little heat to the room.

Thorn crossed to the fireplace and built up a new fire, putting on the worst-seasoned logs in hopes they would keep up a loud, long snapping.

The sorcerer looked a few years younger than Frost. Thorn would be surprised if he had passed twenty-five. Both his eyes were blue, but it was not hard to imagine that Frostflower had stared up at her captors with just that same scared look last summer. The thick copper clamps around his wrists and ankles were crusted with verdigris.

Thorn walked to the bed's head, careful not to brush against the sorcerer. He turned his face to keep watching her. She thought of the first time she had ever seen Frostflower, sitting huddled at a table beneath the inn stairs to drink her milk in very little sips. Maybe this fellow had been sitting still like that, eating a meatless supper late at night, when the townwarriors clumped in to corner him at spearpoint.

His face was thin, but it would have been strong if his eyebrows had been darker and his expression less frightened. His eyebrow ridges jutted very slightly, his nose was straight and smoothly tipped, and he was smart to stay clean shaven since his chin was cleft and just about the right size, neither large enough nor small enough to need hiding under a beard. His hair was buttermilk blond, clean and fluffy except near his face where perspiration had matted it. What a waste! the swordswoman thought wryly—this bastard of a sorcerer's better looking than I am.

Chances were he intended to follow the usual practice of his kind—use the last of his power to blast his rapist into premature old age. Thorn had seen that happen. Twice. It helped keep people cautious about molesting other sorceri, and the raped ones thought they were about to lose their power anyway, as soon as they got their first milking or pricking. Was he planning to wait until he actually felt her slide down around him, or might he start withering her at once, even before she took off her trousers, if she accidentally brushed her lips against his ear?

Crouching, she leaned as close as she dared and muttered, "Keep your voice down. Quiet. I'm not going to milk you."

He turned his head towards her so quickly that his cheek scratched her nose. She jumped back, terrified, and fell with a thump. She sat on the floor a moment, trying, even while she cursed herself for a clumsy, skittish cow, to feel her face for premature wrinkles. Then she saw the sorcerer was still watching her with that identical look of fear and nothing else.

She grinned, imagining how the listeners outside interpreted that noise she had made falling. Quiet, she had told the sorcerer? Well, thank the gods the one concession made to a sorcerer for his maleness was to give him his milking in private. Sorceresses were usually power-stripped with as many looking on as cared to.

Rolling back up to her haunches, she leaned toward him again, not quite so close this time. "I said I'm not going to touch you," she whispered.

A pucker appeared between his eyebrows, but otherwise his expression did not change.

"Don't you believe me? . . . Whisper, mutter—just so you keep your voice down—but answer me!"

He shook his head slightly and moved his lips. At that momen.. the fire popped loudly.

"What?" said Thorn.

He whispered, "Closer!"

"You want me to bend down closer?"

He nodded.

"My ear to your mouth?"

Another nod.

"Unh." She thought it over. His head was not clamped down. She could picture a sudden movement, his teeth in her ear, the contact giving him his chance to shrivel her into a crone. She shook her head. "You can whisper loud enough to let me hear you where I am."

He turned his head away from her and stared up toward the ceiling. A tear slanted down his temple.

"What the Hellbog is it?" Thorn's whisper almost broke into

a full voice. "Mumble up, will you? Don't you *want* a friend? Would you rather have some big cow falling down on you right away?"

"Yes!" He spoke aloud. "You filthy trickster!"

"Shut up!" she exclaimed. "Azkor's talons, sorcerer, I'll get you high enough for one good, wet ride anyway!"

He shuddered. She thought for a moment he was going to break a few hand bones, pulling at his clamps. She stood back and let him pull, watching the bed quiver beneath him. His face was tear-stained and his nose clogging now. He breathed heavily through his mouth, choking on sobs. His prick was pointing straight up, and he probably hated it.

"All right!" Thorn leaned forward and spoke in a low, harsh mutter. "Gut you, there are people listening outside that door. You *made* me say it!"

"Trickster!" he repeated. But at least he used a whisper this time.

"What?"

"You won't—I won't—you won't catch me—with your soft words—then down and off again before—farmers' bitch, I'll shrivel you! Oh, no, you won't trick me and escape!"

"Warriors' God!" Thorn stood back and rubbed her chin, staring at him. Well, they were still talking in whispers. That was something. Even as his words gained strength and coherence, he had kept his voice down. She stooped to make one more attempt. "Listen, you idiot, I'm trapped here with you. Now do you want to trust me and relax, or do you want—?"

"Trust! You will not trust me!"

So that was what he had wanted, trying to get her to put her ear within reach of his mouth. To test whether she would trust him, and, if she did, that meant he could trust her. Or was he playing the kind of game he accused her of?

She found his black robe lying on the floor, picked it up, and spread it over him. Gods, what a simple thing to forget to do for the poor bastard! No wonder he did not see any reason to trust her, lying there cold and naked all this time. "Warmer?" she asked.

"You have some hatred for your comrades?" he whispered. "You hope to make them think I am stripped, so that I will blast them instead of you as they torture me? Is that it?"

Grinning, the warrior got a stool and sat down near his head. "Not a bad idea, at that. But I'd prefer to save both our guts. Can you think of any way to do it?"

He closed his eyes. "God, you people are subtle!"

Apparently she would have to do everything else and the brain-work, too. Aware she did not have much time left before they got dangerously restless outside, she put another ill-seasoned log on the fire and tried to weigh all possibilities. It would have helped if there had been any possibilities.

"Afraid of him, Third Keeper?" came Strongneck's voice from the other side of the door. "Want me to come in and drop you down on top of him?"

Thorn walked to the middle of the room before answering. "Want to get blasted with me, Second Keeper?"

Someone else said something. Thorn could not hear many of the words, but it seemed to be about her having bolted the door from inside. The door clicked and thumped once or twice against the bolt. "Damn you, Thorn," called Strongneck, "nobody bolts herself in!"

"Relieved, Second Keeper? Now let me alone if you want the job done! Azkor's claws, he's limp as a raw egg yolk! You think it's easy to get him up? Well, you don't make it any easier with your bloody banging, you stupid cow!"

"He was up when we left him," protested one of the guards. After clamping him down with gloved hands, they would have tickled and thumped him with leather swafflers on the ends of long copper-plated sticks.

"Well, he's down now! So go eat stones and let me work in peace!"

"Get the dice, Clampen!" This time it was Eaglesight talking. "You have as long as it takes us to play one game of Falling Doubles, Thorn."

Thorn picked up one of the swaffling-sticks, which had been left in the corner, and hit it twice against the door so that it made its distinctive, doughy sound.

Then she returned to the bed, laid the stick gently on the floor, straightened and showed the sorcerer her empty hands. He stared at them, shuddered, and looked away.

She tried to joggle his brain. "Any ideas?"

"No. There is no way." He closed his eyes once more. "What will they do to you if you do not . . . enfold me?"

"Probably peel me, at the least, if they find out. Cold weather to go around without your skin, eh? Unless I climbed out the window and . . ." She stopped and pondered that last idea, not too enthusiastically.

"If you mean well," he murmured, "trust me . . . touch me. My hand. Only for a moment."

Well, that was the only way out she could see for both of them—through the window. So she would have to touch him sooner or later.

"Remember," she whispered, "blast me and you lose your powers. Trust me and we may both have some chance." She set to work on the clamp that held his right wrist. Even now, as she wiggled the pin out of the hasps and lifted away the wristlet, she avoided contact with his skin.

He lifted his arm up, elbow resting on the bed, fingers fluttering eagerly for a moment before he spread them out and waited, gazing up at her. When the fire was not cracking or hissing too noisily, she thought she could hear the roll of dice in the hallway outside. Crouching, she wiped her right palm and held it up to the sorcerer's.

They meshed fingers and held for a few moments, Thorn relaxing as her heartbeat steadied. If he had been aging her, her heartbeat would have raced into a pumping whir while she touched him.

Then he sighed and ruined the moment by murmuring, "Farmers' woman, go ahead. I will not wither you."

"Gods and demons!" Breaking the handclasp, she set to work on his other wrist clamp. "You think we've got time to screw? Just get your stinking robe on and around your stinking body." Freeing his left arm, she moved to the foot of the bed and began unpinning the clamps around his ankles. He sat and gathered up his robe clumsily to pull it on as best he could. She got another glimpse of his groin, cursed her foolishness, said "Finish this yourself," and went to the window.

The hardest thing about taking down the fur drape and winterboard was doing it quietly. But the lattice was heavy pine, interstices too small for her hand to have reached through and almost as deep as the length of her little finger, the screen set at least a hoehead-length into the windowframe all around.

"Sorcerer! You can rot through wood, can't you?"

He joined her at the window, tying his robe together in front, his fingers shaking. He looked through the screen at the wet, thickly falling snow and nodded.

"How long will it take you to rot out this bloody lattice?"

He slid his hands along it, feeling inside the interstices. "Soft pine . . . wetted before the freeze—mild freeze, almost at thaw point . . . Not long. Not as wood goes. I'm good with vegetable matter, even dried."

"Can you work with a little noise in the room?"

"I . . . think so."

"Get started."

He nodded, put one hand on each end of the screen, and closed his eyes. She turned back into the room, rolled up her sleeve, got the swaffling-stick and began to slap it noisily against her arm, meanwhile whistling between her teeth, and bouncing on the bed until the straw mattress rustled and the withies squeaked.

"Game!" cried one of the dicing warriors. She sounded more nervous than joyful at her win.

"Game, Thorn!" repeated Eaglesight. "Will you—?"

"Smardon gut you!" Thorn shouted. "I almost had him up!"

"All right, two more games," said Eaglesight.

Thorn glanced around to see whether the noise had disturbed the sorcerer. He seemed to be deep in his concentration, or trance, or whatever it was. His fingers, though pale on the cold wood, were not trembling. Thorn returned to making diversionary noises, meanwhile looking around the room to see if there was anything useful they could take with them. She saw nothing except the windowfur, a good piece of drapery about two strides long, made of white rabbit skins sewn into a square. And the lamp, or the candles from the gods' niches? She looked up at the statues and saw that one was the Great Giver of Justice and the other was the First Townmaster's favorite, the many-mouthed God of Words. If they had been others, she might have robbed their niches and promised them four candles and a few drops of blood in repayment at her first safe opportunity. But she did not quite dare risk angering the Giver of Justice or even Master Youngwise's favorite. (Chances

were that your favorite god or goddess took you for a favorite
human, and Youngwise was shrewd enough without extra help
from his god.) As for the lamp, it was too likely to slosh its oil.

"Warrior!" whispered the sorcerer. "Shall I rot it entirely,
or . . . ?"

She went to examine the lattice. "Fine. Should be enough."
A good shove or two and the lattice ought to pop out. The snow
had been almost knee-deep when Thorn plowed through it from
the warriors' barracks to the Townmasters' Hall a while ago, and
that was where the older drifts had been cleared away. "Go bounce
on the bed a moment," she went on, thrusting the swafflestick into
his hands. "Moan, squeal, slap yourself, make some kind of noise
that sounds good."

He obeyed, choosing to groan. She put both hands on the lattice
and shoved. The lattice made a muffled plopping as it hit a snow-
bank below the window.

Thorn took the lamp and leaned out. The old snow drift, with
its deep layer of new fall, looked almost chest deep, and Back
Mastershouse Street was deserted all the way from the lantern at
the corner of Featherweavers' Street to the one that marked the
pissing-alley near the curve around the back edge of the barracks.
The three lanterns between were unlit; Master Youngwise believed
in saving oil on nights like this, claiming that cold and bad weather
discouraged robbery in the streets. Thorn suspected bad lighting
did almost as much as bad weather to keep honest folk inside, but
tonight she blessed the old townmaster for his thrift.

Gathering up the windowfur in her left arm, she waved her
right for the sorcerer to come. He came.

She pulled him up on the window-ledge with her, the rotted
edges of pine splintering beneath their knees. Once there, he
jumped first. She landed half a heartbeat after him.

"Here," she said, shaking out the windowfur as they waded
from the drift.

He shrank back. His sorcerous distaste for anything that came
from dead animals. "Listen, you horsenut," she whispered, "all
you've got on is that damn black robe that shows up like a belly-
mole in this snow—if you don't sneeze us into the nightwarriors'
spears first. Now we're going to go under this fur together,
or—"

"I can keep up a wind," he said, "to fill in our tracks."

"Fine. You'll do it from under this fur with me."

He shuddered as she threw it around him, but, finding he could still keep up the wind to wipe out their tracks, he seemed to become a little more reconciled to the touch of fur, maybe even to enjoy its warmth, and Thorn's, as they plowed side by side through the snow. He has it a lot cozier than I do, she thought; he's better off than he was a log-burning ago—now he's even got some hope of living through all this. And I'm a bloody outlaw again! Twenty-four years an honest woman, and then outlawed twice in the same year, for a stinking sorceron both times!

Chapter 2

From this distance, the wall of Elvannon's Farm looked barely taller than an infant's hand. The open gates showed a post of brightness... but was the light within those ancient stone walls any clearer than that outside?

Here, at the start of the wheelpath, Frostflower shivered. Perhaps it was only from the mountain winds of earliest spring. Breathing deeply, she snatched the wind with her mind and directed it around her body, putting herself in the quiet center of a large, very gentle swirl of air.

Although a farmer-priest, Elvannon was a gentle man. So Frostflower had known for most of her twenty-eight years. Twice or thrice a year sorceri would come down from Windslope to trade with Elvannon's people; Frostflower had first come here with her parents when she was seven years old.

But always the trading was done in the field of wild grass between the edge of the wheelpath and the farmwalls.

Refolding the blanket across her arm, carrying it before her like a kind of safe-passage token, Frostflower approached Elvannon's gates.

They were open—she assumed because it was day and because no other priest was likely to raid Elvannon's Farm, which was too poor and too far removed from the nearest neighbors. But when the watchgirl called in an interested voice, "One from the north," a pair of spearwomen came out and stood in the opening.

"Sorceron!" said one, raising her spear. But her companion stopped her.

"We don't..." (some words that did not reach Frostflower) "...at everything in a black robe, not up here." Lounging on her weapon, the second warrior raised her voice and called to Frost-flower, who had halted in the field, "Don't worry about Quick-shaft, sorceron. She's new here—came up late last fall to get over a chest wound, and still skitterish as a damn sweat-bee."

The sorceress walked toward them, keeping her head prudently lowered. Life must seem slow to Quickshaft this high in the edge-lands, especially when Elvannon, who was known to support more warriors than he needed, put them to such token work as guarding his gates.

"Little early for trading, sorceron," said the friendlier spear-woman, whom Frostflower recognized as Coarsecut, Elvannon's chief warrior for more than thirty years. "Haven't had any midlands merchants up here ourselves yet, not since meat-drying last fall."

Frostflower had resolved to use a traditional greeting of farmers' folk, but, despite long practice, she faltered a little. "All...gods guide your priest, and prosper his people."

"Blasphemy!" cried Quickshaft, raising her spear again. Frost-flower shrank back.

"Go stick your tongue in your navel, younghead," said Coarse-cut.

The watchgirl giggled in her tower. Quickshaft thumped the end of her spear on the ground, and Coarsecut grinned.

"Raidleader Coarsecut!" Frostflower lifted her head for the first time to look straight at the old guard.

At sight of her eyes, one blue and one brown, the midlands warrior thrust out her left hand in a gesture to ward off evil, and a low whistle came down from the watchtower. Even Coarsecut looked startled for a moment before she grinned.

"Well, well, little Frostflower," said Coarsecut. "We haven't seen you for—must be five or six years. So you were traveling around the midlands, hey?"

"Last summer only. Before that I was secluded in preparation."

"Secluded in your mountains? In preparation to travel? You'd do better to spend a few years in Elderbarren or All Roads South before heading into the rough country," Coarsecut remarked.

"Seclusion has been our custom for generations, and our ancestors must have had good reasons." Frostflower smiled. "But I think, Raidleader, your plan has much to recommend it."

"Relax, Quickshaft, they haven't grown any wasps in our bellies yet," Coarsecut told the fidgeting midlands woman. "Well, Frostflower, why did you come down this morning?"

Frostflower drew a deep breath. "I ask to speak with His Reverence." She held out the blanket. "I have brought him a gift."

"Poison!" cried Quickshaft. "You see, Farmkeeper? She wants to poison—"

"Demons' farts!" Coarsecut reached out and felt the blanket appreciatively. "Fine work, sorceress. Never could figure out how you people can spin wool as smooth as velvet. Why don't you bring it back later in the summer when we can afford . . . a *gift*, you said?"

"Yes. For His Reverence. I—I would speak with him, as a . . . a friend."

"She'll poison him!" Quickshaft repeated. "Take the bloody thing and burn it!"

"Did Smardon squeeze your brain, or could he even find it? We don't burn woolwork like this."

"You're not going to let her speak with His Reverence?" Quickshaft demanded.

"That's for His Reverence to decide," said Coarsecut.

For a few heartbeats there was silence, as the younger spearwoman gaped and the older one seemed to enjoy her astonishment. Then Quickshaft said, "At least get the sprunging-stick and strip her first—"

"Azkor's talons!" This time Coarsecut sounded more angry than amused. "We don't have any sprunging-sticks here, you midlands bitch! We got one once from some clod of a merchant who didn't have anything better to trade, and we melted it down for the metal. Besides, if that trinket-seller's ballad was—"

"That trinket-seller's ballad was lying nonsense!" said Quick-shaft. "A sensible priest would have skinned his throat for singing it."

"Please," said Frostflower. "I will wait here outside, and I will speak with His Reverence through a copper screen if—"

"No, you won't," said Coarsecut. "You're not waiting here to inhale any more of this bloody lackbrain's stinking breath. Come on, little Frostflower!"

"You're taking her inside?" Quickshaft seemed genuinely dismayed. She stepped between the gateposts and stood with her legs planted wide and spear held sideways, blocking the way as if she intended to protect the dull edgelands farmer from the stupidity of his bumbling raidleader even though she thought none of them were worth a nest of wasps in her belly or her heart sucked out of her chest and set spinning in midair before her face.

Frostflower realized that the midlands warrior was admirable in her way—brave and unselfish. All this courage and selflessness called into action against a timid woman who had much more cause to fear the warrior's weapon than the warrior had to fear her sorcery! Frostflower laughed until she bent over, hugging the blanket close to her ribs. When she straightened again, she saw that Coarsecut was laughing with her. So was the watchgirl—giggles mixed with whistles came down from the tower.

Quickshaft still stood in the gateway, looking angry and befuddled, but Coarsecut knocked her spear aside. "You midlands idiot, stop insulting our sorceri, or next time you come up here with a chest wound, we'll send you on up to them for healing! Come on, sorceress— Shortlashes! Stone that youngster!"

The watchgirl had swung down from her low tower and darted away into the Farm, apparently to alert Elvannon's people. "Then tell 'em, 'Welcome!'" Coarsecut shouted after her, meanwhile waving for the sorceress to follow.

Frostflower had much reason to be grateful to Quickshaft. She had hardly dared think she might be taken inside to speak with the priest in his hall. Surely not even Coarsecut would have made such a decision on her own authority had she not been angered by the younger spearwoman. And the surface turmoil Quickshaft caused had helped distract Frostflower from the inner struggle of walking between a farmer's gates.

"So tell me," Coarsecut said as they walked, "what kind of troubles did you have in the midlands last summer? Was it you in the ballad, or someone else?"

"I have not heard the ballad."

"Unh? Well, you probably ought to hear it. If it was you, you've got a right to know what the trinket-and-ballad merchants are singing about you, and if it was someone else, maybe it'll teach you not to go wandering around in the bloody midlands again."

They were approaching a grove of fruit trees, still bare but beginning to give off the feel of reawakening life. A few farmers' folk were gathering near the orchard, peering down the wheelpath as if ready to hide among the small, gnarled tree trunks at the first sign of gale or skyfire. As Coarsecut sang in a voice few would have paid to hear, she held her weapon up by the middle of the shaft and twirled it round in circles to reassure them there was no danger. Once, when Coarsecut paused to grope for a line, a young fieldboy finished the verse for her.

Frostflower did not enjoy hearing the harsh song. But, although it was disturbing to learn she had gained such a reputation among farmers' folk, it was also somehow satisfying. Fortunately, the ballad named no one, but the fact that the sorceress in the song had mismatched eyes might as easily work for her future safety in the middle Tanglelands as against it.

On finishing, Coarsecut said with an apologetic grin, "I'd have sung you the priests'-hall version, but I know the barracks one better. Well, Frostflower, was it you or not?"

The sorceress nodded. The warrior stopped in the path and whistled. The fieldboy gave a soft whoop that might have been of either delight or dismay and scuttled back to the other followers. At the murmur which rose among them, Frostflower glanced around.

"Don't worry," said Coarsecut, stepping forward again. "That's pride they're mumbling, sorceress. And so it really was one of our own sorceri who earned herself a reputation down there?"

"The reputation, it seems, may be greater than the

earning . . . Raidleader, this ballad is no more than a shadow of the truth. I think whoever made it had no more idea than I had a year ago of what it is to be a farmer's prisoner—I am surprised a merchant would sell this ballad to priests and farmers' folk. You could not see the discrepancy between this underground prison room in the ballad, too cramped for sitting, standing, or lying, finger-deep in muck, and the ways of your own Reverence?"

"Midlands priests," said Coarsecut. "Not true, you say? Hellbog, if we can't even trust the ballad-sellers, how can we know what's going on more than a spear's-throw from our own walls? Come to think of it, of course, why do we want to? What about the scaffolding—was that true?"

"Yes. That much . . . was accurate." Frostflower lowered her gaze, thinking that the balladeer might have been in the crowd of onlookers that day. "But my friends cut me down that same night."

"Well, the good gods prosper 'em for that, anyway," said Coarsecut. She seemed not to notice any incongruity in asking farmers' gods to bless farmers' folk for kindness shown to a sorceron.

We have kept aloof too long, thought Frostflower, her face aching with tears. Why did our visits stop in the time of Elvannon's great-grandfather? Was it that they seemed unfriendly, or that we ourselves feared contamination from their beliefs?

"At that, you're lucky you're small, Frostflower," said Coarsecut. "Hang a big, solid old cow like me up for half a day with a rope beneath the armpits, and my arms would stagnate and rot off afterwards even if some friend cut me down. One reason I'm such an honest bitch. How about the sprunging, then?"

"Yes." The balladeer had actually softened the details of the rape.

"Really stripped and didn't lose your powers after all, hey?" The raidleader chuckled. "That's the part makes that young midlands cow Quickshaft call it all a lie—she says no sorceron could keep power afterwards."

"Yes, such as my powers are, I retained them."

"And you really blasted that midlands priest in the end, hey?" Warriors sometimes spoke of their priests in a way no other farmers' folk would have dared; but even Coarsecut lowered her voice to a murmur. "If I'd been you, sorceress, I'd have done it sooner!—Gods forgive me."

"But I did not blast him! The priest's own silver dagger drew the bolt before I knew I could still guide lightning through air and ground. I . . . would have saved him, had I known in time."

"Unh? You're a better gods'-pet than I am, then, sorceress or not." Coarsecut touched her left fist perfunctorily to her forehead.

Frostflower imitated the gesture. Once she would have considered it blasphemous, but now she felt only a passing twinge of conscience, less than she had felt at mentioning the farmers' gods in the formula of greeting. Does corruption grow so quickly and easily? she mused. Why, I have made the sign with more respect than Coarsecut! Aloud, she went on, "Nor did the lightning flash crimson and blue, with the sound of devils' flutes instead of thunder, nor did it loop along the ground like a fiery snake."

"No? Just plain lightning bolts, hey? Well, plenty to turn the battle for you, at that. . . . You know, sorceress, old Featherfingers—the farmerlings' nurse, she came along with Lady Coarvedda—says her grandfather used to tell about a time when his mother's priest was raided—I guess the land's better in those western foothills—and a couple of their sorceri came down from the mountains and helped defend the farm."

Frostflower shook her head. She had never heard of such a thing. Nevertheless, if it were to save a kindly disposed priest like Elvannon from losing his farm . . . "If His Reverence should ever be threatened," said Frostflower, "you will send to tell us?"

Coarsecut laughed. "Who's going to raid His Reverence? Nearest farmer's two days away and not likely to want our land when he can look south. This farm hasn't been raided by anyone but a few bloody outlaws since the walls went up, and the last outlaw pack that got big enough to try it was before my time—Even the rats go midlands these years. They say His Reverence's ancestor only built the walls because he kept having nightmares about the raid that drove him up here."

They were in sight of the Hall by now. It looked much like Maldron's Great Hall, the ancient pattern for a priest's dwelling in the center of his farm: the long, tall white rectangle with a pillared front facing south, a row of alcove chambers cupping out on each side, and part of the long curve of the garden wall visible in back. But while Maldron's garden wall had risen almost as high as the building itself, towering well above a person's head, Elvannon's appeared hardly waist-high, offering all his people a view of his herbs, flowers, and small inner Truth Grove. Elvannon's whole dwelling seemed smaller than Maldron's, and lacked the mosaic that had decorated Maldron's even on the outside.

Elvannon's winter door was open wide. The priest and priestess stood on the small porch, between the pillars, with two younger priestesses behind them. At least thirty people waited along the wheelpath—workers and children in faded green and orange garments, six or seven warriors, one in a blue tunic and another wearing a short, fur-trimmed cape, two houseservants and a child whom the sorceress mistook at first for more priests because they wore farmers' white, though yellowed and decorated with strips of green and russet cloth. Together with the ten or twelve who already followed Frostflower and Coarsecut, this must be the entire population of Elvannon's Farm, gathered to see how their priest and the sorceress would face one another.

For the first time since passing out of sight of the midlands warrior and her spear, Frostflower trembled. The meeting no longer appeared easy and long overdue. And the smell of cooking meat was in the air. Frostflower had not smelled it since last summer, and the tolerance she had acquired then was now gone.

The raidleader halted and lifted fist to forehead in salute. There could be no form for the sorceress to follow now. Hugging the blanket, she left Coarsecut's side and walked the remaining twenty paces, between the lines of farmers' folk, to the door of the Hall. One baby, who seemed to be smiling in its father's arms, gurgled and waved a knotted rag toy at her. Otherwise, all were silent.

She reached the porch and stopped. She did not quite dare look up and risk startling the priest with her eyes, nor, after the reaction of the midlands warrior, did she quite dare use a priestly formula of greeting.

"Frostflower, is it?" said the old farmer-priest.

She glanced up and saw, in the many fine, soft age wrinkles about his mouth and eyes, an expression that seemed to reflect confusion equal to her own, even mixed with the same apprehension.

"Reverence." She held out her blanket. "I come in friendship . . . if you will have it . . . in trust between us, if you will accept it."

The words seemed stiff and proud as she said them. Nervousness gave them a defiant sound far from what she wished. With one priestess—Inmara—she had formed a bond of trust and sympathy; but that had been more than half a year ago, and Elvannon was not Inmara.

After a moment's hesitation, however, he lifted the blanket from her arms, unfolded it, and touched the crossed blades of grass and the five eggs arranged like petals. "You have woven our symbols into it?"

She nodded. "It was not a presumption, Reverence? I meant no presumption."

"It is . . . unexpected. We did not think you knew our symbols so well."

"I saw them last summer. Perhaps they are clumsily done? I tried to weave only the ones I remembered best."

Refolding the blanket and draping it over his arm, he reached down and took Frostflower's left hand between his own, enheartening her to look up. "So your eyes *are* of different colors," he said, and smiled. "The symbols are not worked as our people would work them, but the weaving, in itself, is far from clumsy. And you have made the half-day's journey in the lingering chill and mud in order to bring us a gift, Frostflower?"

"And . . . and to ask you a favor of you, Reverence. A great favor, perhaps too great." She drew a deep breath. "I would ask you for learning."

"For our learning? For priestly learning?"

"For priestly learning, Reverence. If . . . I will ask for no more than you teach your common folk. I can read my own people's writing, Reverence, but not your signs. I . . . I ask for only what you might teach a weaver, or a warrior, who had a great desire to know as much as possible . . ."

By everything her own people believed, reasoned, and thought they knew of the One God and the One God's creation, she should not have kept her powers after losing her virginity. A winter of debate with her own people in Windslope Retreat had given her no explanation. So she had come to look for an answer in the farmers' creed, among the beliefs she had once called superstition,

but some of which had seemed to prove valid. She risked losing
what remained of her own faith. But not even the sorcerous creed
was worthy of belief unless it was true.

At last Elvannon said, "You have eaten, Frostflower?"

She shook her head. She had tried, three or four times on her
way down, to eat the cold corn and honey-meal cakes she carried
with her, but had only succeeded in swallowing a little milk from
her flask. Nor had she been able to breakfast before leaving the
retreat.

"You must be hungry, then. You will share our meal?"

She did not yet feel hungry, but she realized that in a few
moments, as the tension eased, she might be very hungry indeed,
even despite the smell of boiling meat in the air. "We do not eat
flesh, Reverence," she said apologetically.

"No? Well, well, it's not the only food we put on our table,
even at this season. Will you take dried fish? Locust paste?
Cheese?"

"The cheese, yes, with thanks. Not the fish nor the locusts,
Reverence. But milk and eggs we eat, and what can be made from
them." The Windslope sorceri had never acquired the skill of
making cheese, but Frostflower had developed a strong liking,
almost a craving, for it during her travels last summer.

"Well. Come in, then, eat what you will and leave what you
will." The old priestess glanced at Elvannon. Some unvoiced question and answer seemed to pass between them, for the priest nodded
and gave the blanket to the priestess. She, in turn, gave it to one
of the younger women who stood in the doorway behind. Then
she extended her hands to the sorceress. "I am Coarvedda, Frostflower, and these are our daughters, Enelma and Velcora. Come
eat with us, and perhaps we can talk further of this . . . this price
you ask in return for your . . . gift." She spoke the last words with
humor, but it seemed a friendly jest, not a mockery nor a thinly
veiled refusal. Frostflower took Coarvedda's hands and mounted
the porch's single step.

Someone gave a loud yawk of disapproval, and someone else
exclaimed, "Great Seven Names!" Glancing back, Frostflower
guessed the sounds had come from the warrior in the blue tunic
and the warrior with a fur-lined cape—their rich dress suggested

that they, like Quickshaft, were midlands women come here to mend their wounds.

Elvannon looked steadily at the one with fur-lined cape. "Hatchslices?"

"You're taking in a sorceron for a guest?" the warrior replied. "Azkor's talons, Reverence, do you want the gods to scald us all?"

Elvannon stood a little straighter. "Would you speak in such a voice to one of your midlands priests, warrior? We of the edge-lands live in peace, and our peace allows us time for study. We may own fewer scrolls than your wealthy farmers of the midlands, but perhaps we know the few we own more thoroughly. And if I, a priest of Voma and Aomu, Elraec and Deactire, a guardian of the Ten Candles as well as of the Hollowed Sun, the Crossed Wheat, the Fertile Wreath, and the Bare Tree—aye, and one who keeps a special altar to Great Jehandru of the Seven Secret Names—if I see no reason to withhold welcome from any person who comes in peace and friendship, who are you, warrior, to instruct me in the will of the gods?"

Frostflower suppressed a shudder. Although Elvannon's voice was raised in her defense, it had much the same sound as the harangues that other priest had raised against her and Thorn last summer. For a moment she faltered; but Coarvedda's arm was gentle around her shoulders, and after a short pause Elvannon spoke again, more quietly, addressing all his folk this time.

"Three generations ago, my great-grandfather, one of those who wore the name Elvannon before me, entertained a sorcerer several times—a man whom he called friend—in this same Hall. Eanalda, the grandmother of that Elvannon, had entertained two friends from among the sorceri of Windslope. Back to the year when our ancestor first walled his farm there have been generations when certain of the sorceri visited us freely. Nor have our visitors ever corrupted our faith. Have not our rituals remained as pure as those of the very centerlands? Walls would not keep us safe from the powers of sorceri. It is living in friendship that keeps us safe."

An approving murmur went up, and Elvannon's raidleader began to sing one of the last verses of the ballad, several voices joining in. Coarvedda and her daughters turned and led Frostflower through the vestibule into the long hall.

Inside as well as outside, Elvannon's home lacked splendor.
The mosaic was entirely chips of local stone, with more gray than
white. The designs were in browns, black, and muted reds; there
were no flecks of gold or silver, and only a few bright gemstones
of the more common varieties. Whatever the mountains yielded
of value must have gone into trade with the midlands. Although
decorated with its own cleanness and simplicity of line, Elvannon's
ancient home was less richly embellished even than some of the
buildings at Windslope Retreat. There were many wood panels,
carved with painstaking care, but they lacked paint, though some
of the lighter wood had been stained with cloth-dye beneath its
coat of resin varnish. The floor was tiled, not with tiny chips no
larger than those of the wall mosaics, but with slabs of granite,
some the length of a forearm, cut into geometrical shapes and so
deeply worn that more recent stones had been laid over the original
flooring along the most often used paths.

Elvannon, who was still on the porch, raised a chant in the old
language, the priests' ritual language, with his folk chanting a few
words of ritual agreement in the common language. Meanwhile,
Coarvedda walked to the dais, took a pinch of powder from a
stone box in a wall niche, and sprinkled it on the brazier. A cloud
of incense rose from the glowing coals. The priestess held Frostflower's blanket in the incense while she chanted, hurriedly and
emotionlessly, a few verses in the old language.

"We trust your gift, Frostflower," she explained when this brief
ceremony was finished. "We do this only for the sake of visitors
and traders, so that we can truthfully assure them all the goods
we have from your people are purified. Now come." She smiled.
"We'll spread it out on my bed and talk for a few moments until
they're through out there and ready to lay the meal."

Chapter 3

In a sunny area of her private garden, between Hall and Truth Grove, the priestess Eleva rose from her knees and kicked the side of one of her steambeds.

The flowers had begun well enough when they sprouted in their new, circular beds almost three hen's-hatchings ago. The thin parchment coverings had seemed to let the sun's warmth through and keep it in; the soil had remained loose and soft under gentle, frequent sprinklings with warm water; in especially cold weather the priestess herself had built small fires around the outside walls of the steambeds and heated small rocks to arrange in the top layer of soil between the rows of seeds. She had felt like dancing as recklessly as her small children Evron and Evra on the day they found the first new shoots of violet and goddess-tears in the steambeds, while the rest of the garden still lay under snow.

But as the spring warmed and the other plants began to bud and blow as usual, more and more of the steambed flowers browned and shriveled. Eleva transplanted some of the survivors with her own hands, nursed and coddled the others as desperately as if they were sick babes, all to no avail. At best, she would gain a few plants almost as good as those grown in the regular way.

Yet she was sure the idea was sound—the steambeds should work. She had developed this plan for nine years, since the goddess Raellis had first shown it to her in a dream during her seventeenth winter. If her parents had given her a corner of their garden for her scheme, if her brother and sister had not laughed, or if her husband Deveron had let her try it here during those years of their marriage when he ruled the farm and she had so little to do besides bear him a son and daughter and watch him marry again and give the greater part of his affection to the younger wife and her son. . . . Eleva had not been permitted so much as a major share in the raising of her own children, for Creamybosom used the fact that she had nursed Deveron since his mother's early death as authority to demand almost total care of Evron and Evra—but when Intassa's son was born only a year after Evra, Deveron had told Creamybosom she was growing too old to care for three babes at once, and preserved his younger wife's child for her own care.

And now that at last I have the power to do what I would, thought Eleva, I have the farm to rule and not enough time for anything else! Sweet Raellis, why did you waste your inspiration?

She kicked the steambed again, hard enough to hurt her foot and make her catch her breath.

"A priestess does not show petty anger, sister."

She turned at the familiar, disliked voice behind her. Had he not made free to enter her garden, had she still been alone, she would have sat on the knee-high steambed wall, removed her sandal, and rubbed her tingling toes. As it was, she remained standing. "The days when you could teach me worthless things and laugh at me are past, Rondasu. I am a ruling lady now, this is my own Farm, and I did not invite you to visit me today."

"It will not be your Farm long, little sister, if you squander your time and effort on such heretical stupidities as this." He strolled to the steambed and put one foot negligently up on the wall. "Trying to grow flowers in the winter! It's almost sorcerous."

She made a sound like a warrior grunting.

Rondasu shook his head and pulled one of the healthier irises up by its stem. "No wonder the gods are blighting your plants."

"Out!" She could not keep her voice from shaking. "You have not even the excuse of visiting Intassa now!"

He shook dirt from the roots of the iris and examined them. "Ungenerous of you, sister. You are always welcome back in our Hall and garden."

"By the Seven Secret Names!" she whispered. "I think if I were not your sister, you would try to marry me, too!"

That, at last, seemed to annoy him. "I married Intassa for love, Eleva. Love of herself and love of my sister's husband."

"Of course it was for love of her—since she could not bring you your sister's husband's farm! How unfortunate for you that I remain Intassa's elder."

"By the gods, Lady Eleva, I think I could bring you before the High Gathering today and have you deposed as mad, heretic, and unfit to rule!"

"Aye, perhaps you could, if you cared to leave your Farm for that length of time. But remember, brother, I can claim my own seat in the High Gathering now, and my own place in Center-of-Everywhere! Meanwhile, I tell you to go!"

He sat on the wall of the steambed. "Will you push me through the door, down the wheelpath, and out the gate with your own arms, little sister?" He shook his head. "And even if you had the strength, would you show your people such a spectacle of one priest disrespecting another's body?"

She stared at him for a moment. "Never invite me to your Hall, brother," she said. "Not if you wish to eat your food in safety."

She strode away from him, back through her garden, through the Hall, to her office beside the front door—the special alcove of the ruling priest, Deveron's office until his death. When the doorcurtain was closed, not even another priest could lawfully draw it aside and enter without the permission of its rightful occupant. Rondasu might break in upon her almost anywhere else, not excluding her very bedchamber, but even he must respect her privacy here.

She waited, gripping the large, round, wax-coated agate that had served the priests of this farm as a tablet-smoother since the time of Deveron's great-grandparents. Had she clung to the thin silver stylus or one of the pens, she might have driven the point into her hand; had she touched a tablet, she would have spoiled its wax layer beyond smoothing; had she picked up a sheet of parchment, she would have tried to tear it.

At last her brother left. He paused in the entranceway, turning, perhaps, to look at the curtain. She stared back as if they could see one another clearly through the thin, bleached wool.

He went on out, mounted his horse—probably Rastar, the last and best offspring that Eleva's own old rust-red stallion Pride had sired in her father Rondrun's Farm before she rode him through Deveron's gate. Rondasu usually rode Rastar when he paid his unwelcome visits, as if to tempt Eleva into offering once more to buy the mare, now six years old. Rondasu's price was outrageous.

When she could no longer hear the sound of his mount's hoofs, Eleva put her head down and wept for a few moments. With some effort, she wept very quietly, to guard against anyone overhearing. Then she sat up, wiped her face, and busied herself with the task of deciphering her dead husband's records. Deveron had kept them in a fashion he claimed was traditional on his Farm; Eleva suspected that in reality he had devised it himself to prevent her understanding it. Whenever she had asked Deveron to instruct her in the mysteries of his office, he had laughed, telling her their son Evron would be grown and fitted to rule the farm well before he himself was dead. Neither had Eleva's father ever given her more than whimsical instruction in such matters, pointing out that even if she were to remain unmarried and Rondasu were to die before his time, the rule of their Farm would fall to Shara as the elder daughter.

Well, they had been wrong, and Eleva would hold rule of this farm—her Farm now, Eleva's Farm—in spite of dead husband's superciliousness and live brother's malice, in spite of the very gods themselves, if necessary! She had begun making her own records, setting her chief farmworkers to inventory everything anew, speaking with them about past and future. She no longer had much need of Deveron's old records, but, because continuity should be preserved and because simply to ignore them would be to admit a kind of defeat, she still attempted now and then to untangle them, especially when she was too vexed for other, more immediate work.

And yet, despite everything, Deveron had been a good friend to her, and, she supposed—although she had never felt any other man except in dreams—a good lover, even after his second mar-

riage. The children still cried for him sometimes, and more than
once Eleva herself had wakened from a vivid memory of him and
beat her pillow at the realization that he had died a terrible death,
that his body had been chopped and plowed into his favorite field,
and he would never again give her his seed.

Chapter 4

They looked like two crummy beggars climbing up into the mountains as a last resort after being chased out of all the respectable
towns and even the ratholes like Sludgepocket and Last-of-the-
Worst. They had both been beaten out of Jagrock on suspicion of
outlawry, for no other reason than the way they looked and
smelled. But at least, for all the accusations, suspicions, and evil
names that had been thrown at "Bluntend" and "Wedgepopper,"
they had never been called a warrior and a sorcerer. The only time
anyone had seen Slicer was when a sneakthief in Last-of-the-Worst
tried to rifle their one long bag, so grimy and battered that only
someone in a rathole like that town could think it might contain
anything to make life easier. The other lousehosts who woke up
accepted Thorn's story of having stolen the weapon herself.

Cleaner disguises would have meant staying too long in one
decent town or other. No respectable folk traveled any distance
in winter without some desperate reason, and the few respectable
folk who did move around through the snow were longer remembered as individual faces, while begging vagabonds were remembered as rag-covered backs not worth any more concern than the
hope they would get out of town again quickly. Besides, Wind-

bourne seemed to want the lowest disguise possible.

Thorn had refused from that first night to go to the cloth merchant Spendwell, who was also in Five Roads Crossing for the winter. She already owed him more than she had yet been able to pay back for his help in the summer. Besides, she had ridden into town with him, so his small, rented house might well be the first place Master Youngwise would think of looking for the fugitives.

Fortunately, Windbourne had a secret friend in Crinkpetal the flowerbreeder, one of the richest merchants in Five Roads. Windbourne had raised a thick cloud of swirling snow around them when they opened the hidden door in Crinkpetal's garden wall even though no one was within sight, and the family was influential enough—Crinkpetal's wife had been a cousin of the second wife of a priest near Center-of-Everywhere—that the townwarriors never demanded to search the house, only stood outside, asked the flowerbreeder if he had heard anything suspicious, and warned him of the dangerous escaped sorcerer and warrior.

In fact, Youngwise had not seemed to make much of a search. He only needed somone to lay the blame on for the death of a local priest who had most likely been assassinated by someone in his own family; it suited the purpose as well to have the guilt-offering free and nominally being hunted down as to have him actually hanging with a bellyful of stones.

They had not been able to stay more than a hen's-hatching in the flowerbreeder's house. As the townsfolk began to calculate how soon it would be until they could plant without too much risk of the flowers freezing, more and more of them would be coming to Crinkpetal's shop and browsing through his show-garden beside the house, and the fugitives would be in more danger from their host's customers than from the townwarriors. So Crinkpetal found them their beggarly clothes and smuggled them out of town at the bottom of a wagonful of flower bulbs and special loam, which got them off to a good, dirty start.

Normally, the wagonload would not have been sent out at that time of year. But the priestess Eleva, Deveron's older wife and now ruler of the farm, had made a special visit to Crinkpetal to arrange for its early delivery. Hidden in an upper room, the fugitives had overheard part of the conversation. Eleva had somehow conceived the idea of growing plants in small, walled areas warmed by steaming water and covered with parchment. She would try it with flowers first to save precious foodseed.

Windbourne had seemed impressed; he had smiled with eyes as well as mouth for the first time in Thorn's acquaintance with him. Crinkpetal, however, had afterwards called it nonsense—"Just a poor young widow's first fluster of activity to forget her husband—happens to priests and priestesses as to the rest of us—as if the little priestlings and that helpless younger wife wouldn't keep Lady Eleva busy enough. Well, I've known Her Reverence from a priestling, and she's got stuff in her that may surprise them all yet, if she can grow out of these silly whims in time to take hold and keep that farm from rotting away inside and falling to the first raid like a loose grape from the cluster." He shrugged. "But she's always had these whims, too. Family drove her into them, I suppose. I wouldn't have liked to grow up with her parents and sibs—gods forgive me for saying it about priests." He slapped left hand on right in an arbitrary version of one of the favorite prayer gestures.

"Who would raid Her Lady Reverence?" Windbourne had asked.

"No one, most likely, with the only other farm north of town her own brother's, and all the southern farmers too small and timid. Meanwhile, this gives me more business and you a way to get out of town."

Given the time, Thorn thought, they might have been able to locate a thieves' tunnel beneath the town wall, which would have been slightly cleaner. But thieves' tunnels were not easy to locate (if they were, the townwarriors found them and closed them off) and Windbourne had obviously welcomed the chance to ride beneath a pile of dirt and burrow out like some mangy mole when Crinkpetal, as if by accident, backed the wagon into a huge, slowly melting mound of grainy snow along the wheelpath.

And so they had begun the cold, grimy, itchy, snuffly trudge north to the mountains. Once, while Thorn was sitting on a rock surrounded by empty weedfields and patches of snow, watching Windbourne cook the vegetables he had just grown for their meal, she had asked him how, fastidious as his kind was, he had been able to take on so filthy a disguise, even seem to relish it, and go on living in it for two hatchings or so.

"A disguise is a lie," he had answered. "For lying, I deserve the shame and discomfort. I wonder that I can still speed the growth of this food."

"Unh. You're sure it's not to protect yourself from my earthy advances?"

She sat and whistled for a few moments, idly enjoying a daydream in which Windbourne made up his mind that procreation was better than power and asked Thorn for instruction so that he could glide easily and neatly into some little like-minded sorceress when he found her. A basin and a large rinsing-can of warmed water, several brushes, and two or three jars of scented soap were an essential part of the daydream, almost more appealing than what followed them . . . and, as long as she was musing on the near-impossible, she imagined herself and Windbourne washing each other in the fine, smooth-tiled, well-steamed ablution room of a wealthy priest. That verged on sacrilege, but she had reached the conclusion after last summer that the gods were more lenient than most folk thought. Sometimes she put the coupling in the ablution chamber, too; sometimes she moved it upstairs to a priestly bed, stuffed with wool and covered with satin and velvet bedding.

"If you young sorceri never even think about it," she had asked Windbourne at last, "how can any of you ever decide to marry? How do you know what to do when you do marry?"

After a bit more badgering, she had finally made him confess that sorceri, like other men, did sometimes have shameful nightmares, though he had discussed them only to reassure himself that he was not alone in suffering them. Thorn had remarked that, in her experience, no man but a sorcerer would talk about having those dreams as "suffering nightmares." As nearly as she could tell, males were lucky to get it so cheaply and easily.

She must have frightened him, because he changed the subject and began talking again about Lady Eleva's scheme of growing plants beneath parchment. "I doubt she will succeed. With thin-cut quartz or gemstones, instead of parchment, perhaps— She may scald the young plants with this use of steaming water. . . . Still, what a mind to glimpse in a priestess! . . . And she has a lovely voice."

"Ha! So that's what you young sorcerers dream about, is it? Humping priestesses, hey?"

"The unwilled nightmare is not a sin," he had replied, looking down and blushing angrily.

Or maybe they had said all that in several conversations, spread out over the days that had grown into a monotonous round of itching and smells, broken by half a score of bad incidents, the last being a late-season ice storm that kept them holed up in a hastily dug burrow in the woods, Thorn sleeping from boredom and discomfort while Windbourne concentrated on warming the air around them and keeping off the sleet.

Well, it was over now, at least for a while. Having taken more than two hen's-hatchings to make a journey that in good weather and under better traveling conditions should have taken only one, they were finally in sight of Windslope. Thorn might have preferred to get the sorcerer back to his own retreat first, but she had not been able to make him tell her what it was called or where it was located; and she had promised Frost last summer that she would be back at Windslope in the spring.

There was no ice damage to the fruit trees and small patches of cropland below the sorcerous settlement. Many of the trees bore ripening fruit and some of the fields showed signs of having already been harvested this spring. Folk who could manipulate both time and weather never had to worry about having enough to fill their insides . . . and it took a lot to fill your insides when you refused any kind of meat. Thorn cast a hungry glance at the cows grazing in a small field beside one of the outlying cottages. The pasture was not much larger than the cottage, but the cows were almost knee-high in rich green grass, and they were fatter than farmers' cattle in midsummer. They were also unslaughterable. The warrior sighed. At least on the way here she had been able to get a little stringy, dried winter-meat, when she could pay for it without too many questions as to where a ragged beggar had found the money.

No meat and no humping! Whatever she did, she could hardly spend the rest of her life in a sorcerous retreat. But for now, a good wash and clean clothes would be worth the privations.

The sorceri were starting to come out of their cottages. In the

Tanglelands proper, they were forbidden to wear any outer garment
except the long black robe, and maybe an extra black cloak in cold
weather; but in their own retreats they bloomed out in all the colors
vegetable dye could produce, sometimes with woven or embroidered patterns. Some of them wore trousers and midlength tunics
instead of long robes.

Thorn was not yet close enough to see their expressions, but
she grinned, imagining they must be pretty damned surprised.
They were going to be more surprised when they found out who
their visitors were beneath the dirt and rags. Picking out Frostflower—the one in green and saffron who was holding a baby—
Thorn waved one arm above her head and called out a cheerful
whoop.

Frostflower did not stir. Well, she needed both arms for the
brat, and it was expecting a lot to think she would know her friend
so easily in this disguise. A couple of the other sorceri waved back
and hailed the newcomers, and a big reddish-brown mongrel left
the side of a white-haired sorceron in blue and came down the
trail, wagging its tail eagerly and whining in welcome.

"Dowl, hey?" said Thorn, glad, for once, to see a dog. She
reached down and slapped his head. He let out a bark and tried
to sidle up to her, but she shoved him away with the side of her
leg. "Hey, get off, you stupid mongrel, or they'll have to scrub
you, too." She cupped her hands and shouted, "Heat up the wash
water!"

"Friend?" A bearded sorcerer in a plain pale-yellow robe came
to meet her halfway. As they neared each other, she saw he was
old Moonscar, the master of Windslope—as nearly as the warrior
understood how sorcerous retreats were governed. As he came
closer still, she saw a few fresh milkstains on his robe. He must
have been working in the dairyhouse. With only nine sorceri here,
not counting the baby, even the ruling ones worked. Besides, they
had some idea it was healthy to spend part of their time working.

"Don't recognize me yet, old Reverence?" said Thorn. "Give
us a wash, and maybe you will. How's the brat?"

"Thorn?" Moonscar nodded. "Aye, friend, there is always
water in the bathhouse, and coals banked beneath the trough."

"And a good, big loaf of your hot bread afterwards, hey?"

"It will go into the oven as you go into your bath."

Other folk would have been clamoring to know all the whats, whys, and hows of the situation, but most of the sorceri Thorn had met personally, especially the older ones, were content to wait for new arrivals to volunteer information.

Thorn glanced around and saw Windbourne staring at the muddy path. It looked as if the introduction was up to her. "Grandfather Moonscar," she said, remembering this time that sorceri did not like such priestly titles as "Reverence," but unable to think of what equivalents they used, "this is Windbourne, one of your people. He won't tell me where he's from, but I found him in Five Roads Crossing."

Tearing off his hood, Windbourne fell on his knees and began to rub icy mud and old, grainy snow into his hair. "Aye," he said. "A sorcerer—a sorcerer wearing disguise!"

Dowl padded over to him and began trying to lick his face.

"Oh, get up," said Thorn in disgust. "That's no bloody way to wash your hair. He's in disguise, Grandfather, because he'd be rotting on a gibbet if he weren't, and me rotting beside him."

The old sorcerer nodded to her and joined the dog in comforting Windbourne and getting him on his feet. Scratching herself, Thorn walked on up to Frostflower.

But the sorceron holding the baby was not Frostflower—it was her younger brother, Puffball. The facial resemblance was close, and sorcerous clothes tended to disguise sex, but Thorn realized the difference well before she saw that both this sorceron's eyes were blue.

She looked around again and counted only eight Windslope sorceri, Frostflower not among them. "Well, Puffball, where's your sister? Nothing wrong?"

"She stayed the night with Elvannon. At first we worried—she had never stayed the night before. But early this morning she free-traveled to Moonscar and explained; she stayed yesterday afternoon to save their fruit groves from the ice storm. She'll be back again this evening."

"Elvannon. The farmer just half a day back down there? So she's really done it, hey? Gone down and made friends with a priest. He teaching her anything?"

"She can read their scrolls and write their letters now," said the young man. "And sometimes they let her listen to their hymns.

I heard her humming one in the wheatfield once—at least, I think it must have been a priests' hymn."

"And if she wasn't your sister, you wouldn't approve, eh?" Thorn laughed. "Well, if we'd known, we could've waited a few hours and climbed up together. How's the grub?"

"Healthy. Beginning to take cooked food. Sometimes wails very loudly at night." Puffball seemed a little apprehensive, as if he feared Thorn might have come to reclaim Starwind.

She laughed again, louder. "Seems to be sleeping all right this afternoon." Forgetful of the dirt on her hand, she laid her thumb on the baby's silly tip of a nose and left it smudged. He opened his eyes, twisted up his face for a wail, then seemed to change his mind and started gurgling instead. "Don't worry, I don't want him back," the swordswoman went on. "If he takes after his mother, in a few years you'll probably wish you'd sold him while he was still young enough to attract a buyer."

"Never!" Puffball hugged the brat as close as Frostflower ever had.

A couple of other sorceri had joined them by now—Thorn did not remember all their names, having spent only a few days with them last summer. Most of the Windslope population had gone partway down the path to stand ready if Moonscar wanted help with Windbourne.

Good. The warrior had had her fill of trying to comfort and bully the sorcerer out of his fits of remorse all the way up. Let his own kind take care of him now! She followed Puffball to the wash-house, a building shaped like a couple of giant domed ovens pressed together, closely resembling the dome-shaped dairy house, kitchen house, a couple of the storage houses, and two or three of the small dwellings.

Puffball quickly cleaned the infant's face and left Thorn alone. Even though the long trough was in the back dome of the building, no one else would come into the bathhouse while she was using it—except, she hoped, to leave clean clothes at the door. She doubted that any two sorceri ever washed themselves at the same time, even if they were of the same sex. Windbourne would not be able to clean his body until Thorn had finished, and he needed it as much as she did. She shrugged and decided to take her time anyway. She would have let him bathe first if he had not chosen to wallow in self-accusations down on the path; but, now he was among his own kind, he might go on confessing for a quarter of the afternoon.

Where farmers' folk preferred splashing and sprinkling, the sorceri washed their bodies, like their clothes, by immersion in a trough. Since the bathhouse was also the laundry house, the same trough probably served both purposes. It was carved from mountain stone, the outside sanded down into smooth, gently curving shapes. The inside was set to within half an arm's length of the top with glazed tile, the same sort farmers used except that the colors were arranged in a plain spiral rather than in symbolic designs. The tile had surprised Thorn on her first visit, as had the short copper tube that connected the trough's central drain, now stopped with a plug of linen-wrapped wood, to the clay pipes that carried the water down to a dugout pool below the bathhouse.

Well, there were the few merchants who peddled wool, linen, and cotton cloth so finely woven it could hardly be distinguished from silk. (Only farmers in the southern Edgelands could hope to grow cotton, and only the richer ones tried, since it needed a long, fortunate summer and the saying was that the cotton harvest failed two seasons out of three.) There were the gemstones from the mountains; when you thought about it, who else but sorceri would gather them, with the mountains so full of sorcerous retreats? And there were the dreamberries—more of the damn things for sale in large towns like Five Roads and small, lousy ones like Sludge-pocket than honest farmers' folk could have found if they combed the woods for a year. All these trade items were whispered to come from the sorceri; often the midlands merchants themselves, while avoiding any actual mention of sorceri, would assure buyers that such goods had been "thoroughly blessed and incensed" or "purified by untold generations of honest handling."

The copper was more surprising than the other evidence of wealth and trade, with the way priests and farmers' folk used that metal against sorceri in the midlands. But then, no warrior would have hesitated to eat stew from an iron kettle because she had been sliced by an iron sword, and sorceri turned out to be as practical as warriors in that respect.

Carefully depositing Stabber and the bag that contained Slicer on a long table used for folding laundry, Thorn ripped off her clothes, wound them up into a lumpy ball, and hurled them out the door. If the sorceri did not understand that as a signal she needed something clean to put on after her wash, they would have to risk seeing her come out wrapped in a couple of towels. She tested the water, stirred up the charcoals on the ledge beneath the trough, felt the tiled bottom to be sure it was not overheating, and jumped in. She regretted the lack of hard scrubbing brushes, and to her there was something not quite right about trying to soak clean in still water—the trough was warmer than a river or lake, but it did not flow, it held you trapped in your own dissolved dirt. Nevertheless, it was relaxing in its way. She wondered if any sorceron had ever relaxed to the point of sleep and drowned in the water, chest-deep as it was when you were sitting up in it.

She filled her palms with soap and massaged thought away for a few moments by scrubbing her hair until the scalp slid back and forth on the skull. The last time she had gotten her hair cut to a decent warrior's length was in Five Roads, at least ten days before the priest's death. By now it was long enough to stick on her shoulders when she turned her head, long enough that she could pull a handful of it into sight and make sure it was washed back to its natural tawny color.

So little Frostflower really had carried out her intention to learn priestly writing and study the ways of the gods and goddesses. She may know more about them by now than I do, thought the warrior with a mental laugh. Wonder if she's chosen any favorites yet?

Draining the dirty water, Thorn knelt and poured dipperful after dipperful of clean, cold water from a nearby stone jar over her hair, her body, and the tiled interior of the trough. When satisfied that all were clean, she replugged and refilled the trough, stirred up the coals again to start the new water heating for the sorcerer, dried herself in a cotton towel almost the size of a blanket (simply as they thought they lived, in some ways sorceri enjoyed as much luxury as the richest priests) and found a pile of clean clothes left at the very end of the laundry table, just inside the door: gold-colored trousers and knee-length red tunic, both of velvet-soft wool; linen undergarments of the kind a sorceress wore—the bodice was impossible to tie as firmly as a good warrior's halter, but it would do for the soft life of the retreat—a pair of boots made of sev ral layers of linen and wool quilted together and coated on the outside with some sort of wax or treegum, and a long, blue cloak of heavier wool. Thorn would have had to save most of her wages as Third Wallkeeper of Five Roads for a year before she could have bought clothes like these in the midlands.

She recovered her sword and knife and strolled outside, picking the dirty wax off Slicer's sheen-amber. She might need to disguise the pommel stones of her weapons again when they left Windslope, but for now she wanted to show off her two gems against the beauty of her borrowed clothes.

Windbourne was sitting alone on a stone bench, shoulders slumped, eyes staring down into a cup that tilted unsteadily in his hands. At least his face and hands were wiped clean, and a crust of bread lay on the bench beside him, all of which suggested that his people had been able to talk a little bit of sense into him, not merely given up and left him to welter.

"Trough's waiting for you," said Thorn, walking over and putting one foot up on the bench. "Water may not be very warm yet, but you look as if a cold dousing might do you more good than a hot one."

"It's all so easy for you, isn't it, warrior?" he said without looking up. "A little water and soap, clean skin and clothes, and you think all your disgrace is washed away in the sight of your gods, such as they are. And I suppose it may be—a few rites, a few words, a little ceremony...I could almost envy you your superstition."

Thorn shrugged. "I wasn't washing away disgrace, I was washing away dirt. And yes, I feel a lot better for it. So will you if you stir your...legs and get in there. As for disgrace, I was hoping your own kind might finally convince you—"

"God!" He set down his cup with a thump, sloshing its contents.

Thorn jerked her leg out of the way. "Watch it! That stuff's wine!" Blasted winestains were worse than mud.

"What sort of retreat is this?" he went on. "Sorceri who let one of their own go to study the gods of the farmer-priests! What cleansing can I find here?"

"You can start by scrubbing the stink off your skin. Smell less like bogbait and you may feel less like bogbait. And then you'd better stick to milk and water. All this damn wine inside you to simmer your brain—no wonder you can't think right!"

He finally looked up at her. "Because you saved my life, does that give you the wisdom to explain the state of my being to me? God, warrior! I think your own farmer-priests would call you heretic!"

"I had to put up with your damn moods all the way north," said Thorn with another shrug. "But now I'm going to see if my bread's baked yet."

There were a number of small outdoor ovens in the retreat, but only one of them seemed to have a sorceron sitting beside it— Starsinger, recognizable by her strange, rounded lute. Her high-backed wooden chair was placed near enough to the oven for the heat to warm her old blood, but her voice still sounded like that of a woman thirty years younger. She acknowledged Thorn's approach by nodding without interrupting her song. Returning the nod, Thorn sat in another chair nearby, relaxed in the sun, and listened to the music.

She had been surprised last summer when she learned that sorceri, like farmers' folk, commonly judged time by singing songs when they had food to bake or other work that entailed waiting in comparative idleness. The songs were different, both in melody and subject matter; sorcerous ballads tended to be boring tales with no fights, no lovemaking, and long descriptions of the mental growth someone had enjoyed by watching a butterfly's wings in the sunlight. The only exciting one the warrior had yet heard was about a young sorcerer who saved a traveler's life by crumbling away a boulder that had fallen on his leg—seemingly a difficult feat even for a skilled sorceron—and even this ballad went on to tell how the traveler converted to the sorcerous creed, which took much longer to recount than the rescue. Thorn preferred to daydream about her meal—a loaf of hot, brown, crusty bread almost as long as her lower arm, stuffed with vegetables, some of them maybe fresh-grown.

Once she opened her eyes to look across the footpath at Windbourne, still sitting hunched over his wine. There'll be a loaf of bread in the oven for him, too, she thought, and the bastard had better get his rump into that bathhouse pretty soon if he wants to eat his meal hot. She closed her eyes again and thought it was inconvenient that sorceri could not hurry the cooking of a meal the way they could hurry the growing of one. As she understood it, they had to let things cook at their own speed because they could not touch cooking food without burning their fingers like everyone else; the most they could do was increase the heat of the air in the stove or above the fire, through a process somewhat like the manipulation of weather, and they preferred not to do even this much. "Why do you prize your powers so much if you're so stingy about using them?" Thorn had asked Frostflower; Frost seemed to have an answer to that in her mind, but she had never been able to explain it to the warrior's comprehension.

So Frost was free-traveling now? Well, that was good. It was the reason she had been wandering around in the middle Tangle-lands last summer like a stray piglet squealing to be skinned and roasted—seemed the old sorceri did not teach the young ones this third power of theirs until after a period of real travel, something like the way a warrior could not become a raidleader in a farm without having wounded or captured an enemy in a real raid, nor wallkeeper in a town without having caught a thief or brought in an outlaw's head, with or without the body. Frostflower had been afraid her people might refuse to teach her free-traveling when she came back to them raped and full of doubts about her own god (or goddess? Thorn had welcomed the God of the Sorceri into her own group of favorite deities, and it would be nice to know whether to think of this new one as a He or a She).

Windbourne had probably been traveling around for the same reason. Frost had come back determined to find some sorceron in another retreat who would teach her free-travel if her own com-munity refused; but Windbourne acted as if he himself would now refuse to ask for the instruction. For Frost, Thorn would go through everything again, several times over; for Windbourne, she some-times regretted having gone through it once.

The swordswoman pressed her finger to her chest, between collarbone and left breast, where the brandscar that canceled out last summer's outlawry lay hidden beneath the tunic. Get far enough south or west of Center-of-Everywhere, someplace where Maldron's symbol, now Inmara's symbol, was less known and where it was less likely that both tales would come up in the same time and place, and she might be able to make the first scar do double work. But if she wanted to stay anywhere in the northeast, even to breathe easily in the south, she had to get a second brand somehow from Youngwise or Eleva. The priestess' would carry more honor, show a higher degree of forgiveness; but the town-master's would have just as much practical effect and might be easier to get.

Without that second brand, she would always know herself an outlaw. Even if she escaped discovery in life and Hellbog afterwards, she could never again think of herself as an honest woman. Azkor's talons! she thought, I'm almost as bad as that sorcerer, in my way. I just don't make myself and everybody else suffer about it, that's all.

Chapter 5

Frostflower found Dowl waiting at nearest curve. After his initial outburst of leaping up on her, pawing at her waist, licking her face, threatening to overturn them both with the force of his tail-wagging, the dog was content to sit with his head in her lap, letting her fondle his ears, while she rested a few moments on the old boulder, chiseled into a chair so long ago that now only tradition reminded them its shape was artificial rather than natural.

She did not often stop to rest this close to the retreat, but the climb had seemed especially hard this afternoon. Yesterday had exhausted her, with the work of preserving Elvannon's orchards from the ice storm, the need for spending the night in the farmer's Hall, and the unexpected temptation to read one of his scrolls of secret knowledge, guarded from all but ruling and a few scholarly priests.

Yesterday's crowning triumph had been the ease of her free-travel back to Moonscar's cottage. Her progress in the skill had been very slow throughout the winter, much slower than her ability to manipulate time and weather would have suggested. Moonscar, Silverflake, and Windspur, the other three sorceri of Windslope who had developed the third skill, had assured her it was almost always difficult at first, but, after a period of staggering as if the disembodied entity were drunk or moving through liquid—suddenly the consciousness would break free, the vision would clear, and all would be simple from that moment on, with only the finer gambols and embellishments left to learn. This might happen at any time, even during the night, when it might be mistaken for a dream, until at the next effort free-travel came easily.

But as spring approached and Frostflower still labored as if swimming through mud, she knew even Moonscar had begun to share her fear that the losses of her virginity and certitude, though leaving her other skills untouched—perhaps stronger than before—were hindering her progress in free-travel. Windspur and Ringwood had frankly advised her that if she ever hoped to free-travel easily, she should give up her studies at Elvannon's Farm.

And now, at last, it had happened . . . in Elvannon's home, shortly after her decision not to use her chance opportunity to read some of his people's secret knowledge. Had it been a reward for her decision to keep faith with a priest, or for her turning away from the deepest parts of the priestly creed? Or had it been mere coincidence? Even in her triumph, she was left with doubt. Moreover, free-traveling to Windslope and back had taken the same time it would have taken in the body, and once in Moonscar's cottage, she had had to wait some time before he woke and entered the free-traveling state, as he did almost every night. She had not returned to her chamber in Elvannon's Hall until nearly dawn, and then she had risen with the farmers and spent the day in the study alcove until her usual departure time after the midday meal. Her flesh had rested, true enough, as thoroughly as in sleep, but her mind had not rested for two days and a night.

Sighing, she gave Dowl's head a final pat, rose, and started around Nearest Curve and up the last four hundred paces. She was glad the first cottage was Puffball's. With luck, she could see Starwind again at once. No matter how healthy he was at each of her departures, no matter how safe she knew him to be in the keeping of Puffball and Silverflake, she still must always see him on her return. And she could share Puffball's supper before climbing the hundred paces further to her own cottage and bed.

She rounded the curve. The buildings of the retreat, which were visible from lower down on the slope but hidden from view for long, winding stretches of the path, would now have come back into sight. She lifted her head to look at them—she always liked them in the heavy golden air of near-sunset—and saw Weatherwatcher waiting for her less than a hundred paces further up the path.

No—not Weatherwatcher, only wearing a red tunic like his!

"Thorn!" cried the sorceress, beginning to run despite her weariness.

The warrior dashed down to meet her, caught her up, swung her round, set her down again. "Knew me right away, did you? Claws and tails!"

"I had not expected you for at least a full hen's-hatching yet!"

"No? Well, we can thank our gods I made you that promise last summer, or maybe I wouldn't have gotten back at all."

They were both laughing, but suddenly—from the warrior's words, not from her tone—Frostflower realized something was wrong. "Thorn, you found good work and left it again only to keep—"

"Gods, what a lovely thought! Here, you look worn out—lean; that's the way. Your brother's house?"

Nodding, the sorceress accepted her friend's support, with Dowl running before and around them. "But what did you mean, Thorn, about your promise?" She would have said that she did not wish to hold her back from any plans she might make among her own kind. But to put such a thing into spoken words seemed ungrateful.

"There has to be at least one god—yours or mine, I'm just as thankful—who doesn't want me breaking promises and is helping me stay alive long enough to keep them. Otherwise..." Thorn shrugged. "Well, I'm here as I promised, but if you're still set on another trip through the midlands this summer, maybe you'd better not plan on my company.... I'm an outlaw again, Frost."

They walked in silence for fifty paces, Frostflower leaning heavily on her friend's shoulder and wondering if in some way Thorn was leaning on her for support of the mind. "I do not know all the laws of all the priests in the midlands," the sorceress said at last, "but I know it was not for dishonesty, Thorn." Some things,

even if understood without words, gave additional comfort in the
speaking and hearing.

"I sort of hope it's my own Warriors' God looking out for me,"
said Thorn. "No lack of gratitude to yours, Frost, but I've lived
a lot longer with mine, and I think I know him a little better, what
he likes."

"The questions they have brought to us," said Moonscar, "are
what penance Windbourne may deserve for traveling in disguise
and for certain thoughts he has had since his capture and escape,
and what Thorn should do, now she has been outlawed this second
time for her friendship to us."

They sat around one of the tables in the cloth-house; with
Windbourne, Thorn, and all the sorceri of the retreat except Starsinger and Windspur, who were taking care of the infant, the group
was too large for any of the cottages, and Windbourne had re-
quested they not use the House of Gathering, as if he were ashamed
to sit in its unadorned austerity.

Ringwood rubbed the callus on her left forefinger. "Stay with
us, Thorn. We'll soon wean you into the true creed."

"Thanks, Ringwood," said the warrior with a grin, "but if you
can't come up with any better suggestions that that, I'll just handle
my problems alone."

Frostflower sighed. Ringwood, like Windspur, never let slip
a chance to urge a visitor's conversion.

"Thorn knows," said Moonscar, "that our retreat is ever open
to her. She may rest with us as long as she wishes." He looked
directly at Ringwood. "We will not press our beliefs upon her,
and should she hunger for her own kind of food, we will not
complain if she hunts, cooks, and eats it in the woods—shall we
give that privilege to our dogs and cats and withhold it from our
guests? Unless one of us can suggest some way to help her regain
her honor among her own people, we will say no more."

Thorn grinned again. "You wouldn't want me around here too
long, anyway. Better get on to Wedgepopper's problems—
sorry—Windbourne's. Spiked tails! After almost a quarter of a
year, I think of myself as Bluntend more often than Thorn."

Spiked tails? Frostflower smiled. The warrior was clearly making an effort to soften her speech, at least among sorcerous friends.

"We suggested no penance for Frostflower last summer when she had traveled in disguise to save her life," said Silverflake. "Shall we suggest one for Windbourne? If his own retreat thinks differently, let them measure his guilt. I say he has none."

Windbourne looked up at her. "Your hair may be silver, and mine still yellow, but I say I have great guilt."

"If the guilt exists in his mind," said Wellgiven, "is it not as real as if it existed in fact?"

"I doubted," said Frostflower. "I did not go in disguise without misgivings."

"Doubt is natural," said Puffball, who was just emerging from the everyday scruples of youth through which his sister had passed some years earlier. "If we sinned whenever we doubted, we would never be guiltless."

"Doubt prevents pride," said Moonscar.

"Keeps you humble, hey?" Thorn put in. "The way a little nick every now and again in practice keeps me from going into a real fight with too much confidence."

Windbourne started up. "Why did you bring this priests' woman into our circle, with her foul tongue and talk of fighting?"

"This foul-tongued priests' woman," said Thorn, "saved your blasted guts, Wedgepopper!"

"As she saved mine," Frostflower said quickly, reaching across the table for Thorn's hand. "As she saved Starwind—as she would save any of us. Warriors' skills may have no place in our own thoughts, but when they are used to save our lives, shall we despise them?"

Windbourne sat sullen.

"Well, I say if Windbourne feels all that guilty and wants a punishment, punish him," said Thorn. "It'll do him good, and we can get on to more serious problems."

"Our penances are not like yours, Thorn," said Frostflower. "Not quite. Your hour of suffering at Inmara's Farm last summer canceled out your . . . I cannot say guilt . . . your lawbreaking, simply by the ritual and the bodily pain, did it not?" The priestly creed had great advantages, the sorceress thought, for active, practical people like Thorn. (And yet it was also adaptable to those like Elvannon's older daughter, whose study seemed to approach sorcerous meditation.) "Our penances are meant to purify from within," she continued. "We must not attempt to purify where there is no real guilt."

Thorn shrugged. "Let him go back to his own retreat, then. I suppose he can find it safely enough alone, now we're back in the mountains."

"Frostflower doubted," said Windbourne. "I have never doubted. I recognized my sin from the beginning. If you will not choose a penance for me, let me choose one for myself. I must travel back again to Five Roads Crossing in my own garb. At the farmer-priest's gate, I must push back my hood and proclaim my innocence of his death. Afterwards—"

"Afterwards!" cried Thorn. "You rotbrained bogbait, you won't get much of an afterwards! If they don't spear you down before you have your hood off, you'll wish they had by the time they gibbet you."

"Afterwards," said Windbourne, who by tradition must be allowed to finish before any other sorceron spoke, "I must return to my own retreat crawling on my knees."

Moonscar shook his white head. "This last alone would be far too much. But the other . . . Even those sorceri of the early generations who died of self-imposed penances in the mountains at least left themselves the chance of survival. No, Windbourne, you must think of this not as it concerns your pride, but as if you were choosing the penance for another who had done what you have done."

"The priest," said Frostflower. "Deveron. Can it be that somehow his death distorts Windbourne's thoughts?"

Ringwood slapped her hand on the table. "The coincidental death of a farmer-priest?"

"They are people, Ringwood," said Frostflower, "not so greatly different from us, despite their creed. Such a death as Deveron's must bring sorrow, wherever it falls. He may have been as gentle a farmer, in his way, as our own neighbor Elvannon. Might not the very accident of Windbourne's being suspected of his death have created a link that sharpened his sense of guilt without his understanding why?"

"There may be something in Frostflower's thought," said Wellgiven, who had made his decision ten years ago to give up his own chance at learning free-travel rather than risk seeing widespread suffering among farmers' folk tnat he was prevented, by their suspicion of sorceri, from helping to relieve. "Deveron's death sounds like the result of a fever, perhaps one of the spreading sicknesses."

"Deveron's death," said Thorn, "was probably caused by poison."

"Poison!" cried several of them.

Thorn leaned her chin on one hand and looked at them meditatively. "The people who poison priests are other priests, maybe sometimes an old-fashioned warrior who thinks she's still half a priestess."

Frostflower felt a pain almost of hunger so great it had become sickness. "Thorn, you do not mean that among themselves, they . . . kill . . . murder one another?"

The warrior glanced at her friend. "Sorry, Frost, they do. It's secret knowledge, of course. Some priests don't even think warriors should know it. I've heard of a couple who killed good women for knowing it, not talking about it, just for being aware of it. But I don't see any reason to keep it secret here."

Frostflower covered her face with her hands. Was this the kind of secret to be found in Elvannon's forbidden scrolls?

"Don't take it so hard," Thorn went on. "It doesn't happen all that often. And most farmers don't like it any more than you do. I've heard that the High Priestly Gathering in Center-of-Everywhere executes the ones who do it, when they find out and can get hold of them."

Moonscar nodded. "If it were known that priests did not always guard one another's sanctity of person, could they retain that sanctity among the common folk? And charging such deaths to our people is a part of covering their own guilt; who else but a sorceron would dare strike a priest? But your townmasters also know these things?"

"I imagine Youngwise suspects. He's a shrewd old prick— sorry, a shrewd old geezer. That's why he wasn't particular about what sorceron he had dragged in for the blame-catch."

"But why not pass it off as fever-death?" said Wellgiven. "Do they hate us so much?"

Thorn shrugged. "I suppose there wasn't any other fever sickness in the farm, and His Reverence must have died pretty damn spectacularly. Anyway, I suppose they could have poisoned a few farmworkers and tried to make it look like a spreading sickness that way, but a stray sorceron and one townwarrior or merchant wasted by stripping him or her would be cheaper than three or four farmworkers. Keep the farm and the town happier, too."

"Her . . . Her Lady Reverence Eleva?" said Windbourne. "Like all the rest of them? Another—another farmer-priest?" His emphasis on the last word had more force than most of Thorn's worst epithets.

Thorn slapped the table. "Windbourne, you made her some sort of goddess—or maybe I should say sorceress—because of her nice voice and her plans for steamgardens. If you want to change your mind now, it's your own pretty notion of her you're changing, not the priestess herself. But there are farmers who are just as innocent as you are, a few priestlings and even a few grown wives who don't believe in the poisonings—or at least don't believe it could happen in their own farms—and Her Reverence could be one of them. There've been priests who died suddenly and nobody got the blame. I suspect a few of them were murdered, a pillow over the face or a better poison than someone used on Deveron, and it passed as a natural death. Lady Eleva may have sent Youngwise instructions to look for a sorceron in order to cover her own guilt, or whoever really poisoned her husband may have persuaded her of sorcery to keep her from realizing the truth."

"And why did you not tell me?" said Windbourne. "In all those hatchings we spent together . . . God! You could have told me that I . . . I might be creating a false idea of her."

"You're a sorcerer," Thorn replied. "She's a priestess. What difference would it make what you thought of her?"

"But why was Windbourne in Five Roads during the winter?" asked Weatherwatcher.

"I was traveling in preparation for my study of the third skill."

"In winter?" asked Wellgiven.

Gripping his hands together, Windbourne leaned his upper arms heavily on the table. "The skills do not come easily to me. To such as I, the most difficult preparation is the best."

"Perhaps not," said Moonscar. "It may be that the skills do not come easily to you because you will not let them, because you prefer the most difficult way."

"I could go to Five Roads," said Frostflower. "I am not known there. I could learn what's happened."

"Alone?" said Thorn.

Frostflower gazed down. Her hands looked strained and somehow unreal spread out on the dark wood of the table. She put them into her lap. "If I must," she said. "I traveled alone, with only Dowl, to Three Bridges last summer."

Windbourne shook his head. "It would not lessen my guilt, my cowardice."

"Warriors' God! I should've just gone myself and left you behind, clamped down on that bed!" Thorn exclaimed. "Well, maybe it won't help *you* to know, Wedgepopper, but maybe you're not the only creature interested." Speaking softer but no slower, she went on, "How about free-traveling, Frost?"

Frostflower shook her head. "How long is the journey to Five Roads Crossing? A full hatching in good weather, is it not? Bad weather, night, or bodily fatigue do not stop free-travelers, but to go and return would still require a hatching, and we do not know how long I might need to wander in the town, unable to ask questions, able only to listen for chance talk of last winter's events. You could keep my body safe here from outside danger, but not from the inner dangers of long idleness and lack of food."

"Why not slow time for your body?" asked the warrior.

"That would also affect the free-traveling entity. Not to so great an extent, perhaps, but still . . ." Frostflower paused. Her own need to know was great—she could not say as great as Windbourne's, for no one could be sure of gauging another's mind accurately—but great enough that learning the truth of Deveron's death might be worth the risk. "Yet free-travels of such length have been accomplished," she said. "And I am young and healthy."

Silverflake covered her left hand with her right in negation. "Now that you have found your power for it, I think you may become one of the farthest free-travelers of all, but your body is not yet prepared to lie dormant so long. At the end of the summer, perhaps, with diet and exercise aimed toward that one goal. But even then, the risk would be terrible. None of us could be sure of reaching you in time to summon you back. Moonscar and myself are too old to think of leaving our bodies so long, and in ten years of practising the third skill, Windspur has not yet made so long a journey as you did last night."

"Teach me the third skill, and let me go," said Windbourne. "If I become a wraith wandering alone with no flesh to return into, that will be no more than fitting penance."

"Talk sense or keep quiet," said Thorn. "If we got you to Five Roads in body, Frost? You could free-travel right into the priests' private alcoves?"

Wellgiven asked, "Are there friends near Five Roads who will keep her body safe?"

"The flowerbreeder Crinkpetal," said Windbourne. "He has long been an unsuspected friend, as well as a rich merchant. Baconcrunch of the Fat Suckling Inn—but that was where they seized me, so it might be best to avoid her house. Leatherhands of the western townstable. Others I'd been told of but did not have time to meet."

"Our old friend Spendwell may still be there," Thorn remarked. "But more likely he'll be off in his wagon again before we can get back. I'd say Crinkpetal's our best choice, though I'm not sure he'll be overjoyed to see us again."

"Us?" said Frostflower. "Will they not still be watching for you?"

"If I've got any chance at all of making myself an honest woman again," said the warrior, "it's by proving I ran away with an innocent man."

"But if Deveron was killed by other priests," said Silverflake, "what good would the knowledge do you? Would they not kill you to keep the secret from the common people, rather than lift your outlawry?"

"They might," said Thorn, "if they can get me. Or I might be able to buy another brand from Youngwise or Eleva in return for my promise to keep quiet. Anyway, I'd rather die fighting back— as a really dangerous someone to them—than as a poor, common outlaw scud."

"Thorn," said Frostflower, her mind cringing from the thought of her friend dying either way, "your gods know how I've looked forward to traveling with you this summer. But it might be safer for me to travel alone this time, on this journey."

"Teach me free-travel," said Windbourne. "I must retrace this winter's journey in my own rightful garb—the black the priests have imposed on us—and with my own name. Only thus can I hope to cancel out the lie of living disguised. If they scaffold me, I will leave my body to die and return in free-traveling essence to tell you what I've learned."

Moonscar shook his head. "You have asked for a penance, young sorcerer. As the first part of that penance, I instruct you to advise no grim and deadly penance for yourself. Do you accept this from me?"

Windbourne stared down at the table in silence.

"Don't give him the choice, Moonscar," said Thorn. "Just command him. He's been begging for it, hasn't he?"

"To command is not our way, Thorn," replied the old First Sorcerer. "But unless you accept this penance, Windbourne, you must hope for no more suggestions from me."

Windbourne slowly turned both hands palm up. "I . . . accept it, Moonscar," he said, his head still bowed.

Thorn grunted. "Now maybe we can get somewhere. Let's see. The robe might just pass, if he keeps his hood over his face, but the name's out. Then we'll just call him 'The Silent One.' I'll do all the talking—I don't mind putting on a disguise and getting away from the truth if necessary—oh, don't worry, Wedgepopper, I won't lie about *you*. All you'll have to do is keep quiet and I'll say 'The Silent One' doesn't talk and let 'em draw their own conclusions as to why not."

"Thorn—" said Frostflower as the warrior paused.

Thorn held up one hand. "Wedgepopper and me are the ones in trouble this time, Frost, you're not. So it's either you going alone, or us going, and since he insists on going, teach him free-travel and let him do the work. As for me, I want to be right there when he finds out something, not sitting up here flattening my . . . well, lolling in the sun. All right, how long will it take to teach him free-travel?"

"It varies," said Silverflake, "but I fear it will take a long time in Windbourne's case. If the first two skills have never come easily to him, and if he feels this guilt out of measure . . . he may not be able to learn to leave his body until the guilt is lifted to his satisfaction."

"What?" Thorn struck her hands together. "Demons' claws! And we can't lift his guilt until he learns the skill!"

Frostflower smiled. "So you must let me go, after all. And since you were only two when you left Five Roads Crossing, a group of three will be all the less likely to draw suspicion. What disguise will you wear this time, Thorn?"

The warrior shrugged. "The likeliest one you people can put together for me. Anything but those filthy beggar's rags I wore up here! How'll you travel, Frost?"

"In my black robe, of course. Why not?"

Thorn laughed and slapped the table. "Then I'll go as a sorceron, too! That is," she added, as Ringwood and Silverflake looked doubtful, "if you don't have any scruples about lending me a robe?"

Moonscar cleared his throat and folded his hands on the table. "Our own ancient custom and the priestly laws—there is argument, Windbourne, as to which came first—say that we are to wear black, hooded robes in the midlands. I have never heard of any custom on our side or any law of the priests to forbid anyone else to wear the same kind of black robe." He smiled and nodded, then grew serious again. "But this further penance I would like to give you, Windbourne: that during your travel, you submit yourself to the judgment of your two companions. Do you accept this?"

The young sorcerer looked slowly from Thorn to Frostflower as if caught in a trap. "I accept, Moonscar. But I accept on condition that Frostflower try to teach me the third skill as we go."

"I've never taught," said Frostflower. "I have only learned. . . . But I will try, Windbourne." She, with her own doubts, to be set as guide over another! She was grateful that Thorn would share the burden. But was not the idea of authority different among farmers' folk? Yet Moonscar had been born and raised to young manhood among the farmers' folk, only coming to the sorceri when he had reached the age of firm decision. If he set a warrior to guide a sorcerer, he must think her idea of command would be to his benefit, helping, perhaps, to form again the self-control of prudence, which Windbourne seemed to have lost.

As she made the descent alone for the last time that season, Frostflower pondered how best to take her leave of Elvannon and his family. Though far from satisfied with her thoughts when she reached the Hall, she asked to speak privately with His Reverence before going to the study alcove. He took her into his office at the front of the building.

"This is the last midday I will spend here, Reverence," she began. "At least until the autumn. Soon I begin my summer's traveling."

His white brows contracted very slightly. "Your warrior friend has already arrived?"

"Yes."

"Strange that no one saw her pass. We would have welcomed the opportunity to greet her."

"She wanted to find me again as soon as possible." Frostflower gazed down at her lap.

"You'll bring her here for a meal with us on your way to the midlands?"

"I...don't know." If her own safety alone were involved, Frostflower would have entrusted it to Elvannon, told him of their need to learn the truth of Deveron's death, even asked him, perhaps, whether he could tell her if the forbidden scrolls contained such secrets as this. But she could not risk the safety of two friends to a farmer-priest, however much she herself trusted him.

"Our scrollcase may grow dusty if your visits do not start again in the fall. Will you also accept a token?"

A priest's or townmaster's safe-passage token did not have the same force when carried by a sorceron as when carried by one of the farmers' folk; it meant only that the sorceron who bore it had never been known to work any mischief in the neighborhood of the one who gave it. But it could turn away suspicion that would otherwise fall heavy on anyone in a black robe. "I would be honored, Reverence."

"It may be a small, unnecessary thing now. I've often regretted not having given you one last summer."

"You could not give when you were not asked, Reverence."

He smiled. "Don't be so aloof up there in your retreat. Whenever any of you plan to travel south, tell me. We can spare metal enough for a few tokens. Is anyone else traveling with you?"

Frostflower nodded. "Two."

"Your warrior friend and another sorceron?"

Warriors did not carry safe-passage tokens; if they were wounded, their wounds were token enough, and if they were not wounded, they considered that tokens limited their freedom. But it had been decided that Thorn would wear her disguise from the very outset. "There will be three of us in black robes," Frostflower said carefully. "Windbourne, Rosethorn, and myself." Rosethorn had been the warrior's childhood name, and, fortunately, it sounded not too unlike that of a sorceron.

Elvannon calmly printed both names beneath Frostflower's on his old limestone tablet, darkened by thousands of notes made with his charcoal pencil and rubbed off again when their usefulness was past. "We've grown unneighborly indeed," was his only remark. "I would not have recognized either of these as belonging to Wind-slope folk."

"They are both visiting us, Reverence."

"Ah." He nodded. "Yes, you have your own ways through the mountains from retreat to retreat, have you not? Well, Frostflower, perhaps you have the equivalent of our tokens to tell your people which of us farmer-priests are friends?"

He spoke lightly, but she cringed at the small hint that, for all the closeness they had found, even Elvannon shared the priestly mistrust of her people. "We injure no one, Reverence . . . not unless driven to it. Those strange symbols found now and then on farm walls are not our work."

Elvannon drew a box around each of the three names on his tablet to complete the guide for his coinsmith, who must engrave the letters without knowing how to read them. "It would be as well for you, Frostflower, not to make your knowledge of our scrolls and symbols apparent to any midlands priests. How soon will you leave?"

"The day after tomorrow."

"The tokens will be ready. Will you stop here to share our midday meal, even to spend your first night?"

The sorceress shook her head. "For myself, Reverence, you know how gratefully I would accept your offer. But I cannot speak for my friends."

He enclosed the slate in an old wooden case so that it could be carried without the charcoal marks smearing. "Well, stop at the gate for your tokens, then. It will be a long enough walk to All Roads South without your spending overmuch time here. And . . . we here in the edgelands have little influence on midlands ways,

Frostflower, but my wife's brother once journeyed to Center-of-Everywhere to claim his seat in the High Gathering for half a year. I can promise very little, but at a message of need from you, we will do what we can."

"If I should be in need and fail to send you that message, Reverence, it will be because I had no means nor time." The sorceress held out her hand and the priest took it, so that they sat for a moment with fingers meshed.

And yet, she thought wistfully, they had only mind-danced together over the outer symbols of doctrine and creed, never exploring—perhaps never daring to explore—the depths where truth might be found. She could read priestly writing, but she lacked the inbred perception that might suffuse those parables and rituals with meaning for the soul as well as for the brain.

She envied Windbourne his undoubting belief. But she did not envy him the . . . unhappiness? . . . that drove him to seek deadly penances for what seemed to her very small failings. Windbourne must not die before he had found some surer balance for life and death.

Frostflower no longer breast-fed Starwind; she had begun to wean him well before her first visit to Elvannon's Farm. She suspected the weaning had cost her more than it had the infant, who took readily to goat's milk, cow's milk, soft curds and vegetables boiled and strained to pulp. She had continued to feed him with spoons and pieces of saturated cloth when she was at home in the Retreat—now she must wean herself even from that. She might have had little sleep, that last night she held him in her cottage, if he had not slept with even more ease than usual, so that she soon put him in his cradle and lay down to lull herself with a few slow exercises lest her emotion disturb him.

She had actually felt greater personal misgivings the first time she left him to journey down to Elvannon's Farm, though that had been for a single day's absence. They told her he sometimes seemed to fuss and fret a little for her when she was gone, but on the whole he got along very happily with Puffball, Silverflake, Starsinger, and the others. Now she found herself calculating how much he would have grown by the time of her return in the fall. Would he even remember her after a summer's absence? Musing

on this, she felt the first slight doubt whether she would
return . . . she comforted herself with the reflection that, despite
all experience, a season seemed very long at its beginning, its end
very far off and unreal—it was this natural ignorance of the future,
as much as the specific danger awaiting her friends, that caused
her sudden fear of not returning to the child. But the season would
seem to have been very short, when it was past.

Thorn hugged the baby once just before they left, calling him
"Little Smellybottom" and laughing when he reached for her face.
But she showed no more regret at leaving him now than she had
shown at giving him to the sorceress after his emergence from her
body.

For a while it looked as if neither Dowl nor any other animal
would choose to join them. But at last, as they reached the double-
trunked pine, the dog caught up with them, thrusting his nose into
Frostflower's palm. And when they came to Nearest Curve, the
two-year-old white cat Coyclaws sprang from the top of the boulder
onto Windbourne's shoulders and curled there, *phsst*ing a little
and waving one paw at Dowl, as the sorcerer recovered from his
surprise.

Thorn laughed. "One for each of you, none for me! Good, I'll
share your bloody pets—I get to pat 'em when they're in a good
mood; they're all yours when they get mean and rowdy."

Frostflower smiled. "You must be careful with your language,
Rosethorn."

"Don't worry. Not one 'bloody demon,' not even a 'Hellstink,'
once we're on level ground. Not if I have to tie up my tongue and
go around as a mute myself. Right now, I'm too busy learning
how to climb down this blasted trail in this damn robe without
breaking my nose."

"But you cannot pose as a mute," said Windbourne. "You must
do the lying for all of us, Rosethorn." As if sensing the bitterness,
Coyclaws sprang from his shoulders and began walking by his
side.

When they reached Elvannon's Farm near midday, Thorn and
Windbourne waited on the muddy footpath, she to keep up ap-
pearances, he to avoid the contamination of a priest's outer wall.
Frostflower felt something like shame on his account as she crossed

the weed-field to the gates. Both Dowl and Coyclaws chose to accompany her.

Coarsecut was on guard alone this time; at the busy planting season, Elvannon's warriors took their turns with the work that fed and clothed the farm folk. The last midlands warrior who had spent the winter recuperating in the edgelands farm had departed some time ago, perhaps to avoid being drawn into what she considered degrading work for one of her class. (The sorceress had learned of this warriors' prejudice from Thorn, who shared it.)

"Safe traveling, Mixeyes!" The Raidleader held out three silver tokens, each dangling by its own string. "Yours is the one with one knot in the string, Rosethorn's with two knots, Windbourne's with three. Think you can remember?" Coarsecut winked. Sorceri and most common folk were not supposed to be able to read priestly symbols; they were only for other priests, townmasters, or the rare, eager common scholars to decipher. Nor had Elvannon told his people what he was teaching the sorceress on her visits. But the Raidleader, it appeared, might suspect that Frostflower did not need the knots to remind her which token was which.

"I will remember," said Frostflower.

"Why not call your friends over and we'll make sure they get the right ones? Do they still think we eat sorceri for dinner?"

Frostflower sighed and shook her head. "Some of my people are as strict in their beliefs as some of the midlands priests."

"Unh. Too bad. We had a table set up for you in the east orchard, but I guess you'll just have to settle for that flat old rock in the field out here." The Raidleader reached behind the wall and brought out a large slat-box. "Or you can carry it along."

The box was of cherrywood panels, carefully carved, varnished, and fitted together in such a way that when the container was empty it could be folded into a cube for easier carrying. It would probably bring a good price in the shops of Three Bridges or Five Roads Crossing. Elvannon was generous where he could afford generosity. "I will persuade my friends there is no danger in eating in the shadow of your walls," said Frostflower. "We'll return this at once when we've eaten."

Despite her promise, she might have had difficulty, even with Thorn's help, persuading Windbourne to sit in a field beside farm walls and partake of a dinner given them by a priest. But Coyclaws had lingered with the raidleader while Frostflower and Dowl turned back to the footpath and, on reaching the others, she learned from Windbourne, who spoke in a stunned voice, that "Coyclaws—the cat—she's gone into the Farm. She turned her head and stood stiff for a moment, then she streaked away behind the wall."

"She's gone after a mouse," said Thorn. "Or a bird. She'll be back when she's had her dinner. If you still want a bloody, meat-eating cat climbing on you and sullying your tender skin with the breath of farm air, Wedgepopper."

The young man, who already seemed more attached to Coy-claws than she to him, agreed to wait and eat in the field in hopes she would return by the end of their meal.

Although this was a thin season of the year for farmers' tables, Elvannon and his family had provided more than three travelers could eat and drink in one meal. There were wine, fermented milk, and minted water, each in a container made of tightly woven cloth, oiled and waxed, rather than of leather. Thin brown wafers, the best bread farmers themselves ate in spring; their well-baked crisp-ness helped mask the age of the flour. Two paste loaves firm enough to slice, one of dried vegetables cooked with new spring herbs, the other of dried fruits sweetened with honey. (When made for farmers' folk, they included chopped meat and insects.) Nine hard-boiled eggs and two flattened balls which Frostflower rec-ognized, even before removing the beeswax, as cheese.

Thorn, whose teeth must be aching by now for meat, began by peeling an egg and eating it cheerfully in three bites.

But Windbourne grumbled, "Priests' eggs! The farmer-priests allow as many cocks as they have to run constantly among their hens, do they not? How can we suppose these eggs are not fer-tilized?"

"You've never been inside a farm, Wedgepopper," said Thorn. "The priests keep their cocks separate, all right. They don't want to risk a little sunlight spoiling the eggs for their tables."

"I've heard that your priests consider chicks half-grown in the eggshell a great delicacy," he insisted.

"I'm not going to mention some of the things I used to hear that your people ate. There's no more chick in that egg than there is in your eyeball."

Thorn cut several slices from a vegetable loaf, layered a couple of them between three wafers, and took a large, crackling bite. "Not too bad without meat," she remarked. "Which of those bags has the milk, again?"

"Without meat?" Windbourne picked at a slice of the paste with his thumbnail and frowned. "What are these? Insects—weevils, tiny grubs. God, they're in the bread, too! The priests do not even sift the creatures from their flour before they bake it!"

"Those are seeds and spices," Thorn said firmly. "Eat it or go hungry. Don't pay any attention to him, Frostflower. I'm surprised he chews at all, for fear of biting his lip and swallowing a shred of his own skin."

Windbourne was silent for a time, drinking wine and picking every suspicious black seedlike thing from a slice of fruit paste. Frostflower ate a few layers of paste and wafers, repeating to herself that the specks were indeed merely seeds and spices used for flavoring. Then she peeled one of the cheeses. Here, at least, was safe food, as well as food so delectable, even at this time of year, that she had purposely saved it for last.

"Cheese!" said Windbourne in disgust. "Don't you know how they make it?"

"They cook milk and let it ripen," said Thorn.

"They throw in a piece of cow's stomach!"

"What the Hellstink do you *do* in that mind of yours?" Thorn exclaimed. "They just squeeze soft curds together and let 'em age—we ate soft curds up in the Retreat, didn't we?"

"And how do they make the curds meld and toughen and turn yellow?" said the sorcerer. "It's the juice from the cow's stomach that does it! Why do you think our people don't go on and make hard cheese from soft curds?"

"No!" cried Frostflower. "No, it can't—but some retreats *do* make cheese!"

"Aye," said Windbourne, "to their shame. And some sorceri with more laxity than prudence make leather of their dead cows' skins and white jelly of their hoofs. But you do not suppose the farmer-priests wait for cows to die naturally before cutting up their stomachs?"

If it was true . . . if this was indeed the secret which enabled farmers' folk to make cheese . . .

"I never heard about it," said Thorn, "and I've spent a damn lot more time inside farms than this bogbait has."

"My parents," said Windbourne, "left Southcorner Retreat because of the way they use the bodies of their dead animals there. Aye, they make cheese in some retreats. My mother saw it made."

"Thorn," whispered the sorceress, pushing the cheese toward her, "you must eat it. I . . . have eaten it all this spring—they would think me ungrateful suddenly to return it now." A tear was rolling down from her left eye, and she tried to wipe it away furtively, ashamed of feeling such grief for the loss of so shallow a pleasure.

"Damn you, sorcerer," Thorn muttered. "All right; Moonscar put me in command over you, and I'm commanding you now: If you see her eating anything else you happen to think she 'shouldn't,' keep your bloody tongue quiet about it."

Frostflower touched her friend's sleeve. "We have both been put in charge of guiding him—not of commanding, not the way you understand authority, Rosethorn. Am I to seek for deep truths and hide from minor ones?"

"It's not a question of looking for the truth, Frost, it's a question of finding enough food to fill our bellies. Demons' claws—"

"I will not speak, Rosethorn," said Windbourne. "But if Frostflower wishes to live by her own creed, she might do well to observe me and eat what I eat."

"Addle your brains with wine and then twist back your tongue at a little good, healthy cheese," Thorn grumbled, cutting off a slice of it and holding it out to Dowl on her palm. The dog nuzzled it up eagerly, and the warrior grunted in vindication as she wiped her hand on her black robe. "Maybe you people should take a few lessons from your own animals and not ask so many questions."

Frostflower tried to smile and ate another slice of fruit loaf. When she returned in the fall, she would ask Elvannon how cheese was made. In no other way could she explain her sudden refusal of a food she had enjoyed before . . . and if he lied, as she suspected Thorn had lied, to spare her conscience? —No, whatever he said, she must trust him. Perhaps, after all, there were other ways of making cheese. Meanwhile, for this summer, she would avoid it . . . and at these thoughts she wondered, If I should find the truth I seek, and it does not please me, will I be strong enough to recognize and accept it? Or will I pass it by as ugly and spend all my life searching barren and empty symbols for pleasant false-hoods? Will I prefer cheese to truth?

Coyclaws returned near the silent finish of their meal. She hopped up onto the rock, sat down near Windbourne in a place clear of food, and began washing her face. Thorn cut another small piece of cheese and held it out to her. The cat sniffed it for a moment, ate it, and went back to washing her face. Thorn glanced at Windbourne and started putting the food they had not eaten into their bag so that they could return the valuable box.

Chapter 6

Eleva had started out for the far northeast field to see how the new wheat was growing over Deveron's body; but, passing the forge, she paused to watch Rediron and his assistants at work. When she saw he was forging a scythe, she asked whether he did not have more pressing work at this season. Harvest was several hen's-hatchings in the future.

"Aye, Lady Reverence, but they'll be cutting the first hay before this hatching's out," said the smith.

"Your work is at your forge, Rediron, not walking about the fields deciding when the hay will be ready to cut." That statement sounded in her own ears sterner than she had intended; but although bred a priestess, she had only ruled the farm for a quarter of a year, and she still felt a degree of secret awe that a clean, smallish woman, by virtue of priestly birth, a white robe edged with gold, and a golden wreath on her head, could command a huge, grime-blackened man with a heavy hammer and a pair of assistants almost as muscular as himself. "Besides," she went on, seeking a way to compliment without seeming soft, "I think you can produce an excellent scythe in less than a day, can you not?"

He grunted, grinning. "Less than half a day, Lady Reverence."

"Well, then! Surely you have more pressing work. Our warriors—have they all the good swords and spears they need?"

He grunted again, this time in displeasure. "Most of 'em wouldn't take weapons of my forging, Lady Reverence. Call me 'clumsy plowmaker,' some of 'em do. Like that farting—" he touched fist to mouth in apology for the language "—like Your Reverence's raidleader, that Splitgut. Go buy their weapons from those lazy town weaponsmiths instead."

"I will speak with Splitgut. Perhaps Deveron set their wages too high if they can afford to squander their money. Meanwhile, several of our wagons need new wheelrims. Replace those on my small townmarket wagon first. I will very likely want to visit the flowerbreeder in Five Roads again, if not the townmaster, well before the hay is ready for cutting."

Rediron nodded. Eleva reflected that she knew of very few flowerbreeders who still lived in farms; hence, priests' visits to town flowerbreeders harmed no farm artisans, while the luxury of flowers for decoration was a recognized privilege of even the poorest priests.

Why should it be exclusively so? Many townsfolk, including some of the poorest, indulged in planting purely ornamental flowers wherever they had enough earth around their dwellings or could set a crock of dirt near a window—else the flowerbreeders would not have moved from farms to towns and grown wealthy. Why must farmworkers be content with the short-lived blooms of their useful plants?

Her thoughts were broken off by sight of Sprint, the cobbler's younger son, scrabbling around on the smithy's earth floor, picking up small things and putting them into a large, dirty sack. "What are you doing, young farmworker?" demanded the priestess.

He looked up at her, touched fist to forehead, grinned, and held his sack open so that she could see its contents—little crumbs, splinters, and shavings of metal.

"Ah. Good. But would it not be better to search for them when Rediron and his forgeworkers are at rest?"

"We've got a trade, Lady Reverence. I get to keep the smaller chunks if they get the chance to step on me and make me squeal. I get more chunks than they get squeals."

Eleva forced herself to smile, though she would rather have

frowned. "A rough sport. Well, I'll permit it—but if you should gain a broken hand or rib from this, there will be more than squeals from all who were present. I'll not have my workers maimed in sport before they're even old enough to choose their adult names! And what makes your chunks worth the risk, Sprint?"

Grinning more broadly than before, he held one up to her. "Look at it, Lady Reverence—it's just the right size, and sharp and lumpy and heavy! Lazy old Scratcher won't have enough stones sharpened, no matter how long they take to catch the rotten sorceron who killed His Reverence—but these'll scratch his guts pretty good going down, won't they?"

"Go back to your mother's cottage and have her teach you how to cobble!" said the priestess. "We will waste no good iron for an execution!"

The boy stared up at her open-mouthed for a moment, then got to his feet and scampered away. Eleva glanced at the shortness of the shadows and decided to return to the Hall. She was too discomposed for a reverent visit to her husband's field of burial.

Swallowing sharpened pebbles would be a fitting punishment for Deveron's murderer. Stones were the nearest means that honest people could use to approximate the stomach-grown insects of the sorceri.

There were, of course, natural plant poisons as evil in their effects as sorcery. But the common folk must not be shown that priests knew how to extract and strengthen the natural poisons, nor should physicians be given any plausible reason, such as preparing poison for an execution, to dabble in the wicked skill. So it must be stones . . . if the sorcerer were found. But he must be the same one who had been captured the first time. Rondasu had suggested a purge of all sorceri who might have been seen in the area between String-of-Beads and Fourth Road Ends from the spring before Deveron's death to the spring following it; but Eleva, as Deveron's ruling widow, refused to let more than one person suffer.

And the warrior who had helped that sorcerer escape? No, thought Eleva, she is not my responsibility. Leave her punishment, if she is ever found, to the devising of Master Youngwise.

By the time she neared the Hall, however, satisfaction at remembering how easily she had made both the huge smith Rediron

and the boy Sprint yield to her will had largely replaced less
pleasant thoughts. She was in command of herself and her Farm.
When Evron was old enough, she would find him a young widow
or brotherless daughter for his bride. There was the daughter of
Inmara, near the Rockroots; news had just come a hen's-hatching
ago of the safe birth of this child, the last one begotten by Reverence Maldron before his death—true, Maldron left two sons by
other wives, but the son by the dead wife was said to be ambitious
to wall in a new farm of his own, his full sister was all but promised
to a nephew of Inmara's, Maldron's third wife had returned with
her children to her brother's farm and was not unlikely to marry
again; and thus Inmara's daughter might, perhaps, inherit. Within
the next four to seven winters Eleva must make the journey to visit
Inmara's Farm.

Or there was Amron's daughter Mikka, if the old priest did not
beget a son yet on his younger wife; his land in the curve of the
Western Rushwater was good, though liable to floods. Failing all
else, Eleva might find a raidleader worthy the name and capture
a farm for Evron; after this taste of power, the priestess doubted
that she would be willing to give her own farm over into the rule
of her son and tamely retire to Center-of-Everywhere to claim her
place among the old and landless priests who, in practice, com-
posed most of the High Gathering.

There would be a husband to find for little Evra, too . . . if only,
thought Eleva, I could find her an old priest with no sons or living
older wives—a man still young enough to give her a few years
of pleasure and a child or two, but old enough to die and leave
her the rule of his farm while she is still in her prime! She will
want rule, for I will train her in its skills. As I myself was not
trained.

In the more immediate future, Eleva decided to eat the midday
meal with her children and their young nurse Blowingbud in the
apple-tree arbor. Then, when Evron and Evra were in bed for their
afternoon naps, she would pay her visit to Deveron's burial-field.
Later in the year, when the wheat was heading, she would take
the children; she thought she would be better able to explain where
their father was if she could show them the grain nearing its
harvest.

Eleva's plans for the rest of the day did not include Intassa, whom she found waiting for her on the bench beneath the old peach trees in the walled garden.

"You should have sent Lightheels or Dart to let me know you were here," said Eleva.

"I could not find the pipe. It always used to be in its niche beside the office."

Eleva found it more convenient to keep the small silver pipe used for summoning messenger-servants on her table in the office. "There is no reason you should not go into the office for it, Intassa. You are free enough in the rest of my hall."

Intassa shook her head. "I know you leave the curtain open when you're not inside, Lady Eleva, but Rondasu would not want me to grow into a habit of entering the ruling office. And I never went into it before, you know. I've never been inside a ruling office anywhere, and never wish to be."

"Cows' breath! That's no boast, it's a pity. Every farmer should know something of how to rule."

"Every priest, perhaps. Not every priestess."

"Every priest and every priestess as well! You may think you'll always be safe from it, Intassa. You had—was it three brothers by your father's older wives?"

"Four," said Intassa. "And one older sister."

"And then you became a second wife, and now you have a strong, young new husband, a good, healthy son, and a husband's sister old enough to take over rule from you if anything should widow you again."

Intassa made the circle against evil.

Eleva ruthlessly went on. "But suppose some accident were to take Rondasu and Shara both, before Invaron grew old enough to rule? Almost thirteen years, and Invaron your only child. Or suppose Rondasu and Shara should both be called from their farm at the same time? You ought to be able to take the governing for a few hen's-hatchings, at least! Sweet innocent, with so few of you in the hall, either you should learn how to govern at need, or else you should persuade my brother to marry two or three more wives, each one older than you."

Intassa held her palms out helplessly, her pale gray eyes seeming to symbolize the utter impossibility of her ever managing the rule of a farm. "Rondasu would not teach me. And he will not

marry anyone else—he says so often that between Shara and me
he has all the women he needs. Her to see to the household and
me to give him a bed and children."

Eleva sighed. "You're right, Rondasu would not teach you.
And as for marrying another . . ." She paused. That Rondasu had
never seemed desirous of even one wife used to worry his father
and mother. Once, when Eleva was old enough to know and have
witnessed the birth-end of procreation but not old enough to witness
the mysteries of Aomu and Voma, she had awakened at night in
her bedchamber and heard her father shouting at Rondasu, threatening him with a dangling lustration and other harsh purifications . . . in the morning, she had not dared question her father, but
her mother said she must have dreamed it, and her sister Shara
had said their father was angry because Rondasu had "tried the
bald god's harrow." (Shara would not explain what this meant;
the elder by seven years, she rarely spoke to Eleva except to tease.)
"As for Rondasu's marrying another," she went on, "it's good that
he so loves you as to want no other now, but if he wants children
of his own . . . He does know of the difficulties of Invaron's birth?"

"He knows." Intassa's smile lent a sheen to her eyes. "He says
it need not mean there will be danger with the others, especially
if the father is different."

"And so you would risk it again? On Rondasu's confidence
and prayers?"

Intassa nodded.

A wave of hot fear went through Eleva's mind. "You really
love him so much, Intassa?"

"Yes! Oh, Eleva, I love him, because he loves me—he is the
first man to love me for myself. Forgive me, I know how you
loved Deveron, and I loved him, too, but it was always you he
loved best, you, his first wife. I was merely for variety, an extra
ornament for his ceremonials, a bed to come to when you needed
to rest alone. Rondasu . . . Rondasu is to me what Deveron was
to you. I suppose it can only be so between husband and first
wife."

Eleva shivered. This was not how their household had seemed
to her. She would have said it was herself whom Deveron had
married for convenience—a priestess for his ceremonials, a pro-
genit is for his heirs—and Intassa whom he had married for pure

love, to whose bed he had gone the more gladly.

Intassa apparently saw the shiver and misunderstood it. "Oh, forgive me, Eleva! I had almost . . . it's wicked to flaunt my happiness when you've lost—"

"No! Your happiness is mine." It was a formula response, nor could Eleva so much as utter it sincerely—not because she envied Intassa now, but because she could not believe that Intassa's present happiness would prove solid. "Nevertheless . . . Intassa, it may not remain so smooth. They say every priest needs two wives, even three, or he grows weary, irritable."

"No," said Intassa. "Not Rondasu. You cannot understand him as I do, Eleva—being his sister, you can hardly see him as a husband."

"True," Eleva said dryly. And yet she had often sensed a power in Rondasu, as if he might prove strong and supple as Aomu or Raes, with the right bedfellow. Sometimes the sense of it had been so strong as to make her uneasy when with him, grateful but at the same time a little regretful that she was his sib. This supposed fear for Intassa's happiness—might it not, after all, be mere envy? "Well," she went on, "enjoy him then, Intassa. And if you are willing to bear again, Raes and Aeronu bless you, Aomu and Voma make you fertile. Shall I arrange a small ceremony for you here?"

"That . . . that's very good of you, Lady Eleva, but . . ." Intassa lowered her gaze.

"But? And I hardly see why you should call me 'Lady,'" said Eleva, annoyed at the formality. "Rondasu never does—not in earnest. He seems to think I'm playing at rule. He'd rather I gave my Farm into his capable hands and spent all my time studying the scrolls." She forced a laugh. "I suppose, if I find it difficult to see why you love him, that's the reason."

Intassa picked at the cloth of her skirt as if trying to work a snagged thread back into place. "Are you sure you would not be happier, Eleva?"

"Happier? To sit forever combing out where Voma's work ends and Aeronu's begins, how many talons Azkor has in his left front claw and what the middle letter of Jehandru's Seventh Secret Name may be?"

"Rondasu says it might be best if you did spend more time

reading the scrolls, Eleva. He says—"

"Ah. Rondasu the learned and virtuous still fears for his poor little sister's destiny at the Harvest Gate, does he? So that's the reason you're shy of accepting my prayers—Rondasu the beloved of the gods has told you about the sorcery of my steambeds."

"They . . . they really do seem . . . impious somehow, Eleva."

"Aomu and Voma are the same in my steambeds as anywhere else on the surface of the Tanglelands, and if my attempts to start their spring labors early are impious and blasphemous, so is every cartload of manure and compost we spread on our fields, so is the pulling of every natural weed that threatens to choke a planted sprout—so is all cultivation!"

Intassa had risen, her face pale. "Eleva, have you—will you bring down the gods' blight on Deveron's Farm?"

About to respond that such a blight would no doubt please Rondasu, justifying his opinion and laying her farm open to his taking, Eleva choked back the words and instead replied, as gently as she could, "So you have come to beg me to return with you, as your husband wishes?"

"No . . . no, only to ask you, on his behalf, if you will not open your hall to his brotherly visits again."

"*Brotherly* visits! Rondasu's word, or his wife's?"

"But I—speaking for myself, Eleva, it would complete my happiness if you were to return. Shara is kind to me, but she is . . . too kind, I think—too constantly polite. We need your leaven, your honest speaking, your—your roughness, sometimes. And I think Invaron misses the other children."

"The widowed sister in the older brother's household!" Eleva drew a deep, shuddering breath. "You would not have me with you for long, Intassa. He would find some distant priest for my new husband, so as to have me far away and his claim to this farm settled beyond dispute. And I would accept the new marriage, even as the third wife of some doddering old fool, only to be away from my sibs. No. I will never remarry, and I will never go back to my brother's farm."

Intassa came forward and laid her hand on the other woman's arm. "Deveron was a wonderful mate. Even Rondasu, to whom I am more, who loves me better, cannot surpass him in coupling, and I know what he must have been to you, his first wife. But is it not better, Eleva, to have a mate than the rule of a farm?"

Eleva rose. She was the shorter of the two by half a head, but she felt immeasurably the stronger. "You made your choice. I would have given you a share in ruling this farm; but perhaps, for you, a husband is indeed the better choice. For me, it is the farm. If ever I do take another husband, he will be a commoner."

Intassa's fingers closed tightly around Eleva's wrist. "A commoner? A common worker or merchant to sit in Deveron's office?"

"Of course not! A commoner to warm my bed and leave me my ruling office." Had Intassa never heard of such marriages, or was she so fully imbued with the idea that the husband must rule that she discounted all tales to the contrary? "Yes, perhaps I'll marry my smith Rediron! That will stop Rondasu's schemes to find me a husband and take away my farm."

"Your smith?" Intassa recoiled. "Oh, no, Eleva, not that huge, grimy creature to—to sleep where Deveron—"

"Why not? By the Seven Names, Intassa, sooner than give up this farm, I would marry the sorcerer himself!"

Intassa shrank from her as from a rotted corpse. "Deveron's murderer?"

Eleva regretted her words. When Intassa told Rondasu and Shara that her sister had said such a thing . . . "I said that only for emphasis." She tried to laugh. "A priestess marry a sorcerer! See to what foolish statements conversation leads when it is not kept strictly polite." She extended her palms for the parting gesture. "Return to my hall whenever you wish, Intassa. Bring Invaron— stay the night if you will. I want neither Rondasu nor Shara within my walls again, but you and your child will ever be welcome."

Intassa hesitated, then laid her palms on Eleva's too lightly and quickly for full contact before she hurried away. Watching her go, Eleva guessed that she would not return.

Chapter 7

Windbourne had grown milder toward his companions as the days went on, but he seemed also to have grown even more bitter, perhaps because more silent and inbrooding, toward himself and his own supposed guilt. Once, waking before dawn, Thorn had found him squatting beside the remains of their forest campfire, holding an ember to his thigh—he had peeled off a small piece of his own skin and was cauterizing the wound. When they reminded him of Moonscar's instruction to inflict no grim penances on himself without first seeking their opinion, he had protested that he needed to purge himself at once of an evil dream, that he had not wanted to disturb their sleep, and that this was no grim or deadly penance—he had appealed to Thorn if it could not be meted out to a warrior and she consider herself fortunate at getting off lightly. Replying that it all depended on the offense, Thorn had given him a warrior's command to do no such thing again; but after that morning they had considered it wisest to allow him whichever of his self-punishments seemed least likely to injure his health, hoping this would be enough to drain off some of his desire for pain before it built up too dangerously inside him. Several times Thorn had yielded so far to his pleas as to whip him with her belt or a thin tree branch. "I never wanted that kind of boggy work before," she had confided to Frostflower, "but he drives me so itchy it's almost a pleasure."

The first clear hint of increasing danger came when they reached String-of-Beads, a small town only a quarter of a day's walk north of Five Roads. Windbourne knew of one family here, a widowed potter and her children, who had been friendly to sorceri; but he and Thorn had not contacted them on their way north in the winter, and when Frostflower approached the shop window now, the woman frowned, shook her head slightly, and dropped the shutter.

Perhaps the widow was simply overcautious. They had better luck with the old innkeeper of the Silver Pear, who sold them the use of the room above her stable with a grin and the cheerful words, "If the warriors come, it's between you and them. I'll neither warn you nor deny I'm keeping you, though I won't help them much, neither—thank the gods, the time's past when anyone could have pressed my old undermouth into service against a sorcerer . . . gone now, like the best of my eyesight . . . and as for the stable, you wouldn't hurt me by blasting it—needs a new upper part anyway, and they say Their Reverences are generous enough when it comes to repaying folk for sorcerous damage. Meanwhile, I've always found blackrobes' pay as solid as any and more solid than some. And likely you'll be safe enough here. Wise of you three to stop in String and not in Five Roads, though. Aye, if you'll listen to an old innkeeper, you'll go past Five Roads by the Western Footaround and on through Fourth Road Ends to Epplewhim."

"I fear we have an errand in Five Roads," said Frostflower .

"Oh, aye? Well, like as not it's safe enough if you mean no mischief. But I'd sit up above my stable awhile and think about how important my business was. Especially if any of you should happen to be a young sorcerer with buttermilk hair and a cleft in his chin, as might be mistaken for another young sorcerer they caught in Five Roads last winter and let slip loose again."

Windbourne was enduring another self-imposed penance that day, a sunrise-to-sunrise fast. He asked to add an hour of kneeling with arms outstretched, and they left him in that posture while they went down to the inn's mealroom, a little after the townsfolk's usual suppertime, to eat bread and porridge. A small storm arose while they ate. Frostflower hoped no one would learn of Windbourne's kneeling and blame the weather on his sorcering rather than the season. Fortunately, the storm was short and mild, and soon settled down into a soft, thunderless rainfall, which Pear-keeper remarked would be welcome on the farmers' fields.

It was not so welcome on their robes as they returned from the main inn building to their room above the stable. They found Windbourne already asleep, exhausted from his penances, and Thorn remarked that was just as well, since they had to take off their outer robes before the wetness soaked through to their un-dergarments. (But Windbourne could not have seen much more than a few blurs of light cloth in the dark room. String-of-Beads, like most other towns, allowed sorceri no fire, at least in the warmer seasons—no lamp, candle, nor brazier, nothing except a few pots of smudge-incense to keep away the insects.) The two women spread their robes on chair and table, then wrapped them-selves in fraying blankets for warmth and sat talking a long time, while the full moon, rising higher, infused the thinning clouds with a glow that gradually brightened the chamber, the stable animals occasionally stamped or snorted below, and Dowl and Coyclaws alternately napped and roamed about in search of a caressing hand or other entertainment. Eventually the cat curled in Frostflower's lap, while the dog nosed her and the sorceress tried to stroke both at once.

"I wouldn't walk beside you." Thorn was arguing. "Nobody'd guess we were together, but I'd be where I could look out for you."

"You must not think me so incapable of avoiding danger when left on my own." Frostflower left off stroking the animals to grope for Thorn's hand. "And where would we find the clothes for your change of disguise?"

"Oh, Hellbog!" said Thorn. Coyclaws was now twining her paws over the women's arms, seemingly intent on wrestling Frost-flower's hand back to herself.

Dowl was thrusting his nose into Thorn's hand. "Why not just free-travel all the way there and back?" the warrior went on, absently tugging Dowl's ear.

"Deveron's death was almost five hatchings ago, Rosethorn. Folk no longer talk of it constantly, even here; how much more seldom will they talk of it in a large and busy town like Five

Roads? Free-traveling, I would have to depend entirely on chance-heard conversation. In the body, I may be able to ask a few questions—"

"Better be pretty damn careful about that!"

Frostflower smiled. "We live by a vow of prudence, Rosethorn."

Apparently Thorn tugged too hard, for Dowl gave a little yelp, ducked his head, and shook it. "Why not send Wedgepopper in alone?" said the warrior, ignoring the dog. "He'll insist on going in sooner or later anyway—let him do it now and take the danger."

"He has not quite found the third skill yet. He can sit up, out of his body, and speak with my entity, but he could not free-travel back to us here from Five Roads to tell us what he's learned."

Thorn shrugged. Dowl, as if impatient with both women, trotted across the room to curl on the floor beside the sleeping Windbourne.

"And you must remain here with him, Rosethorn," Frostflower continued. "If we leave him alone . . ."

Coyclaws jumped down from Frostflower's lap, bounded across the room, and sprang upon Dowl. After a brief spat—more of surprise than resistance on the dog's part—Dowl left the place beside Windbourne to Coyclaws and trotted back to the sorceress. Windbourne had not stirred. Possibly he was in trance.

"All right," said Thorn. "I don't like it, but all right. Find out what you can; we'll see that Wedgepopper waits out for you tomorrow night. I'll expect you back in the body the night after that, or we come in after you. Will the mongrel go with you or stay with us?"

"As he chooses."

In the morning, Thorn grumbled that Frostflower had won her consent to the "woodbrained plan" by catching her tired and off-guard, but she kept her word and let her friend go on alone. Dowl glanced from one to the other of the humans several times, as if puzzled by this friendly separation here in the midlands, but at last he loped after Frostflower. She was grateful for his companionship; it cost her more than she would admit to leave Thorn now, even for Thorn's own safety.

It was a relief, however, to be free for a time from Windbourne, who seemed in his very silence to reproach her thoughts, doubts, and actions. Was that, she sometimes wondered, how I seemed to Thorn last summer, before I lost my certitude?

She had long known that different retreats had different practices and different interpretations of creed and religion; but she had always thought the differences of practice were minor and those of interpretation theoretical. She had had little direct contact until now with the sorceri of any other retreat except Mildrock, the home of her almost-lover Wonderhope and her sister Cloudbird. In some ways, Windbourne's attitude shook her faith in her own creed almost as much as what had happened to her last summer.

He had asked her once whether the ballads sung of her were true, and she had told him the tale stripped of its exaggerations and misconceptions. She had vaguely hoped that with his strict faith and stranger's impartiality he might succeed where even wise Moonscar had failed, and find a satisfactory explanation for how she had retained her power after losing her virginity. He seemed not to have looked for an explanation; he had merely said that, in his opinion, she was wrong to continue practicing her skills. She did not understand how a man of his strict conscience could have dismissed her problem as easily as he seemed to. She suspected he thought of it more than he let her see. She had not gone on to tell him in words that this was the chief reason she now studied the priestly creed, so perhaps she was as shy of thought-sharing as he.

Five Roads Crossing had ten gates, two for each of the roads of its name (though one "road" was more accurately a wheelpath). The Northwest Gate that Frostflower approached was set in a new section of the wall.

Long ago, towns, like farms, had been subject to raids by farmer-priests or rival townmasters. The Town Truce of the High Priestly Gathering had stopped this more than two lifetimes ago, and many towns, like String-of-Beads, had let their walls fall into disrepair. Most of the smaller towns built since the Truce had never had walls, and larger towns that still kept their walls in good repair rarely enlarged them. Some of the wealthier families preferred to erect new houses outside the walls, though such houses frequently had their own small walls surrounding the gardens, with a few hired warriors to guard against thieves.

Five Roads, however, still took obvious pride in its walls, enlarging them so that only a few of the poorest folk lived outside and a very few of the richest, who built against the town wall so that their private walls bulged out here and there like warts. Nor was this town pride entirely archaic. Thorn said that town walls still served two practical purposes besides showing off prosperity: to keep wildland outlaws shut out in the open where the occasional peace-guarding patrols of spearwomen could skewer them, and to keep town lawbreakers inside where townwarriors could catch them.

As the sorceress came nearer, she saw two warriors in the open gateway, apparently leaning against the posts. According to Thorn, the swordswoman or axewoman was supposed to stand in the gateway while the spearwoman walked back and forth. Would Thorn frown and call this spearwoman a loafer?

"Sorceron coming!" the watchgirl whooped down to the warriors in a much less pleasant shout than Elvannon's watchgirl had used that first time. A brief conversation followed between watchgirl and warriors. Then all three faces turned toward her—one warrior at each side of the gateway and the watchgirl above in the frame of her cupping tower with its pillars and tiled roof. The sorceress was still too far away to read their expressions. Surprisingly, since it was not long past midmorning, no other folk were within sight. She went on towards the gate with head bowed, one hand stroking Dowl, the other in her pocket, closed over Elvannon's safe-passage token.

Thorn had made Windbourne bury his token at a distinctive oak between All Roads South and Elderbarren; the coinlike bit of metal bore his name, which might be known. The warrior was not eager to use her own token, for she said that the similarity between "Rosethorn" and "Thorn," which might slide by well enough when the name was only spoken, would probably look obvious when someone who could read saw it in engraved letters. It would have seemed strange if not all sorceri of a group had tokens, so the women had carried theirs out of sight, Rosethorn's with the string broken and Frostflower's without the string, to show why they were not being worn, if the need to show them should arise. So far, it had not arisen.

When Frostflower came within five paces of the warriors, she stopped to be hailed and questioned, the customary procedure for commoners and sorceri alike.

"What are you, sorceron?" said the axewoman.

"Frostflower, from the northern mountains."

"Not who. Hellbog, names are just names. *What*—an ''er' or an ''ess'?"

Frostflower lifted her hand from Dowl's head lest she grip his fur too tightly. "I am a woman."

"Vuck's claws!" said the spearwoman. "Better feel it and make sure."

The axewoman guffawed. "Feel her yourself, Whistlepoint! ''Er' or ''ess,' she's too small to be the one that killed His Reverence, anyway."

"Oh, yes, you can laugh, Splathandle. You don't stand to lose three kips!"

"The more fool you, to bet on a sorceron's sex with Fleaglance— I tell you, the brat never misses."

"Come on, Whistlepoint," the watchgirl shouted down, "either feel her or pay me now!"

There was a thin, rushing sound, and Frostflower glanced up just in time to see the watchgirl catch the coin Whistlepoint had thrown up to her.

"Malice, malice, hang for spite!" chanted the watchgirl. "Tried to catch me offguard, hey? All right, let's have the other two!"

The spearwoman threw both coppers at once. The watchgirl gave a cry of outrage. "Stone you, Whistlepoint, one of 'em fell—"

"Look for it when you're off duty!" said Splathandle with a laugh. "You gamblers deserve each other. All right, sorceress, go on in."

"Are there any special restrictions I must know?" said Frostflower.

"Don't try to sell anything," the axewoman replied in a quick monotone. "Don't buy anything sharp or made of metal, don't get drunk, don't come closer than three paces to a fire, lamp, or candle, and if you buy a sleeping room to yourself, no flame or constant-wick allowed—smudge-incense, all right, if somebody else lights it. Don't stand within four paces of a statue, don't enter a holy hall." The monotone broke. "And don't put wasps in our priests' bellies."

Frostflower nodded and went in. She walked ten paces down the street and paused, struck by the near-desertion of the area. A few pigs, their ears clipped to show they belonged to the townmasters, scavenged the street. A cat who was dozing in a window woke long enough to spit at Dowl as he stopped to sniff her. All the doors were closed and the shop windows shuttered. From the middle floor of one of the houses Frostflower heard someone trying to lull a wailing infant.

She turned and saw the gatewarriors grinning as they watched her. She walked halfway back to them and asked, "Is this some holiday? Surely it is not a sickness in the town?"

The axewoman chuckled. "Not a holiday, but might as well be one. Our local Reverences are holding solemn ceremony—a quarter of the day in each holy hall, fines for not attending. You came to the wrong gate if you hope to get a meal, 'ess. This part of town'll be empty till midday. You might try the Fat Suckling Inn, a hundred paces from South Center Gate, but you'd better walk fast if you want to eat your porridge before Their Reverences move on to the South Holy Hall."

"You are permitted to tell me the reason for the ceremonies?"

"Nothing that'd interest your kind," said Whistlepoint.

"Nor us, neither," said Splathandle. "Gate duty's a pleasure when it looses you from solemn harangues. Thank your demons you're not allowed in the holy halls, 'ess."

"You told me nothing of this before."

"They had another bet, these two scramblebrains," said Splathandle, "whether you'd come back to ask. The watchbrat won again."

"Better hurry on to the Fat Suckling, you and your mangy dog," the watchgirl shouted down, "if you want to fill your bellies before that side of town shuts up!"

Frostflower glanced up. "Can you not shout more softly to one who has brought you wealth today?" Then, to the axewoman, she added, "How is it they lock their doors here beneath your very eyes?"

"Vuck's claws!" cried Whistlepoint, thumping her spear against the ground.

But Splathandle laughed. "They lock their doors out of pure kindness, so the thieves won't come around to be caught and gutted, and so we can spend our time making silly bets instead of watching shops."

Frostflower touched her fingers to her lips in a peaceable imitation of the warriors' salute. To return a strange warrior's jests was to strain her vow of prudence, but at least she seemed to have gauged Splathandle's temper correctly—condescending but far from malicious.

The wagers of the spearwoman and watchgirl, the axewoman's lack of malevolence, suggested that the general attitude toward sorceri was much more relaxed here in Five Roads than their experiences in String-of-Beads had led them to fear. Might the fact that Deveron's murder aroused no greater nervousness toward black robes indicate that other townwarriors, like Thorn, secretly disbelieved in Windbourne's guilt? Might Splathandle's "Don't put wasps in our priests' bellies" have been meant as a friendly caution? Yet the warriors were still watching for a sorcerer of Windbourne's description—she must warn him of that. She wished she could warn her swordswoman friend directly at the same time, for she could not help but mistrust Windbourne's prudence; but her free-traveling entity could not touch Thorn's senses.

Here in the town's edges, the streets were curving, with numerous sudden angles and unexpected alleys. The oldest part of Five Roads, that which had been in the center of the area enclosed by the original walls, would probably have straight streets, but for now Frostflower's attempts to proceed toward South Center Gate were often baffled, as if she were in a maze.

Doubting that she could reach the inn before the people of that part of town began to gather in their holy hall, the sorceress reconciled herself to the prospect of an empty stomach until midafternoon. "Poor Dowl," she murmured, pulling him away from some budding rosebushes beside a shop that looked as if it had once belonged to a wealthy family.

Why did towns like Five Roads grow so large? Frostflower found nothing appealing in them. If I were of the farmers' folk, she thought, I would prefer to live in a cottage in some good priest's farm. Yet folk left smaller towns like String-of-Beads and Frog-in-the-Millstone to settle in larger ones. And not all the in-

crease of a town's size was due to the increase of its population;
as folk grew rich enough, they built larger houses with more garden
land around them. Frostflower passed several of these luxurious
homes, walled about like farmers' personal gardens to shut them
off from the shops and dwellings of poorer folk. The flowerbreeder
Crinkpetal lived in such a house. He might give her clearer information than Baconcrunch of the Fat Suckling Inn could provide,
and a safer place to leave her body while she free-traveled back
to Thorn and Windbourne tonight.

In winding through the tangled streets, she chanced on the holy
hall for this section. The folk gathered inside were beginning a
hymn, all of them lifting their voices at once in one of the priestly
melodies. The sorceress paused. A year ago such music had
seemed alien, disturbing, and unlovely to her. But she had heard
much of it in Elvannon's Farm; he and his family had sung some
of the more informal hymns and hymnlike ballads of their class
for her, and even allowed her to witness, from a little distance,
part of the Unblanketing of Aomu and Voma—the celebration of
the melting snow—and some of the Planting Rites. Now she could
hear beauty in the mysterious minor keys and patterns in the fluc-
tuating rhythms. And, when she heard so many farmers' folk
singing at once—their voices reverberating through the great, high
temple almost as through a very small valley—she seemed to feel
for a moment the same impulse that led so many people to live
close together in a crowded, malodorous town.

Drawn by the reverent majesty of the hymn, she crossed the
open yard and sat cross-legged at one side of the temple's gauze-
curtained door. Dowl lay beside her with one soft sigh and a few
thumps of his tail.

This hymn was in the ancient language of the priests. As spoken
and explained by Elvannon and his family, it seemed to bear some
resemblance to the ancient language of the sorceri. Frostflower
caught the word for "seven," and soon afterwards a sound that
resembled the ancient sorcerous word for "tree," and from these
she guessed it might be a hymn to Jehandru of the Seven Secret
Names, often depicted in priestly statuary as a tree.

When the hymn was finished, three women, almost certainly
priestesses, read a long passage from the Second Scroll of the
Afterdeath—a dialogue in which Jehandru's intermediary Maejira

the Merciful and the demon Azkor took turns describing to the Death Goddess Eshesha the rewards and punishments they would mete out to the good and the guilty after death. Frostflower thought it varied slightly from the version she had studied in Elvannon's copy of the scroll, but she could not be sure.

On two occasions during their journey south, Windbourne had surprised her by asking what she had learned of the farmer-priests' religion. The first time, she had tried to explain their idea that all plants and many insects were generated by the constant coupling of the Earth God Aomu and the Soil Goddess Voma, but he had quickly cut her short. The second time, guessing that what he really wanted was to hear something that might help him think gently of the priestess Eleva, she had spoken of the farmers' conception of "the Glorious Harvest," which did not differ so greatly in its essentials from the sorcerous belief of afterdeath. But she had not added particulars of the farmers' Hellbog, for which sorceri had no parallel idea, nor had he asked for any, although he had heard Thorn and other farmers' folk refer often enough to Hellbog and its demons.

After the reading, a man's voice took over the ceremony. This would be the presiding priest, probably Rondasu, who Thorn said was the nearest male priest left within a few hours' travel of Five Roads. His voice was rich and deep and might have been pleasant, but for his words:

"Children. No, not children—fools and idlers. Almost half a year ago, a priest was murdered almost in your midst. A great priest, my own brother by marriage. You allowed the murderer to escape from your very town. Does the Great Giver of Justice smile on you for this?"

Frostflower's eyes remained shut, but her back stiffened and her muscles tensed.

"True," the farmer-priest went on, "Deveron was not your master, nor am I, nor is my sister, the Lady Reverence. You live under townmasters, and some of you take pride in that, as if it made you stronger in yourselves, less dependent on the Gods and their priests. But it is to priests alone, not to townmasters, that the Gods reveal their laws! Your townmasters receive the laws from the priests, and so you, towndwellers, in return for some fancied increase of freedom, receive the laws and wishes of the Gods only

at third remove. Can you remain complacent? Or should you not
bestir yourselves to greater efforts, lest you lose what little you
have?"

Dowl began to thump his tail against the pavement. The sorceress became aware of footsteps walking towards her across the
yard. She opened her eyes and saw a swordswoman approaching.

"Dare you allow a priest's murderer to escape, in your laziness
and cowardice," the priest went on inside, "and not fear that He
of the Seven Secret Names will strike down your town walls,
destroy your proud wealth and make your boasted freedom like
stones in your throats?"

The swordswoman was now close enough to question Frostflower in a low voice. "Didn't they warn you to avoid holy halls,
sorceress?"

Frostflower crossed her arms over her breast in a gesture of
submission. "The gatewarriors warned me not to go inside, warrior. I did not think it would be unlawful to sit quietly outside."

Undisturbed by their soft exchange, the priest's voice continued. "Some of you must have connived at the sorcerer's escape—
an act so abominable in the sight of the Great God of Justice, so
abhorrent to all the deities—"

The new warrior had gray hair and lines of weariness around
her eyes. At her waist hung a tubular copper sheath, half an arm's
length long, tied by a copper chain. "What interest would a sorceron have in listening to a priestly ceremony? Aren't you committing some kind of sin by your own notions?"

"—only by coming to the priests can the guilty townsman or
townswoman be purged," the priest was saying. "Only by confessing in secrecy and submitting to purifications."

"They were singing when I first sat here," said Frostflower.
"It was so lovely that I saw no harm in listening."

"Well, they're not singing now. I suppose you find His Reverence's scolding lovely, too? How much have you heard?"

Frostflower shrugged and shifted her legs. "Enough to know
it lacks the beauty of the singing." Dowl got up and walked to the
warrior, who gave him a few pats. "If you'll tell me which part
of town had the first ceremony this morning, warrior," Frostflower
went on, "so that I may go there and buy a meal—"

"I'm afraid not, sorceress." The warrior unchained her copper sheath. "Stand up and put your hands behind your back."

The sorceress rose, trembling a little, but did not turn. "Warrior, I promise you, I will not venture near a holy hall again—I will not even step into the yard before one, if you will—"

"Sorceress, I'm not a young woman. You could blast me into the grave in a puff. But I've lived long enough in this rotten world not to care that much, and I can throw my knife better than some of my spearwomen can throw their spears. Now turn around and put your hands behind your back." She slipped one end of the copper chain through the hollow copper tube.

Inside, the priest was saying, "If you wish the most stringent purification, the purging likeliest to make the demons let you slip by in pity, as one already punished in full, go to the widow of the murdered priest. If you wish a milder purification, come to me...."

"Warrior," whispered Frostflower, "I have already been power-stripped." Since that term had always been the exact equivalent of rape, she judged it no lie to say this.

The swordswoman raised her eyebrows. "Unh? Well, I'm not equipped to strip you myself anyway, sorceress, and if you don't give us any trouble, it might not come to that. But Townmaster Youngwise will have a few questions for you. Probably the priests will, too."

"I have a token from Elvannon—a priest in the north...."

"Good. That should help you, at least with Master Youngwise. Where is the thing?"

Frostflower took it from her pocket. As she held it out, she tried her last resource and looked full at the warrior with her mismatched eyes.

The warrior blinked, shook her head, and made a noose in the end of the copper chain. "I'll deny this if you repeat it, sorceress, but between you and me, I don't believe much more in your bloody power than I believe any of the gods would save me from it. But I do believe in what Master Youngwise and the priests would do to me if I let you go and they found out about it. Now turn around."

Frostflower repocketed her token, turned, and put her hands behind her.

"You wouldn't want to wander around Five Roads today anyway," said the swordswoman, coming closer. "When His Reverence gets through with them, the town idiots are more likely to give you chopped quills than good food. Cross your wrists."

Frostflower crossed her wrists and felt metal touch them. Dowl whined and tried to nuzzle their hands; the warrior seemed to nudge him away. Frostflower turned her head to try for a glimpse of what her captor was doing. She could see nothing, but the warrior noticed her effort and explained.

"Never saw one of these before, huh? Chain goes through the tube and loops around your wrists, then I can hold the other end of the chain and push you ahead of me with the tube without ever touching your myself—a good little length of copper to protect me from you. Master Youngwise invented 'em last winter. You know, this may be lucky for you. If you can clear your motives with Master Youngwise this evening, maybe get his token and string it around your neck along with that northern farmer's, you'll be a demon's-reach safer for the next few days then you might have been otherwise."

Perhaps the warrior was right. Inside the temple, the priest was now saying, "Whoever has sheltered the murdering sorcerer— whoever has even seen him pass and kept silent out of fear—in the sight of the Gods, that cringing sorceri-lover shares his guilt and the guilt of all his kind. Will you allow this evil, this rot, this sin, to remain in your town, infecting it like some foul disease, threatening at every moment to bring the rage of Azkor untempered by the mercy of Maejira—the devouring justice of the Seven Secret Names?"

Frostflower tried not to shiver. If they should ask her directly whether she knew the sorcerer supposed to have killed Deveron . . .

The warrior drew the small-linked chain only tight enough to keep it from slipping off and used the tube less to push than guide her through the streets. The sorceress took courage—this was far different from the roughness of her capture last summer.

"I owe you some thanks, sorceress, for not disturbing the ceremony back there," the warrior said when they were well away from the temple, Dowl padding patiently beside them.

"Would the farmers' folk not have come out in a mob to tear me apart?"

The warrior chuckled appreciatively. "'Farmers' folk.' Yes,

it's not a bad name for the gobbers, even if they are townspeople. What's your name, sorceress?"

"Frostflower."

"Ever been in Five Roads before?"

"No."

"Unh? Thought maybe I knew you from somewhere."

"I traveled between All Roads South and Three Bridges last summer; I do not remember seeing you, warrior."

"Never out of your hole before that?"

"No."

The warrior must have shrugged, for the copper tube dipped briefly. "Haven't been farther east than the Wendwater for twelve or thirteen years myself."

"What happened here, warrior," Frostflower ventured to ask, "to bring forth words like that from His Reverence?" Perhaps she should have asked sooner, not only in the hope of learning what she had come to learn, but because not to ask might be to advertise that she already knew much of the story.

"I'd better not tell you that yet, Frostflower. By the way, I'm Eaglesight—Wallkeeper, if you'd rather use the title."

At length, following a tree-lined avenue that led through a sizable garden, they came out into a round yard similar to the one before the holy hall, but thrice as large and ringed by important-looking buildings with trees planted between and in front of them. Eaglesight directed Frostflower to one of the most plainly designed of the buildings, standing three stories high. Before they entered, the wallkeeper paused to point out the sights of her town's center. "The ancient Holy Hall," she began, indicating an oval building ringed by trees and surrounded by garden on all sides except that facing the open yard. "Now Their Reverences use it mostly for a Truth Grove away from the farm, their own little token tighthold in Five Roads. With luck, you'll never see the inside of it, Frostflower. The gardens used to be priestly territory, but Master Youngwise made a deal in his youth, and now they're free to anyone who walks in them respectfully."

"Except sorceri?"

Eaglesight rubbed her chin and nodded. "Youngwise never laid down any rule against your people enjoying the place, so long as there's no ceremony going on in the old temple, but you'd be smart to keep to the path through it. Amazing, the things we can call disrespectful if you people do them." She pointed to the next building, which resembled the priests' dwelling in a farm and was surrounded by its own garden wall. "There's the priestly alcove-hall across from us, where Their Reverences sleep when they deign to spend a night in our stinking town, which one or other does once or twice a year, to keep up the form. Every Hatching-Day a squad of pious townsfolk go in and spend their holiday keeping the place clean. That next building's where the undermasters live. Then the front end of the warriors' barracks—looks pretty good from the front, doesn't it? When the wind blows from the south, they light incense around the rest of this yard to keep the smell of the hinder parts from their dainty noses. Then there's the First Townmaster's dwelling on our left; doesn't look so fine as the priestly alcove-hall from the outside, but probably a lot more comfortable inside. And this one we're going into is the Town-masters' Hall, where the real governing of the town, such as it is, is supposed to go on. Ordinarily, one or other of our frigging undermasters should always be sitting in the front alcove or the judgment hall, but today they're both in attendance at the cere-monies, along with the First Master, and Wallkeeper Snagcut's sitting delegate this morning, the bloody cow. So we'll just go in by the side door without telling her you're here."

The side door was a descent to the cellars. Though dry and not ill smelling, these were dark, lit only by a few constant-wicks and an occasional small candle before the niche of some god or god-dess. What Frostflower thought at first was an unusually wide passageway cut here and there by a partition she soon realized was in fact a maze of rooms opening into one another.

Eventually the women reached a brighter area, lit and ventilated by a ceiling screen through which sweet fragrances and sun-dappled shadows penetrated. "Are we below another garden?" Frostflower asked.

"A little one, for summer council meetings. Behind the judg-ment hall. In their own humble way, our townmasters manage to rival the priests. Want to use the close-room over there? Have a drink of water? It'll be a boggy long afternoon for you, but I can't do anything about that."

"Thank you," said the sorceress. Eaglesight freed her hands and let her go into the close-room. When she came out again, the warrior had produced dried apricots and cold water from a stone cupboard at one side of the room.

"I wouldn't drink too much," said Eaglesight, picking up the copper chain and tube again. "Have to immobilize you for the afternoon. It'd be skin off my back, First Wallkeeper or not, if the priests or anyone else found you loose here."

Frostflower nodded and turned, holding her hands behind her back. "Should you have shown me so much kindness already?"

"Now you ask, no. I should've hooked you right away, like this." Eaglesight fastened the end of the chain to a copper hook in the wall. The height of the hook, combined with the length of the chain and tube, made it impossible for the sorceress either to stand without bending her knees or to sit on the floor. Eaglesight moved a small bench over for her to sit on, then frowned at Dowl, who waited just out of the way, wagging his tail trustingly.

"Must you immobilize him, also?" said Frostflower.

Eaglesight shrugged. "Better. I can see he's gentle enough to roll eggs, but if Their Reverences get the notion he's trained to go for their noses at your command..." Returning to the stone cupboard, she untangled a variety of chains, ropes and straps until she found a thin iron chain several strides long. She secured one end to the cupboard and hooked the other end rather loosely around Dowl's neck, patting him as he tried to lick her face. "Anything else before I go? I can give you a cushion or two, but they're pretty damn greasy. Might have a few creatures living in 'em, too."

Frostflower shook her head. "I am to be alone the entire afternoon? You will not return?"

"Probably not. It's a big town, and a good day for robbers."

"Is it not unusual that a wallkeeper should walk patrol in a large town like Five Roads Crossing?"

Eaglesight raised one eyebrow. "Never knew sorceri were so interested in warriors' work. No, it's not usual, but any woman not on other duty today has to make the rounds of the holy halls with Their Reverences and the townmasters, and I'd rather look for the robbers. So I named myself to street-guard for the whole blasted day. . . . Are you really harmless, Frostflower? Or just kind to an old swordswoman?"

Frostflower lowered her gaze. "It would be very difficult for me to harm anyone, I think, even with such weapons as are available to all folk."

"Is it common for you people to wander around loose after you've been power-stripped?"

"Is it common for us to escape death after the stripping?"

The wallkeeper laughed. "Well, sorceress, if my opinion's worth enough, by nightfall you'll be out looking for an inn. One friendly warning: If the priests come, be careful how you answer their questions. His Reverence Rondasu would have purged the whole damn neighborhood last winter, Lady Shara is her brother's bitter little echo, and I think Lady Intassa may be out to prove her early remarriage doesn't mean she's any less eager to punish her first husband's death, for all her silence and meek manners. Master Youngwise will probably be on our side, if only to cross His Reverence while pretending not to. You may end up for a while like a bone with two dogs fighting over you, but if the right dog wins, there are worse ways to get out of trouble. And Lady Reverence Eleva may—just may—be on your side, too. I'm not sure why, and I'm not sure I'd trust her very far, but she does things just to show her power and annoy her brother, and she purrs right along with Youngwise most of the time. That's the main reason we didn't have the purge when Reverence Rondasu called for it. As for our noble undermasters, they'll probably wiggle out of coming if they can, and since Smoothermore's a priests' paw and Clearthinking goes along with the strongest blast of mouthair, Master Youngwise usually prefers to cross wits with Their Reverences alone. Well, I'd better go look for the real criminals— they could've strolled off with half the stinking shopgoods in Oldcraft Street by now."

Solitude made up a large and cherished part of Frostflower's life, as it did the lives of all sorceri . . . but not the kind of solitude that remained after Eaglesight had left. Though the wallkeeper had seemingly done her best to soften it, Frostflower's present confinement much more closely resembled the tales she had heard from childhood—and which she had come to believe approximated the wild rumors farmers' folk told of her own people—than had her imprisonment last summer in Maldron's Farm. (Yet her folk dared to enter towns, and shunned farms!)

Dowl put his head in her lap, gazed up at her, and whined, puzzled as to why she would not pat him. She murmured comforting words, and after a few moments he sighed, snorted, shook his head, and lay on the floor beside her to sleep.

Eaglesight's apparent leniency could, conceivably, have been a trick to make the sorceress trust the wallkeeper further than she should. Frostflower thought over all that Thorn had told her of the personalities and power struggles in Five Roads Crossing. Thorn had characterized Eaglesight as a decent woman predisposed towards honesty, but who had compromised with expediency. Thorn called Youngwise a "slithering old triple-tongue"—but Thorn had special cause for complaint against him, and if he did "shave the dice to please the priests," he apparently did it, from what Eaglesight had said about the public garden surrounding the old temple, for the good of his town.

The two most important farms were those of Deveron and Rondasu. Their forebears had amassed the neighboring farms, chiefly by raidfare, until Rondasu's Farm included all the cultivated land northeast of Five Roads in a rough quarter-circle between the Wendwater, the Mirrel, Mideast Road Straight, and the Dranwoods, which separated his farmwall from the townwall. Deveron's Farm, on the other side of Mideast Road, was somewhat smaller but commonly considered to have richer land. Deveron had organized no raids during his tenure; Rondasu, the younger man by six or eight years, only one—some five winters ago, he had successfully driven out the last priestly family besides his own and Deveron's that remained between Five Roads and the Mirrel River.

South and southwest of Five Roads there remained a number of small farms whose priests raided each other sporadically, but the southern farmers rarely mixed in the government of Five Roads, preferring to dominate the smaller towns to the south. Eventually, some southern priest might succeed in increasing his lands and driving out his neighbors as the forefathers of Deveron and Rondasu had done in the north, and then the power pattern might become three-way and surround the town; but no one seemed to think that possibility near enough to worry about.

Rondasu's father, Rondrun, had sired two daughters in addition to Rondasu, and his neighbor Deveron had married the younger of these daughters, Eleva, as his first wife, while the older daughter, Shara, remained in the farm of her birth as an unmarried priestess. According to priestly custom, the marriage between neighbors had precluded any attempt of one farmer to raid the other, at least for a generation or two, and so the power had seemed to balance peacefully. At Deveron's death, Eleva became ruling lady. Intassa, Deveron's younger wife, had apparently remarried after Thorn and Windbourne escaped the area. If she had married Rondasu as his first wife, the two farms were linked by yet another marriage.

Both priestly families, it seemed, were unusually small: no widows of either Deveron's or Rondasu's father still survived, and the only members of the coming generation were Eleva's and Intassa's children, none of whom were seven years old yet. As far as Thorn was aware, there had been no visiting priests in the area, and Rondasu had not involved himself in the search for the murderer of his sister's husband until the following morning. Thus, if Deveron had been poisoned by one of his own class, it must have been by one of his wives—Eleva or Intassa... perhaps by both of them working together.

The sorceress had only a dim understanding, buried long ago by choice and more recently by brutality, of the emotions that led women and men to marry. She had vague memories of her own parents' happiness before her father's death, which had happened when she was eleven years old, and she knew that here and there other sorcerous couples lived in contentment on the edges of their retreats. But sorcerous marriages were one woman to one man, and entered only for the sake of friendship and mutual regard deep enough to overbalance the loss of sorcerous power that marriage entailed. Priestly multiple marriages might be contracted between strangers for reasons of wealth, ruling power, and policy. Might such household situations not lead to... strange emotions... jealousies strong enough to...

No! The sorceress would continue to assume that Deveron had fallen victim to some sudden disease.

Both to quiet her fears and to take her mind off her constraint, she went through several exercises. When she opened her eyes again, she was breathing more steadily; but she was disheartened to see, by the small distance the shadow of the ceiling screen had moved, how little time had passed.

Well, sorceri had ways other folk lacked of shortening such a wait as this. Frostflower might slow her body's time, watch the sun-pattern slide across the floor as quickly as the shadow of a wind-blown cloud, hear the birdcalls and fountain ripples above merge into a high-pitched whir, feel Dowl's breathing like a rapid quiver against her legs. Or she might put herself into a trance or else—more difficult because of her discomfort—a state of conscious meditation. Or she might free-travel.

It was never wise to change the body's own time without good physical reason.

Either a trance or a state of meditation would allow her mind to ponder in its deepest, calmest reasoning, and her case should not be worsened if they found her in harmless trance.

But free-travel appealed to her most. It had its dangers. If the body were destroyed while the entity was outside, the entity was doomed to melancholy wandering and an eventual fate on which those who had not experienced it could only speculate. She might be very rash to free-travel here, leaving her body in a townmasters' prison. Still, if they found her in that state, they would probably assume it was trance.

She would have time to go to String-of-Beads and return here by evening, but chances were it would do little good since Windbourne did not expect her until midnight and only whim or inexplicable instinct could inspire him to enter the free-traveling state himself at midafternoon today. Moreover, for the maximum prudence, she ought to remain close to her body. But the idea of spending the afternoon in the garden around the ancient temple, in the intangible but unsuffering freedom of the unrestrained entity, was mischievously tempting. She began the preliminary exercises.

She was still rather disquieted to see her own body as it appeared to other folk, so she glanced back only once after leaving it. Some part of her personality, she knew, remained inside with her suspended senses; and indeed, while close to her body, she could almost feel herself in two places at once. As she withdrew, however, all conscious awareness of the part that remained inside fell away.

The most dubious part of her venture was finding her way up. The entity could move a few fingers'-length above ground or floor, and it could jump down from any height and land without injury, but it could not fly, nor jump appreciably higher than the physical body in good health. And it could pass through doors and walls and see a little better in the darkness than the physical body could, but it did not have any surer instinct of direction. Therefore, she followed the regular doorways. Though she tried to memorize her route, she doubted that, after so many turnings and doublings back, she would be able to retrace the path very quickly. Well, she could follow the townmasters' group when it came to question her.

And if she missed seeing it approach? She decided to spend part of her afternoon in the upper floors of the Townmasters' Hall. She could find and mark the way to the small garden above her cell and drop down through the screen to her body.

She finally found stairs that led up to a short interior passageway. Following the sound of voices, she passed through a dark brown doorcurtain and emerged at one end of what must be the townmasters' judgment-hall.

It was large enough to hold the entire gathering-house at Windslope Retreat, roof and all—much larger than the central hall in either of the two priestly dwellings the sorceress had seen, as if by its size the townmasters hinted that their power, at least in town, was superior to that of the farmer-priests. But, as if in apology, it was also stark, with floor of dull-glazed tile, walls of brown clay, and ceiling high but smooth plastered, lacking even the exposed rafters that might have lent a little relief to the eye. There was no dais.

One warrior, her back to the doorway, slouched on a short-backed bench behind a plain, heavy oaken table. Another warrior, a spearwoman, held a thin youth by one arm. His hands were behind him, as if bound; he looked to be in his late teens or early twenties; and he seemed to be hiding apprehension with a display of insolence.

"Napping at home in bed," the spearwoman was saying. "Can't show . s token for missing the ceremonies."

"I was sick," said the youth. "It came on very suddenly."

"And left very suddenly," replied the spearwoman. "I found the brat snoring away comfortable as a bloody wine-nose."

"My father took the fine-money along to the ceremonies for me—"

"Not much point in that," said the warrior behind the table. "Couldn't bring your token back to you in time, could he?" Reaching down, she produced a coil of rope from beneath the table and tossed it to the spearwoman. "All right, Quickarm, spread him out and up with the tunic. No need to chain him below and worry the undermasters with him this evening."

Frostflower fled. To escape the sound of the young man's screams, she hurried along the passage in the other direction. It ended in a second doorway, this one covered with a blue and white curtain that swayed in the air currents and seemed to glow a little as if sunlight were shining through the thin cloth. Passing through, she found herself in a pleasant chamber where three walls were decorated with mosaic done in chips of multi-colored tile and the fourth had large, carved windowscreens on either side of another door. Beyond this door lay the townmasters' small inner garden.

This garden had no trees, but many shrubs and bushes, some espaliered along the walls. Its chief glory and luxury were the flowers—almost too many. She did not regret that the free-traveling entity had no bodily senses except sight and hearing, for she might have found so many mingled fragrances rather cloying.

The ventilation screen to the cell below was ashwood with an upper coating of lead. Though surrounded by a border of prickly leafed teasel as if to prevent its being stepped upon, it was probably capable of sustaining a man's weight. Peering through the interstices of the screen, Frostflower glimpsed her body sitting below, with Dowl still napping comfortably at her feet.

There was only the one door into the garden at ground level, but a stairway with an intricately carved handrail led to an encircling balcony two floors above. She ascended the stairway, entered a passage on the upper floor, and soon located stairs that led down to a back doorway. Whether to keep prisoners in or thieves out, the heavy oak door was still on its hinges despite the season. Frostflower passed through and reached a back street.

Behind her was the comparatively undecorated back of the

Townmasters' Hall. To her right was a high wall with a few
treetops showing above it—that would be the back of the garden
around the First Townmaster's dwelling. To her left was a lower
wall over the top of which, by walking as high as possible above
the pavement, she could see a triangular exercise yard bounded
on one side by the stark wall of the warriors' barracks. Across the
street was an even line of shop fronts, looking little different from
any other respectable street of small shopkeepers, the windows
closed and shuttered today.

Frostflower studied the back of the Townmasters' Hall. From
one of those windows Thorn and Windbourne must have made
their jump into this street last winter when the snow lay thick and
the shopwindows were closed with seasonal shutters to keep out
cold as well as thieves. Here the way began to Crinkpetal's house,
where she had hoped to learn the present situation and be given
a friendly refuge for her free-traveling. If ever she did reach Crinkpetal or some other trustworthy friend, she must ask sure, simple
directions to the townwall before she free-traveled to String-of-
Beads.

She went into the front part of the warriors' barracks. Behind
the pillars that faced the open yard, she found a wide flagstone
walk with a long, shallow rectangular pit in the middle, four steps
leading down on all sides to its slightly uneven floor of brown
tiles. On the other side of the pit, six small alcoves flanked a
leather-curtained doorway. From behind the doorcurtain came the
clash of blades—at least one pair of warriors, probably remaining
to guard the barracks or awaiting a turn of duty. The alcoves were
uncurtained and simply furnished, each with a table and two or
three benches; she assumed they served as offices for the wallkeepers and waiting-rooms for complainants. The pit might be
used for demonstration combats of some sort. She realized she had
told Thorn more about the life of sorceri than Thorn had told her
about that of warriors. But no doubt, thought the sorceress, I have
shied away from such knowledge. Even now, hesitancy outweighed curiosity, and Frostflower did not go into the actual barracks.

Neither Inmara nor Elvannon and his family had forbidden her
any priestly holy places except when they were in use for certain

ceremonies. She explored the ancient temple at leisure. Once, all folk who lived outside farm walls had been expected to go to the nearest farm, or at least to a consecrated place in the open air, for the vital ceremonies of the priestly religion. As towns grew larger, they were allowed holy halls, where neighboring farmers came to officiate; sometimes sending a younger member of the family while the ruling priest led the ceremonies in the farm, sometimes holding the town ceremonies a day or two later. The original theology had allowed only one holy hall to a town, for some of the ceremonies required the whole day. But when too many towns became too large for this system, the High Priestly Gathering had at last allowed each town as many temples as needed for its folk, and permitted priests to shorten or otherwise accommodate the ceremonies. The town's original holy hall must be the site of any opening ritual, but such rites had in many places become brief private prayers for the priest or priests and a few others, like townmasters and lay acolytes, who would move about with them during the public ceremonials. Thus, an ancient temple like this one of Five Roads Crossing could now be turned into a sort of Truth Grove and Holy Glade for the priests alone, used as rarely as their town alcove-hall, and kept as reverently clean between whiles.

Frostflower had learned part of this from Elvannon and part from the books in Windslope Retreat, for sorceri had long preserved their own records of the history of the Tanglelands and the doings of its rulers. Some of it she might have guessed. The oak, beech, and elm trees planted closely around the outside of the temple suggested a grove and, though mature, seemed not to have been planned by the original builders, for many of the trunks obscured weathered images like half-statues carved into the stone walls. Inside, there was only one large chamber, rising to a high vaulted ceiling. A grove of artificial fruit trees filled most of the floor space, leaving a broad aisle around the edge between wall and grove. The trees were statues, carved chiefly from applewood; they were uncolored and stylized, but, as if to compensate for the artificiality, each tree reflected all the seasons, with leaves, buds, blossoms, full-grown fruit, and a few bare limbs. Carved birds poised ready to feed wooden worms to their gape-beaked chicks— a highly symbolic representation, since worms were held to be the

semi-sacred pets of Aomu and Voma, and their consumption by
birds was considered a natural sign of union between the deities
of earth, weather, and harvest.

Within the imitation grove was a marble altar, white with a
black top. Frostflower did not look long at this. Aside from the
altar and the trees, the chamber was bare save for a number of
stone chests that stood along the wall, looking much like small
altars but with hinged lids. Being out of her body, the sorceress
could not have lifted the lids had she wanted to. The building also
had a cellar, entered by way of a small, inset alcove near the back.
The spiraling passageway led to a small ablution chamber. A
second archway showed that the tunnel led further, but Frostflower
decided she had explored enough deserted underground areas.

She had made great progress since last summer in that she
could keep the unpleasant memories under control and appreciate
the beauty and artistry of the holy hall. Pray God these new priests
did nothing to unbalance that tenuous appreciation!

Most of the afternoon she spent wandering in the temple garden,
wishing that her entity could feel the breeze, even at the cost of
also feeling the chill of the air or the heat of the sun. She often
returned to the streets around the central building, but the shutters
remained closed all day. After a long debate with herself, she tried
entering a few of the houses, thinking she might hear conversation
roused by the priest's harangue; but no one was yet home in the
first house she entered, and in the second house, a man was using
the close-room with the door open while he traded jocularities with
a younger man. Her inadvertent intrusion on such easy immodesty
kept the sorceress from repeating the experiment. Better to wait
for conversations in public places.

At last, near sunset, she encountered Youngwise's group on
its way through the garden: a priest, three priestesses, the three
townmasters, Eaglesight, and the two gatewarriors Frostflower had
met that morning, Splathandle and Whistlepoint.

The priest and one priestess walked in front, the oldest townmaster between and slightly behind them. These three were conversing, not loudly, but freely. The other two priestesses, one tall
and golden haired, the other not quite so tall and silvery blond,
followed, saying little, each of them escorted at a respectful half-
pace behind by one of the younger townmasters. The three warriors

brought up the rear, Eaglesight whistling very softly, the other two silent but not, it appeared, overly apprehensive. Frostflower moved alongside the front three to hear their talk.

"I was closer to him than you were, brother," the lead priestess was saying.

"All the more reason, sister, they should come to me."

"I hardly see that. Nor do I appreciate—"

"I simply meant to free you of the extra work, Eleva." The man seemed to have his annoyance under better control than the woman. Or was he baiting her on purpose? "Occupied as you are with your attempts to run Deveron's Farm—"

"It is Eleva's Farm now," she replied, "and occupied as I am, I would still have time to deal with any who knew of the sorcerer's escape!"

"Your Reverences," said the old townmaster with a smile, "do not erode our humble town faith in our priests."

"You mean that we should let our private squabbles fester inside our own farmwalls, Master Youngwise?" said the priestess Eleva. "Yes, I would be content to do that—all the more content if my good brother Rondasu stayed within his walls and left me alone in mine. But when he uses our common ceremony to hint to your townspeople that I am unjust and vindictive—"

"How could I consult with you ahead of time on my wording, sister," said the priest, "and still respect your wishes to be left alone?"

Master Youngwise smiled and folded his hands together in his wide gray sleeves. "Shall you continue this quarrel, Your Reverences, before Eaglesight's prisoner?"

For a moment Frostflower felt guilty. This conversation was not meant for her hearing.

Rondasu said calmly, "A sorceress, caught listening to our ceremonies. We had best make an example of her."

"Aye, an example of my vindictiveness!" said Eleva. "Give her purification over to me, Rondasu, and let me show the townsfolk the truth of what you told them."

"The thing happened within our walls," said the townmaster. "Therefore, I must accept responsibility. Under your guidance, of course, Reverences."

They had reached the edge of the paved yard. "Your Reverences," said one of the undermasters, "and Master Youngwise, if you have no further need of us . . ."

Youngwise waved his right hand. "Yes, yes, Smoothermore, Clearthinking, you may seek your supper. This is a small enough affair that one of us should be able to bear the responsibility alone."

Decreased by two, the group went on across the open yard. "It may have happened within the town walls," said Rondasu, "but it was obviously an offense against us and our ceremonies."

"As also against the folk of Five Roads Crossing," replied the townmaster, "in that your ceremonies today were extraordinary and directed at us. Moreover, she was not actually found inside the holy hall, but on the street outside."

"Wallkeeper!" said the priest, turning to look back at Eaglesight.

"Reverence?"

"The sorceress was leaning with her back against the holy hall?"

The aging warrior glanced at the priest, the townmaster, and Eleva. "That I couldn't say, Your Reverences. She was sitting cross-legged and I approached her from the front."

"You were derelict not to notice this crucial detail, Wallkeeper," said Youngwise. "Well, we shall hope that the sorceress remembers it." His voice was stern, but Eaglesight, who had stiffened while answering the priest, relaxed at the townmaster's rebuke, almost shrugged as she touched fist to lips, and soon resumed her very soft whistling.

The priest fingered his gold necklace. "Whatever the wretch says, she will clearly have been sitting with her back against the wall."

"When one sits cross-legged, brother," said Eleva, "one tends to lean forward, not backward. And these people have their own rules. For her to touch our holy hall may seem as distasteful to her as to us."

"Distasteful?" Rondasu raised his brows. "A mild word for it, sister. And if she does indeed share this opinion, she could have had no other reason to sit so near than to spy for her murdering fellow."

Eleva stopped in the middle of the yard and turned to face her brother. Their kinship was obvious, both in their brown hair and eyes and in the determination of their wills; but their difference was equally obvious, her anger forthright and his half-veiled. "So you intend to trap her whatever she says, Rondasu! As you trapped that sorcerer—guilty of my husband's death because he was captured, and even more guilty because, chained down with no hope of mercy from us, he dared escape!"

"You forget yourself, sister," said the tall golden-haired priestess, who must be Shara. "Our brother did not entrap the sorcerer. The townwarriors of Five Roads Crossing captured him, and he escaped again, with the connivance of that wretched swordswoman, before we had so much as been notified of his capture."

Eleva glared at the last speaker, opened her mouth, then hesitated as if changing what she had been about to say. "Well, then, Rondasu, if this sorceress was touching the wall, she is mine. As the sorcerer will be mine should we recapture him, though he would be a full flask of stupidity if he were ever to come near Five Roads again."

"I was the officiating priest, sister Eleva, you only my acolyte," said Rondasu.

"Aye—on my suffrance, because the ceremonies were your idea. But I am still the one most closely concerned in my husband's death, and by that right I claim the sorceress."

"Someday, dear sister," murmured Rondasu, "you may wish you had repeated less often that you are the person most concerned in Deveron's death."

"If I might venture to suggest to Your Reverences," said Youngwise, "that the sorceress can hardly be questioned while we stand here in the open yard?"

Eleva turned sharply and walked toward the Townmasters' Hall, leaving the others to follow.

Rondasu soon matched her pace. "So, then, sister, you admit the sorceress must be involved in your husband's death, that you claim her although I was officiating priest?"

"If my husband had not died, you could not have played with your pretty ceremony today. That is my claim to the sorceress."

"Someday, Eleva," said the priest, "you'll weave your own bonds with that half-heretical tongue of yours."

Frostflower doubted that any of the others except herself overheard this last exchange. The brother and sister had too far out-

stripped the rest. As for the sorceress, self-concern had finally
outweighed distaste for intruding on privacy, and she felt no com-
punction about listening.

But how much good had it done her? Might Eleva have spoken
as she did because she knew Windbourne had not killed her husband—and might she know that because she herself had poisoned
him? Might Rondasu's sternness rise from a sincere belief in the
sorcerer's guilt, and, if so, might it not be better to fall into
Rondasu's power with some hope of convincing him of the truth?
How far would Youngwise and Eaglesight go to demonstrate their
apparent neutrality? And how could Frostflower use to her advantage what she had learned, pledged as she was to speak truth
or nothing, and more than ever confused where her advantage lay?

Reaching the Townmasters' Hall, Rondasu strode up the steps
without hesitation, pushed aside the brown linen doorcurtain, and
only then paused to look back at the others. Eleva waited at the
foot of the stairs until the rest of the party came up. The tall
priestess, Rondasu's other sister, climbed at once to his side, took
the curtain from his hands, and held it back while he entered. The
silvery-haired priestess, who must be Intassa, looked from Eleva
to the pair at the door, blinked, pursed her lips, and quickly climbed
the stairs. An expression of distaste seemed to cross Eaglesight's
face, one of open and unveiled disgust crossed Eleva's, and Youngwise, pausing beside her, muttered, "They'll make the poor lady
another like themselves yet."

"Not like themselves." Eleva touched his elbow. "They'll destroy her before they can corrupt her completely."

So Frostflower understood that some bond of confidence existed
between Eleva and the old townmaster. But were they disgusted
with her siblings' malice or with some quality that other folk would
not have called "corruption"?

On seeing the priests and townmaster enter, the warrior behind
the judgment table rose and stood with left fist to lips until they
reached her end of the hall. She was not the same one who had
been there at midday.

"It's near enough sunset, Keeper Clampen," said Youngwise.
"You may go. Knot the cords on your way out."

The warrior nodded, staring for a moment but saying nothing

as the party got lamps from a cupboard, lit them, and passed on into the back passage.

Youngwise had now fallen back with Eaglesight. The First Wallkeeper shook her head. "And you call Clampen a Third Wallkeeper?" she muttered. "Thorn wouldn't have let us all get by without a question or two. That bloody cow Strongneck wouldn't have either, whether she could do anything with the answers or not."

"Aye, and see where Thorn's shrewdness brought her," the townmaster muttered in reply. "And Strongneck, too, one might add, may her new employer have better satisfaction of her than we had."

"Strongneck will do for *his* purposes well enough—born to be a blasted farmwarrior, that one. But she was better than Snagcut, and as for this clodwit Clampen..."

"Aye, aye, you'll have more choice in your next underkeepers, Eagle, but we had to give my undermasters some sop. Must I remind you of the grumbling because Thorn had been your choice?"

"So now Thorn was my choice alone, was she?" murmured the wallkeeper.

When they reached the underground area the group walked in silence. Was it part of their plan to take their captive unawares? She would have hurried on ahead, but she could not remember the way.

At last they reached her cell. Dowl trotted forward the length of his chain and stood wagging his tail to greet them. The motionlessness of Frostflower's body was not at first apparent in the failing light, and the priest muttered, "Doesn't so much as raise her head to look at us, the demons'-bait."

The townmaster began in a louder tone, "So, sorceress..."

Frostflower heard no more for a few moments. Of necessity, there was a short interval when she lost all sensual contact with the outside world while reentering her flesh, the sight and hearing of the free entity cut off, the senses of the body not yet touching consciousness. When she opened her eyes, the priestess Eleva was bending over her, holding a lamp near her face and stroking Dowl with her other hand.

"Lady Reverence?" said Frostflower.

Eleva straightened and turned toward the others. "You see? I told you it was merely one of their strange sleeps, just as I told you her dog would not harm us. And small blame to her for sleeping through her afternoon's wait!"

"Admirable indifference," said Rondasu. "I could have thought of quicker ways to awaken her with that lamp than by peering at her. And why do you call this lady a 'Reverence,' sorceron?"

True—there was no way, so far as they were aware, that Frostflower could have known. "The wreath?" she said, looking at the metal circlet on Eleva's head and realizing even as she spoke that its very pale gold was not easy to tell at a glance from silver, especially in twilight.

"You cannot expect these people to know all the intricacies of our customs, brother," said Eleva. "To her, any priestly matron may be 'Lady Reverence.'"

"Then they should study our ways with greater care," said Rondasu, "when they plan to come spying among us."

"Your Reverence," said Youngwise, and added a few words in an undertone, too low for the sorceress to hear. Rondasu nodded sharply, turned one palm up in a gesture of annoyance, then changed it to a gesture of goodwill by laying his hand on the townmaster's shoulder.

Frostflower could not deny forthright that she had come to spy, but she said, "Your Reverence, I have a token from Reverence Elvannon—"

"A priest of your own neighborhood, no doubt?" Rondasu laughed. "An edgelands reverence?"

Shara joined his laughter. "They care little what mischief you people work in our midlands, so that you leave their own small farms in peace."

"Shara," said Rondasu, turning to her. There followed another conference too low for Frostflower to hear; she guessed that Rondasu was transferring his annoyance, along with the townmaster's advice—whatever it had been—to his older sister. Perhaps Youngwise had counseled him to be more subtle in questioning the sorceress; Rondasu now gestured once or twice at the third priestess, as if commending her continued silence. Shara scowled, the silvery-haired Intassa smiled, and meanwhile Youngwise went on to Frostflower,

"Did you find the wall a comfortable backrest, sorceress?"

"Was it built for one, Master?"

The townmaster grinned slightly, then frowned. "In plain words, sorceress, were you touching the holy hall wall?"

She knew why he asked, but not whether she should hope to be put under his judgment or that of the priests. How difficult it was to gauge minds when your natural inclination to like and trust had been overlaid with years of training in the need for caution and mistrust when among farmers' folk! "Master," she said, "I understand that my offense is having listened to the priestly ceremonies, but is my guilt greater or less for leaning or not leaning against the building? Is the very wall consecrated somehow?"

"It is," said Youngwise, "but that's not the reason I ask. According as you touched the holy hall or did not touch it, so you are to be judged by me as townmaster or by Their Reverences."

At least he told her that much plainly and truthfully. "Why should this be, Townmaster?"

"Will you question us, sorceress?" said Rondasu.

"Allow her the natural curiosity of any creature, brother!" said Eleva.

"Curiosity! Does any ruler—priest or townmaster—allow curiosity in an outlaw?" Rondasu slapped right fist into left palm. "Next you'll say it was mere curiosity that caused her to listen to our sacred rites!"

"Your Reverence," Frostflower said quickly and timidly, "if I could unsay my question—"

"You cannot," said Eleva. "It remains in the air, and it remains an understandable question to any but a man who lacks the imagination to see himself ever in the disfavor of anyone with the power to destroy him for his sins. Sorceress, the holy halls are priestly ground, under our governance, but the rest of Five Roads Crossing is profane ground, under the governance of Townmaster Youngwise and his undermasters."

The sorceress drew a deep breath. She must tell the truth sooner or later, be the outcome what it may; they were not likely to let this point rest. "I sat cross-legged, not leaning against the wall, but I will not swear that I never touched it with any part of my body or robe. I did not know it would prove so important, so I did not notice the matter closely enough to remember it now."

"Elegant!" said Rondasu. "Elegant and convenient. See how she tries to escape by throwing us into confusion?"

"If you are confused, wise brother," said Eleva, "withdraw and save your delicate brain for weightier decisions. Master Youngwise and I will judge the sorceress together and satisfy both our gods and those of the town."

"Gods of the town? There are no gods, sister, who speak first to the townmasters and only afterwards to us!"

"Without entering into questions of doctrine, Your Reverence, which are, of course, for you to decide," said Youngwise, "I may point out that while we are in doubt whether she touched the holy hall, we do know that she touched the street."

"The gods of the Truth Grove," said Rondasu, "have power to restore memory, even to heretics and unbelievers."

God! thought Frostflower. Will they torture me for nothing more serious than to learn whether or not I touched a wall? "Your Reverences," she said, "and Townmaster, I will answer your questions as truthfully here as in your Grove. Surely willing truth is better than truth enforced?"

All turned to look at her.

"Whether or not willing truth spoken elsewhere is preferable to truth uttered within the consecrated circle of a Truth Grove," said Youngwise, "is not for an unlearned townmaster to say. But without delving into doctrine, the point that occurs to me is whether it might not be simpler and more convenient, as well as more preserving of life and labor, to question her here first, at a little distance, before arguing which of us should provide a young man for the stripping that would be a necessary preliminary to the Truth Grove."

At worst, thought Frostflower, I can leave my body again before it comes to that! Nevertheless, she could not stop trembling. She glanced at Eaglesight, but the wallkeeper only gazed back as if to say she regarded what her prisoner had told her as a secret for the prisoner to repeat or not. The sorceress bowed her head. "I have already been raped, Master."

Rondasu was first to speak. "I did not know that any of you

people continued to prowl our midlands afterwards."

"There . . . are many things we do not know about each other, priests and sorceri," said Frostflower.

Master Youngwise took several steps forward, patting Dowl as the dog turned to him. "Lift your head and look at me, sorceress. As your dog is doing."

She obeyed the townmaster. He squinted at her face, took the lamp from Eleva, bent closer, and squinted again. She blinked once or twice; he did not.

"Mismatched eyes," he said, straightening at last. "Like those of the sorceress in the ballad."

"Unh?" Eaglesight grinned. "So that's what jogged my memory about her."

Rondasu spoke at almost the same moment. "What ballad?"

"Not, perhaps, the most likely ballad to be sold to Your Reverences," the townmaster replied. "Briefly, it concerns a sorceress who retained her powers after being stripped."

"Impossible!" said Rondasu.

The silvery-haired priestess put her fingertips to her forehead in what might be a gesture to ward off evil, though the sorceress had not seen it before.

"It seems you were mistaken, sorceress, to assume Reverence Rondasu knew little about your ways," said Eleva. "He knows enough to judge what is possible and what impossible touching your powers even though he has always called such matters filthy knowledge—small wonder if no singer ever tried to sell him this ballad! But *I* would have paid to hear it," she went on, with an angry glance at Youngwise. "If such things are possible, we priests should not be kept ignorant of them!"

Youngwise touched palm to chin in another version of salute. "There will be few ballads sung, Lady Reverence, if you take all the singers to the Truth Grove. And that you would have to do in order to sift the true ballads from the exaggerations!"

Dowl whined and looked around. Eleva began stroking him again. "And you are that same sorceress?" she asked Frostflower. "Or is the color of your eyes coincidence?"

"I . . . am that same sorceress, Lady."

Eleva laughed. "Well, then, brother, I see little thrift in doing the thing a second time, and we can hardly take such a sorceron to the Grove. We've no choice but to question her here."

"She lies," said Shara. "She lies to escape stripping, so that she can blast us all."

The silent priestess moved to Rondasu's side. He put one arm around her. "We're not quite so poor in choices as you suggest, Eleva. We have a spearwoman with us."

"Reverences!" cried Frostflower. "I will use no power against you—the ballad is also true when it tells that I used none against the young man—"

"Brother," said Shara, trying to move between Rondasu and the silent Intassa, "if a sorcerer could put wasps into the bowels of our sister's husband at such a distance . . ."

He nodded. "Aye. Intassa, there's no need for you to be here, dovelet."

Intassa looked at him, shook her head a little and opened her mouth for the first time, but he forestalled her. "No. Hurry away, wait in one of the buildings above—don't tell us which one, don't even decide until you reach the yard. For the sake of our son, Intassa!"

Intassa nodded and hurried away. Shara moved into her place beside Rondasu and said, "I have no child, brother. I am free to share the danger with you."

"Nonsense!" said Eleva. "If there were danger, we would have felt it by now."

"Reverences," Frostflower pleaded, "our powers are not—perhaps—what you imagine them to be." How much more could she say without betraying the delicate, carefully nurtured impression of being dangerous that was one of her people's protective devices? "If you do not drive us to—"

"This builds into a denial of her fellow-sorceron's guilt," said Shara, pressing closer to Rondasu.

Youngwise sighed. "Well, Eaglesight, is your woman prepared to throw at need?"

Eaglesight, who had been watching the scene with her arms folded and her back against the wall, shifted her weight from one leg to the other and said, "Well, Whistlepoint, what's your opinion about making a throw?"

The spearwoman touched fist to lips before replying. "It's possible, Wallkeeper. I don't need as much backspace as some. But her Lady Reverence should move a little farther away. And, frankly, I'd as soon you got down Swoop or Quickarm for the job. She seemed like a gentle little bitch, for a sorceron, even if she did cost me five kips."

"So she is the same one you and Splathandle let in this morning, hey?" said Eaglesight.

Both gatewarriors nodded, fists to mouths.

"And you didn't notice her eyes, either of you? I thought you were a keen one for spending your pay on ballads, Splathandle?"

"She looked down all the time," said the axewoman.

"Yes, she has that habit," said Eleva. "Even I, watching her awaken, did not notice the color of her eyes—Well, I was standing to one side and only saw her profile. But have we not encouraged her people to walk with gaze lowered? An outward token of respect for honest folk?"

"Speaking my own opinion, Master Youngwise," said Eaglesight, "I'd say there's no reason to be flitty as flies over this. As Her Reverence says, if the sorceress was going to blast us, she'd have done it by now. But she knows if she does, she sits here in those copper chains and either starves while we rot away around her to keep her company, or Snagcut brings a few more spearwoman and they take off the grate in the garden up there to get a clear throw at her."

"Aye!" said Rondasu. "We cannot depend on hearing anything but lies from her now, and we cannot strip her and bring her to the Truth Garden, but we can leave her here for awhile. Starvation may do what stripping did not, and bring us more truthful answers as well."

"Starvation is not holy ritual, brother," said Eleva.

"Reverences," said Frostflower, "His Reverence Elvannon knew the ballad, and yet he gave me a token. I have it in my right-hand pocket."

Eleva bent and felt Frostflower's robe for the pocket.

"Gods, sister, do you fear neither sorcery nor defilement?" said Rondasu. "To touch the creature—"

"Yes, brother, I fear the defilement of punishing any innocent creature—even a sorceron—for our own guilt." Eleva found the token and waved to Youngwise. He stepped close and together they examined it by the light of their lamps. Eleva nodded and drew back her hand as if to toss the small piece of silver to Rondasu, but clearly changed her mind at the last moment and retained it instead. "Sorceress, what is your name?"

"Frostflower, Lady Reverence."

The priestess nodded. "She's told the same name, both to us, to Wallkeeper Eaglesight, to our gatekeepers, and to the priest who gave her this token. Will you demand to see it, Rondasu, or will you accept your younger sister's word for once?"

"And was it also the name of the sorceress in your ballad?" Rondasu demanded.

"The ballad gave no names," replied Youngwise.

"Master," said Whistlepoint, "that young cloth merchant who rode in with Thorn last fall—Spendwell—well, he got a little drunk on Midwinter Loudnight and boasted he had known the sorceress in the ballad. I remember because I bet on it later with Clampen and Steelsplinter, and then the bastard denied it when he sobered up and cost me half a silver."

Youngwise raised one eyebrow. "Interesting. But since Spendwell left Five Roads two hatchings ago, and since you've just told the sorceress his name, the matter does not promise to be useful at present."

Frostflower offered a silent prayer of thanks. The net was sufficiently tangled without the need to determine whether she should freely confess or try to keep secret Spendwell's true role in last summer's events—on the whole, she thought secrecy best, for Spendwell's role might lead to a revelation of Thorn's identity as the warrior of the ballad.

"Meanwhile," the townmaster went on, "what have we? A sorceress who carries a priestly token of harmlessness and a dog who is obviously harmless. They were found listening to a priestly ceremony, which the sorceress probably understood no better than did the dog, at a time when all the folk in that part of town were attending the same ceremony and she could have little else to do while waiting to buy a midday meal. Otherwise, she has shown us no sign that your fellow Reverence of the edgelands misplaced his confidence. Had she been listening at the door of our own judgment hall, Reverences, I would set her free at once and go to my supper."

"You do not deal with holy mysteries in your judgment hall,

Townmaster," said Rondasu, "but with mere practicalities."

"Frostflower," said Eleva, "why did you listen?"

"The music attracted me, Lady Reverence."

"The same feeble tale she told the wallkeeper," said Rondasu.

"So you yourself find our hymns so dreary, brother," replied Eleva, "that you think no one would sing them nor listen to them but through duty?"

"And the oration?" said Rondasu. "The oration meant only for good, decent worshipers of the gods—as the hymns and readings were also meant?"

"They were public mysteries we celebrated today," said Eleva, "not private, not secret. Very public indeed, when we require every townsperson older than nine years to attend under pain of fine . . . though perhaps the fines were welcome in your town fund, Master Youngwise?" She turned back to Frostflower. "Well, and what did you think of His Reverence's noble oration? Or did you prudently allow your mind to wander, as do more of our decent worshipers than would dare admit it?"

"From what I heard, Lady—I do not think it was a great portion of the whole—I understood that one of my people is blamed for the death of a priest in this area."

"And so you were concerned to hear more," said Rondasu, "in hopes of learning something of use to the murdering cohort of yours."

"Your Reverence, we have learned that when such things happen, they sharpen local feeling against all of us who wear the black robes. If you heard something likely to concern how the folk of a place were likely to treat you, would you not stay to hear more, whether you had had any part in the original affair or not?"

"All sorceri have cause enough for guilty fears," said Rondasu. "All priests are justly honored. I would have no reason to spy on matters in which I had no part."

"Very true," said Eleva. "You do not recognize any matters in which you have no part, Rondasu, even if that part is only the interpretation of Jehandru's justice. Well, we can relieve you of a part of your great burden of judging every creature that drinks of the Wendwater or the Mirrelstream. Go home to your well-earned rest, and leave this woman to my judgment and the townmaster's."

"You've not yet ruled for half a year, sister," said Rondasu. "You have not seen your first harvest stored, and you have no practice in wielding the Truth Knife or the Whip."

"I served as acolyte in the Grove often enough for our father and always for my husband. Oh yes, Rondasu, I know the ceremonies of the Truth Gove, if it should come to that, which I think we've determined it cannot. And I was the only one of us who dared touch the sorceress to examine her token."

Rondasu paused. Shara was pressing his arm. He exchanged a glance with her, turned back to Eleva, and smiled. "Master Youngwise can witness that the more I try to persuade you to prudence, the harder your willfulness grows. Do you intend taking her back to your own farm, or judging her here?"

"In that the offense was committed in our street, Reverence," said Youngwise, "it was committed partly against the town."

Eleva nodded. "I'd meant to visit Crinkpetal again within a few days. I'll finish this matter tonight and arrange my business with the flowerbreeder in the morning."

Shara spoke. "We'll see that the town alcoves are clean to receive you tonight, then, sister, and light candles to the gods for your safety before we go. Which alcove do you prefer?"

"The far southeastern one with the pear tree beside the window. Best not linger too long, and carry along a few lighted candles for your own safety, Shara. And you might wear copper belts."

"And you, Eleva," said Rondasu. "Though any precaution may come too late, now. The gods preserve us all!"

"The gods will preserve the most loyal first," said Shara.

Eaglesight grunted—it might have sounded irreverent, but at the same moment she stood up straight and touched fist to lips. "Whistlepoint, Splathandle, escort Their Reverences, then return to barracks. I think I can handle this one as safely alone as with any four or five of you."

The gatewarriors saluted and followed the priest and priestess out. They seemed relieved—at getting away from the sorceress, or at being held blameless by their wallkeeper and townmaster?

"I would like to hear that ballad in its entirety," said Eleva.

"That could best be done by purchasing it from the ballad-singers, Lady," said Youngwise. "I fear it's neither my business nor my wallkeeper's to remember ballads verse by verse."

"I might be able to whistle you the tune, Lady Reverence," said Eaglesight, "with a jog to remind me which tune it was—I remember it was one of the common ones."

Eleva slapped the wall. "I've had music enough for one day. It's the ballad's story I want to hear."

"And I would prefer to hear the true tale, now we have its sorceress," remarked the townmaster.

"I'd like to hear both." Eleva gave her lamp to Youngwise, bent and fumbled with Frostflower's chain. Her efforts resulted in a slight pinching of links around the flesh. "Cows' breath!" said Eleva. "Wallkeeper, this is your equipment—you unhook her."

As Eaglesight crossed the chamber, now almost dark except for lamp and constant-wick, Eleva found another bench, drew it near Frostflower's, and sat. Youngwise kindled a few wall-niche candles, placed the lamps on stands, and followed Eleva's example. Eaglesight finished unhooking the chain-and-tube device, removed it completely from Frostflower's wrists, then brought dried fruit and four cups of water from the stone cupboard. Last, she filled a bowl of water for Dowl, moved the lampstand into the circle of benches, and squatted between Youngwise and the sorceress.

"Now," said Eleva, "Frostflower, let us hear your story."

The sorceress hesitated, rubbing her wrists and shifting to a more comfortable position on the bench. "Lady Reverence, I would prefer to be judged first and told my punishment."

Eleva chuckled. The townmaster glanced at her and chuckled likewise. Dowl looked at them and wagged his tail.

"She's spent an afternoon chained here," said Youngwise, "and I call that punishment enough for crossing a yard and sitting on the pavement. Her punishment for angering priests and thus discontenting the gods—that I put into your hands, Lady Reverence."

The priestess slapped her palms together. "I think it far from likely that the gods are angered by everything that angers His Reverence Rondasu and the pious Lady Shara. What punishment should I give to a sorceress who had the audacity to find our hymns beautiful for their music? Had I known of this at once when it happened, I would have made her sit outside the holy halls all afternoon and see whether that did not cure her of sharing what we hope to be the gods' taste in music. As it is ... I think I must be content to subject her tonight to the smell of burning incense—pine for stringency, followed by lavender for obliteration, then a cup of honey-wine for deep sleep, followed by a splashing with rose-water at dawn for renewed innocence—if a sorceron may be called innocent, of course. Well, Frostflower, will you submit to all that, or will you wither me and escape?"

"Lady Reverence?" said Frostflower, caught between hope and bafflement. "Is this not incredibly mild?"

"In my own opinion," said Eleva, "it's a rather complicated purification for a singular lack of offense, but I must keep you overnight and do something to you, or His Reverence Rondasu, if he musters the courage to touch you, will do worse."

"And you will exaggerate its stringency when you tell him of it? Lady Eleva, I feel as if I were a ball that you and His Reverence . . . and perhaps Master Youngwise also . . . were throwing about among yourselves, each hoping the other would drop me."

Eaglesight put back her head and laughed. "Child, take off your black robe and become somebody's wisewoman—you might be a townmistress yourself by the time you're as old as I am now!"

Eleva frowned, but not as if displeased with anyone present. "And you feel like that with good cause, sorceress. Perhaps, if you had not pleased me by displeasing my brother, I would incline to greater harshness. Perhaps I am kind for no better reason than the wish to be unlike him. Have you guessed why we sit here so long? My sibs, I don't doubt, are up there pretending to search for dust in the priestly alcoves in hopes of seeing us come up, and I've carelessly trapped myself. If they see me take you into the Truth Grove at once, with only Master Youngwise and his wall-keeper for acolytes, they'll have fuel for a charge of heresy, or at least ritual levity. If they see us go into the Grove alone, or even come into the alcove-hall in friendly manner, they'll have fuel to charge me as a sorceri-lover, or careless in my responsibilities. So we sit here to outwait them."

"But they know we must take one or another of these courses, even though they do not see it?" said Frostflower.

Eleva shook her head. "No. If I keep you long enough, I'll be able to . . . Sorceress, did your question show concern for me?"

Frostflower gazed downward. "Lady, your dilemma touches my fate. Or at least my immediate comfort."

"Well. Five Roads has enough folk who can be consecrated as temporary acolytes—virgins, especially virginal warriors when they can be found—" (Eaglesight gave a kind of laughing bark and fed Dowl a prune when he thrust his nose into her hand.) "—parents of three children, grandparents of seven . . . and I need never say whom I chose of all these townsfolk. Rondasu cannot Grove me. Not without dragging me to Center-of-Everywhere. Give me enough time, secrecy, and shadow, and I can clothe such a scarecrow as to tell my brother to his face that I gave you whatever purification he chooses to imagine."

"Lady Reverence," Frostflower said softly, "I cannot lie."

"Yes, yes," Eleva replied, "we've heard that before. You must say it, of course—"

"It is true, Lady. We can remain silent, unless . . . forced to speak; we can . . . twist the truth to a certain extent, but we may not lie."

"Gods!" said Eleva, annoyed. "Then remain silent. Do you think we make a practice of lying without good cause? As for being forced to speak, if Rondasu tried that, he'd keep on until you said what he wished. In any case, now you've heard this much, my plans would be as damning as my actions."

"Eaglesight and I could play witnesses, if not acolytes," Youngwise suggested. "With Ruling Priestess, First Townmaster, and First Wallkeeper all telling the same tale, who would believe a different one from the mouth of a sorceress?"

Eleva nodded. "So, Frostflower, you will be our guest for a while. Now tell us your story while we outwait my sibs."

Frostflower drank half a cup of water but ate nothing. She told last summer's events very simply, omitting much. She did not tell how Starwind was born, for that would be to confess to illegal sorcering, nor did she identify his mother with the swordswoman of the ballad. Fortunately, the ballad—at least the version she had heard—was vague enough on that point that she could say simply, "The babe was given to me by a mother who did not want him, but the priests could not believe this."

The townmaster and wallkeeper, having heard the ballad before, listened to Frostflower's story with no perceptible change of attitude towards her. The priestess, however, trembled slightly and moved farther from the sorceress.

"So you *can* blast your enemies," said Eleva. "With age, with lightning, or with . . ."

"We can, Lady. But we prefer not to. It costs us a very great price. I did not guide that bolt to the priest."

"And who were they?" asked Youngwise. "The priests, the warriors, the merchant—who were they all, eh?"

"It is not always pleasant to be known as a person in a ballad," the sorceress replied. "Without their own assurances otherwise, I must assume that if they have not already revealed themselves, they prefer not be known."

Eleva shifted back to her old position on the bench. "We'll respect that. It argues well for your predisposal to keep our secret here. Wallkeeper, can you go up and see whether His Reverence and the priestesses have gone yet?"

Eaglesight saluted, gave Dowl a last pat, and left.

"If they are still watching, Lady Eleva," said Youngwise, "I suggest we remove the sorceress to one of the upper rooms in this building and seek our own houses. It grows late, and dried apricots make a poor supper after a day of snatching cold capon and wine between ceremonies. And we all need rest."

"Do you have an upper room more strongly enclosed than the one in which you kept the sorcerer last winter?" Eleva bit into an apricot.

The townmaster took a drink of water before replying. "How will you guard her, Lady Reverence? Will you stay awake all night?"

"I can put a barrier of incantations and incense around her alcove, Townmaster."

There had been no open mockery in his tone, nor any open sarcasm in hers; nevertheless, their words seemed to crystallize what Frostflower had already sensed—despite their alliance against Rondasu, all was not perfect harmony and trust between townmaster and ruling priestess. Was there also a subtle disharmony between Youngwise and Eaglesight? And were these serious, or mere evidences of the fact that no two persons could ever share exactly the same opinions on all points—the fact that kept every person separate and alone even with the closest friends and most beloved siblings?

The bad feeling between Youngwise and Rondasu needed no particular explanation; such feeling was widespread between those townmasters who hoped to see their domains as independent as possible of priestly influence and those priests who demanded to exercise power in the neighboring towns as well as in their own farms. Sorceri had watched such developments through the generations, discussing them thoroughly and keeping careful records, to the best of their observations. As a group they had much the same motive for studying the history and conditions of the other Tanglelands folk as Frostflower had for studying the currents and power-plays of this small area: self-preservation.

The bad feeling between Eleva, Rondasu, and Shara was more baffling. Frostflower was aware that the opposite of friendship sometimes existed between sibs, but her only personal experience was of deep mutual love and trust with her brother Puffball—still, in many ways, her closest confidant. Also, a deep sense of the loss of her other sibs still occasionally twitched her mind, accompanied by the certitude that, whenever she should visit Mildrock Retreat, her emotion and Cloudbird's would immediately flow into the friendship of siblings even though they had been raised so far apart.

The alliance between Eleva and Youngwise was atypical of what Frostflower's people had observed of farmers and townmasters. Eleva's motives might be connected with her effort to retain rule of her farm. Rondasu seemed to be using three weapons: his sister's alleged heresy, her inexperience and youth (though he could not be more than a few years her senior), and her sex. Among priests, according to their curious attitude toward gender, males generally held rule, females only when they had been widowed while their oldest sons were still children, or when a priest produced only daughters, which was rare because most priests took more than one wife. (A very few ruling priestesses had taken two husbands at once, but this was rare indeed.) Such a situation could only rise from a theory that men were better fitted to rule, as women were better fitted to fight—Thorn said men never became warriors because they were too important to risk their lives, but Frostflower thought the ancient reasoning must have been that women were better suited to battle.

Sorceri neither fought nor wielded rule in the same way farmers' folk wielded it, and the only distinction they made between a sorcerer's studies and work and those of a sorceress were that, when two sorceri did marry, the woman bore the children and was usually more successful in suckling them. So her own experience hindered Frostflower's efforts to understand the situation here. But perhaps Rondasu was insisting on his superior qualifications for rule as a male, and Eleva was attempting to shore up her power by attaching the nearest male ruler as her ally, even though he was a townmaster, even though their closeness might throw more doubt on her orthodoxy.

But townrulers shared priestly theories of sex and rule, perhaps carried them still further, since townmistresses were even more rare than ruling priestesses. Why, then, should Youngwise ally himself with Eleva? Congeniality of character? Or did he fear that if the two large farms to the north were combined, the single ruling priest would gain enough power to threaten some of the town's independence, and was he therefore allying himself with the ruler who seemed to him the weaker? Or did Youngwise and Eleva share some secret?

Eleva might have poisoned her husband as the only way she could gain rule of his farm, or Rondasu might have poisoned him as a step toward joining the farms. Youngwise might have learned this or guessed it, and allied himself with Eleva either because he disliked Rondasu as a murderer or because he was able to hold Eleva to his will with his knowledge as with a chain. Perhaps he had even aided one or the other of them in the poisoning.

As far as Thorn knew, the command to find a sorceron as blame-catch had come from Deveron's Farm, presumably from Eleva, on the night of Deveron's death. Rondasu, unless he had been visiting his sister and her husband at the time, would have had no part in commanding the original search. Had Eleva used the ever-convenient excuse of sorcerous evil to cover her own guilt, or had she sincerely believed a sorceron was responsible? If the latter, what had happened in the intervening days and nights to change her opinion? . . . If it was changed—if her seeming kindness now was not trickery, or, at best, a refusal to hold all sorceri responsible without examination for the crime of one.

Or might Rondasu have arranged Deveron's poisoning through another? Might he have conspired with the townmaster, and might Eleva be holding Youngwise with her knowledge of his guilt, rather than the other way around? Yet how could that be, since Youngwise had definitely been in his own house in Five Roads that night? An especially slow-acting poison? Or might the silent, silvery-haired Intassa have administered it? Had she not been Deveron's second wife, and was she not now already Rondasu's first? Might Intassa have been married to Deveron without caring for him? Might she have come to hate him, or might she have felt so indifferent to him that his life seemed less to her than a place as another farmer's first wife?

But Intassa had seemed hardly aware of her own dignity, overshadowed by her husband's sister—indeed, had they not called the tall, golden-haired priestess "sister," and had there not been a certain facial resemblance, a stranger might have mistaken Shara for Rondasu's first wife and Intassa for the unwed sister. Intassa might be as innocent and unoffending as she appeared, or she might be weighed down by guilt.

Eaglesight returned at last. "They took their time, Master and Lady. They even saw to supper. The tables are laden and waiting in the alcoves. But they're gone now. They should be passing the north holy hall by the time we get outside." Eaglesight put away the remaining food and water. "The door's hung on the one for the sorceress. Will you want a few warriors to guard it? I'd recommend myself, Splathandle, Firethrust, and Cleanedge."

"No one," the priestess replied.

"You'll spend the night alone in the same house with a sorceress, no one to guard her even while you sleep?" Youngwise clucked. "Lady Reverence Eleva, you are brave."

"If she's gently inclined as she seems," said Eleva, "I can keep her very well alone. If she's malicious after all, she's more likely to kill your warriors or corrupt them as that other sorceron did Thorn than they are to control her. I am merely realistic and practical."

"Well, and is that not the base of bravery?" said the townmaster.

Eaglesight made no comment except to grunt and give the

copper chain-and-tube device a rattle, as if to ask whether the
priestess wanted it back on Frostflower. Eleva paid no attention
to the hint.

Youngwise led the way up, Eleva following him, Frostflower
coming next, with Dowl beside her where the passage allowed,
and Eaglesight behind. All but the sorceress and the dog carried
lamps. They emerged at a side door, probably the same by which
the wallkeeper had brought the sorceress down that morning,
though in the lamplight it was difficult to be sure. Once outside,
Youngwise bid them good-night and turned toward his own dwelling, while Eaglesight escorted Eleva and Frostflower across the
open yard to the priestly lodging.

"Thank you, Wallkeeper," said Eleva. "You may send a
barracks-girl to wait outside the door at about two long-ballads'
length after sunrise. If I have not come out to give her an errand
by midmorning, you may come in and search for me—you and
Youngwise, and Firethrust if you will—no one else."

"That may be too late to help you, Lady."

"If so, it will have been too late long before sunrise. And let
the girl bring her breakfast out with her."

"As you wish, Lady Eleva, but this may give your brother a
red-hot edge to scrape our skins with."

"I'm confident that Youngwise can find a blame-catch with
very little trouble if you need one," Eleva said dryly.

Eaglesight laughed. "Well, let's hope that somehow or other
he can make it Snagcut. If griefs come, don't let 'em come with
empty claws."

"As Youngwise says," Eleva remarked. "Yes, he knows how
to make the demon give as well as take."

The wallkeeper laughed again. "His Reverence had the door
hung at the next farthest southeastern alcove, beside your own."

"No doubt it gave him an excuse for staying longer, as well
as a chance to demonstrate his great concern for his poor young
sister's helplessness. Though his logic in giving the sorceress the
next alcove to mine seems somewhat murky." Eleva drew back
the doorcurtain. "You do not need your lamp to reach the barracks,
Eaglesight?"

"I haven't been a townwarrior so long I can't still find my way
around stranger places than this, Lady. On darker nights, too."

"Good. Then give Frostflower your lamp."

The wallkeeper coughed. "We're breaking town law as it is, standing here with our lamps closer than four strides from her."

"I want both lamps, and I do not want to occupy both my hands in carrying them. And I doubt you can offer your lamp to the dog! Now, I had almost decided to grant Master Youngwise that the mealshop owners and innkeepers of Five Roads could enjoy the same prices and early choices as the raw-food merchants when buying from my farm. Should I rethink my decision?"

Eaglesight grinned and handed Frostflower the lamp. "We'll just pray to the gods you're still here long enough to write out that agreement, Lady Reverence." Then she turned and started for the warriors' barracks, whistling.

"Let's get inside, Frostflower," said Eleva.

The sorceress went in, shielding the lamp flame with one hand to prevent its setting the doorcurtain alight. Such an accident could so easily seem malice on her part!

She waited, Dowl beside her, in the entranceway between the front alcoves. A few pale blue constant-wicks marked one corridor. Eleva came in, carrying the summer lattice-door in her left hand. She tried to set it into grooves in the jambs, inside the curtain, and Dowl pressed close to her as if to see what she was doing. Frostflower stepped forward to hold Dowl or assist Eleva, and the priestess thrust the lamp at her.

"Here, hold this for me a moment," said Eleva. "It's clumsy enough setting this door in the grooves one-handed even without your dear dog's curiosity. How well does he get along with cats?"

"He used to chase them sometimes in his puppyhood, Lady, but we have not seen him do it for—two years, at least, and he has never fought nor bitten one."

"Good. Though our cats should be able to take care of themselves."

"Cats here, Lady?"

"We have a pair of them to keep our cellars clear of vermin." Having angled the door into place, Eleva held out her hand to receive her lamp again, and made no comment when the sorceress returned it at once.

She is brave indeed, thought Frostflower. By all they know and suspect of our people—part of it from my own story—she has put herself more at my mercy than I am at hers. And if she believes her husband to have been killed by sorcery...but she could not believe it and still treat me like this.

"How thrifty of my sibs," the priestess remarked. "I told them I would sleep in the far southeastern alcove, and they lit only the constant-wicks on this side of the corridor, to lead us there, no doubt regretting I had not chosen a closer alcove to spare them the expense of so many wicks."

"They lit only every other wick, Lady Reverence. But do not the townmasters supply your hall here?"

"No. They did for some generations, but four winters ago Master Youngwise, after working at it all his life, finally persuaded Deveron to release the town from the expense. And I had my part in helping Deveron decide," she went on proudly, leading the way along the corridor. "The chief counter-argument was that it would rob the town of another chance to prove their piety. But we replied that to be supplied by the townfolk was to lose part of our hold on this property—we had supplied it in the beginning, six or seven generations ago, and by continuing to let the town supply it now, we risked it eventually being lost to us as priestly ground and coming to be considered as town property we were merely privileged to use. Rondasu argued against us. He pointed out that the town merchants had bought from us the food and drink they donated afterwards to the cellars of this house. But we replied that by stocking it directly ourselves we would be sure of having the best quality. And once Deveron had decided, most of the small southern farmers voted with him—Rondasu was still too young in his rule to counter our influence. Master Youngwise embellishes his own storage chambers with our left-over supplies, of course. But he does it circumspectly, and shares his servants and stores with us at need. Do you wonder why I explain all this to you, Frostflower? I have a use for you, and it requires that you know something of our ways."

"I am grateful for your confidence, Lady."

They reached the alcove meant for Frostflower. The wooden door stood slightly ajar, a thin bolt leaning against the wall beside it, ready to be slipped into place. Eleva lifted the bolt and dropped it back against the wall. "Light as a kiss without passion! As much as to say, 'Little sister, we know you're too weak to lift a true, useful bolt into place!' By the Seven Secret Names, they'll find I'm strong enough to do more than that!" Pushing open the door, she took a few steps into the alcove and raised her lamp to look around. Near the bed stood a smudge-incense stand and a small table, set with wine flask, cup, two covered dishes, and a constant-wick ready for lighting. Otherwise, the room looked much like a bedroom alcove in Elvannon's hall—bed, one chair, a wall niche with the statue of a god, and little other furniture—comfortable but adorned chiefly by lack of clutter.

"Well," said Eleva, "let's inspect what they've prepared for me."

Except that one alcove was guarded by a wooden door and the other by a linen doorcurtain, there was little to indicate which room had been readied for the sorceress and which for the priestess. Eleva went to her table and lifted the lid of one dish, letting forth a vapor that smelled of stewed meat and spices. She looked down and nodded.

"Lady Reverence, shall I go back to my own alcove now?" said Frostflower.

"Um," said Eleva and made no further reply, gave no further sign of having heard the question; but Frostflower was at once sickened by the smell of meat, aware of her stomach's need for food and her nerves' for a little wine, and not entirely sure the priestess had really meant for her to follow into this room at all.

The sorceress returned to the alcove meant for her. She was loath to close the door, nor did she quite dare as yet to lift the lids from the dishes and learn whether these folk knew and respected her aversion to meat. She put her lamp down on the table and started to pour a cup of wine. Her right hand trembled, and she held the wrist with her left hand.

"Stop!"

Eleva's sudden command made Frostflower upset the cup and sluice a dollop of wine from the flask. She glanced around and saw the priestess standing in the doorway, her lamp in her hand and Dowl by her side. Bowing her head, Frostflower bunched her sleeve to begin wiping up the spillage.

"Leave that!" said Eleva. "Don't dare dabble your robe in it."

"Lady Reverence?"

Eleva crossed the room and looked at the dark wine puddling on the table and dripping to the floor. "You hadn't already drunk any of it, had you?"

Dowl followed Eleva, bending toward the liquid with an inquiring whine. The priestess caught him round the neck and held him back.

"No, Lady," said the sorceress. "I'd only begun to pour."

"Then Maejira nudged me in time—one of the goddesses, Frostflower. Jehandru's great intermediary of mercy. A reasonably sure sign she's watching you, sorceron or not. What urged you to leave me like that and creek back here?"

"I . . . was not aware that I crept, Lady. I made no special attempt to soften my steps—I'd asked first whether you wished me to go or stay, and when you did not answer, I thought . . ."

"Aye, so perhaps it was your question penetrating late into my brain, and not Maejira's nudge, after all."

"Lady, if the wine is not wiped up, it will stain—"

"Let it! Stain or perhaps burn away part of the wood and tile. We'll close the door, of course, to guard against the animals coming in to lap it up while we sleep—convenient that this is the alcove with the door. Although the flask here on your table may have been safe enough, after all."

"Poison?" Frostflower whispered. "Lady, do you suspect . . ."

"Sorceress, I suspect enough danger from my own kind to explain my seeming courage toward you. My wine is likelier to be poisoned than yours—they would blame my death on your sorcery. They half mean you to escape, you know, leaving that puny bolt for the door. Aye, sibs come to know each other's minds to some extent."

Dowl made another attempt to sniff the dark pool on the floor. Eleva pulled him back and said, "Let's leave and close the door before one of the cats finds this alcove."

Frostflower took her lamp and followed the priestess out, holding both lamps again as Eleva closed the door and settled the bolt in place. "Yes, it'll be enough to keep two cats and a dog out," the priestess said with a nod. "If you did escape, Frostflower, they'd have another sorcerous blame-catch to rail against, and if you didn't, they'd most likely have you speared down. Still, it's possible they may have poisoned your wine, too. They could call it the just vengeance of the gods, this time—though Jehandru knows why His justice should strike down one murderer and not another. Well, they'd find an explanation for Jehandru's ways. They're very orthodox, my sibs."

"Lady . . . you are sure? And the food also?"

"No. I can't be sure without consuming the stuff. We may find ways to test it in the morning. But I call it foolish to gamble. Come with me and we'll either find ourselves a supper we can trust or remain hungry and healthy."

Eleva led the way into the long hall and down the stairs behind the dais. To one raised in the small but merrily individualistic buildings of a sorcerous retreat, where many cottages tended to perpetual overcrowded, cozy clutter, the dwellings of farmer-priests remained awesome in their echoing austerity. Frostflower thought she could understand how priests who created and lived in such halls could also fashion a creed that held so many people in its sway.

Besides the ablution chamber, which Eleva mercifully passed by, the underground tunnel led to storage cellars with dirt floors and walls that were plastered and shelf lined, like those of common folk, rather than covered with priestly mosaic.

"They may think I'm pouring myself and you directly into their plans," said Eleva. "Or they may have guessed I would be sus- picious. It hardly seems likely they would have attempted to poison the food in storage; still, best be careful." Bypassing any foodstuffs that seemed ready to hand or easily unwrapped, she selected a small cheese with its beeswax covering unbroken and lightly dust covered, four pears that she dug from several layers down in their pit, and nine eggs. She paused at the shelves holding flour—they were sparsely laden at this time of year—and touched a small bag. "They could have poisoned flour easily enogh," she said, "but I doubt they have. We priests are not taught to cook. They know I cannot prepare my own bread from this."

"Lady," said Frostflower, "I can cook."

"Can you?" Eleva took the bag of flour from the shelf and added it to the other foodstuffs in a basket she had chosen from the hard-to reach corner of a high, dusty shelf.

In another room, she selected a jar of charcoal-filtered water and one of sweet Western honey-wine. Both jars had unbroken wax seals with films of dust.

Frostflower noticed that Eleva had chosen no meat, though a few long, hard-rinded sausages had hung from the ceiling and several wax-sealed jars of insects in brine, each jar marked with a picture of the kind of insect within, stood on the shelves.

How would Eleva have accepted the idea of the sorceress growing fresh, safe vegetables and fruits for their supper? Frostflower did not suggest it. That a strange priestess should entrust her with the cooking—that was a great enough advance for tonight. If Eleva herself were trustworthy, and not playing out a long game to dull her prisoner's suspicions and gain her confidence . . .

At last they came up by stairs that led directly into the kitchen, a small building just inside the garden wall—one difference from priestly farm residences, where the kitchen was one of the cottages well outside the garden wall. The place was dark, and chill with the unnatural cleanliness of a kitchen cleaned more often than used. But it was well equipped, with many implements unknown to Frostflower, for all the skill of retreat cookery. The sorceress kindled a fire with her lamp and set to work, conscious that Eleva, even while lighting the numerous kitchen lamps, was watching her.

Frostflower sifted the flour and Eleva scrutinized the maggots left on the fine sifting-screen. "Most of them seem still to be lively," she said, "but some look dead."

"They might have died in their own natural time, Lady."

The priestess took a large pinch of sifted flour and dropped it onto the open flame. It caused no unusual color. "I've become overcautious," she said with a laugh. "The bag was sewn up and dusty, was it not? And would they have risked spreading their traps throughout the storerooms, with the necessity of removing them afterwards to avoid poisoning themselves or some of the southern farmers or perhaps our good townmasters? But have you any sorcerous tests for poison, Frostflower?"

"There is one way I could test it, Lady . . . but to practice sorcery within your walls . . ."

"It may not be the last time I ask that of you. And I promise you this, whatever I ask you to do here will remain my secret and yours."

Frostflower took a pinch of flour and studied it for a moment. If it were poisoned, the poison would need to be very strong for such a small dose to prove fatal. And if Eleva meant to kill her, she had gone about it in an irrationally convoluted way. But if the priestess were being honest with her, then whatever she could do

to show good faith might be worth the risk. With one thought of
Thorn, of the infant Starwind, of Puffball and the others in Windslope Retreat, she put the flour on her own tongue.

Eleva started and caught her wrist. "You'll test it on *yourself?*
Why not on your dog? Why not on one of our priestly cats, if I
can find them?"

"I dare test it on no other creature than myself, Lady." Frostflower closed her eyes, thought of a single sharp, clear musical
tone in a quick effort to drive away all dangerous imagination, and
speeded her heartbeat until its pitch seemed to blend with the note
in her mind. Feeling no ill effects, no twinge of nausea nor diz-
ziness nor other symptoms that might result from poison, she
normalized her heartbeat and opened her eyes. "It seems whole-
some, Lady."

"What did you do, Frostflower?"

"I sped my body's time, Lady Reverence. I passed the equivalent of a day in those few moments. If the flour were poisoned,
I should have felt some effect of it."

"So this is your sorcery? It seems to depend more on what you
tell me of it than on what I can see. And had you told me what
you were about to do, I'd have found one of the cats—*I* am allowed
to endanger animals in order to protect humans. Though our cats
seem peculiarly shy tonight. Perhaps my sibs took them away to
prevent our testing the food on them. Or perhaps they merely scent
the strange dog." Eleva glanced at the salt and herbs in their
gridwork niches that covered the walls. "We'd best eat bland
tonight."

"Lady Reverence . . . I carry a little salt and a few herbs of my
own."

"Good. I dislike bland food. The well-water will be safe, if
you wish to boil anything. They could hardly poison a common
source."

Frostflower made thin batter for filled flat-breads. Eleva, still
watching her, peeled the wax from the cheese.

"Lady," said the sorceress, "I've heard that a piece of cow's
stomach must be thrown into the milk curds when cheese is made?"

"I don't know whether it must be. It has been, each time I've
seen the process."

Frostflower did not ask whether the eggs had been fertilized.

It was safest to assume that priests would store only eggs laid by hens who had been segregated from cocks. She filled a flat-bread for herself and one for Dowl with beaten eggs alone, then mixed cheese into the filling for Eleva's, as she would have mixed chopped vegetables if she had had them.

"You stuff only one with cheese, Frostflower?"

"We eat nothing that has required the death of a mobile creature, Lady."

"Not even to share my danger, if there is any?" Eleva cut a slice of cheese and held it out on the palm of her hand.

To taste cheese again, and with such a reasonable excuse as that of proving good faith with Eleva, was double temptation. But at last the sorceress shook her head. "Forgive me, Lady. There are still two eggs—shall I mix a new filling for your bread?"

Eleva flipped the cheese round in her fingers, lifted it, and took a bite. "You would have disappointed me had you taken it. Gods, if we were so scrupulous in our creed! Hurry and cook those things, and be sure you remember which is which. Does your dog share your scruples?"

"I do not feed him what I would not eat, Lady, but I do not question any food he finds elsewhere."

Eleva cut more cheese and fed it to Dowl. Frostflower marked her flat-bread and Dowl's with the initials of their names in the sorcerous alphabet, left Eleva's unmarked, and slipped them onto the white stones below the fire to bake. It seemed to her that whenever a test of good faith arose, she was the one asked to undergo it. Yet was not Eleva's entire treatment of her evidence of good faith?

"We won't sleep in the chambers I told them," said Eleva. "We'll sleep on the other side of the hall. In one alcove together, perhaps?"

"Did you lie to them purposely, or have you changed your mind on a sudden?"

Eleva cut another piece of cheese. "You think me overcautious? Likely I am. A woman does not gain confidence by seeing her mate die thrashing at invisible horrors, screaming of thirst and green wasps." She looked down at the cheese in her hand and pressed it back against the larger lump. "Perhaps he did see what he screamed of seeing. For all the lamps we lit around his bed, the pupils of his eyes almost swallowed the irises, as if to enable him to see things we could not. . . . Tell me your opinion, sorceress. Could that have been sorcery?"

It could not have been, but to explain that no sorceron could have caused such a death, nor any death at such a distance, might endanger the vow of prudence. "Lady, we do not harm any creature without reason. Nor would any sorceri do such a thing to the danger of their own freedom and power."

The priestess poured two cups of charcoal-water. "Nor do I believe in that sorcerer's guilt, for my own reason. A reason you might not accept, being atheist, but you could hardly mock it more than my sibs mock it. The gods speak to me in my dreams, Frostflower. Not often, not on every matter, usually not clearly, but truthfully. Maejira has shown me in a dream that my husband was killed by no one who wore a black robe."

"And yet . . . forgive me, Lady Reverence . . . and yet you sent the townmasters word to look for a sorceron?"

"The dream did not come until two nights afterwards." Eleva's tone was bitter. "But I was not the one who sent that message to Master Youngwise: I was still watching at Deveron's bed—he had fallen quiet at last, and I hoped even then to pull him up from the bog of death with a few damp cloths and a little burning incense. Intassa sent the news to Five Roads, under my sister's urging, I suspect, and I have never been able to learn how exact were their directions in my name, whether it was their prudence or Master Youngwise's to seize the nearest sorceron."

"Your sister? Lady Shara? I had thought Shara lived with—"

"With her brother and mine, His Reverence Rondasu. She does. But Deveron insisted on entertaining one another from time to time, in token of kinship. He said that friendliness, even when not demanded by ties of blood, was the surest way to avoid raids between neighbors."

"And you think that your sister may have . . ." Frostflower stopped, uncertain whether the hint, even though it had come from a priestly mouth, might not draw down priestly wrath if repeated by a sorceron.

"I have made no accusation. If they wanted Deveron's Farm without an unfamilial raid, they should have poisoned me as well. We all ate the same dinner and drank from the same flask of wine,

served by Deveron's own servants. As well accuse poor Intassa
as my sib Shara—it was in her bed, Intassa's, that he
died.... Nevertheless, there are certain plants—thornapple, win-
tergreen, no doubt others—that can produce apparently sorcerous
deaths. And if no sorceron had been found that night, they could
have blamed the townwarriors' incompetence."

Frostflower turned the flat-breads to bake more evenly. "Lady,
you said you had some use for me?"

"I had other dreams, too, in my youth," said the priestess.
"Dreams of a young man . . . tall, blue-eyed, hair and lashes golden
as the inner crust of lightly baked bread . . . and always he came
to me in a black robe. I never knew whether these dreams were
sent by gods or demons, or simply by my own desires. Rondasu
always said I was tainted with heresy, even in childhood. I did
not dream of my blackrobe more than twice or thrice in the years
I was Deveron's mate, but this past winter and spring, now my
husband is dead, the dreams have been coming again."

Frostflower shivered. It was not possible . . . and yet, a year
ago, she would have said it was not possible for a sorceron to
retain power after being raped.

"It is true, is it not," the priestess went on, "that you people
send your souls from your bodies and travel in dreams?"

She must have heard some rumor of free-travel; but was free-
travel not a conscious state, however the body appeared to others?
"Lady Reverence, a sorceron could not enter the dreaming mind
of anyone else, not even another sorceron."

Eleva chuckled. "It's not my dreaming *mind* he enters."

"Then it cannot be a sorcerer, and still retain his power.
Your . . . experiences must be simple dreams, Lady, nothing
more."

Eleva detached the piece of cheese she had cut earlier and
pressed back. This time she began to eat it. "Yes, I know your
stricture—we use it against your people often enough. But dream
couplings don't touch the flesh, no more than wakeful imaginings.
No woman ever conceived from a dream—that's simply a rumor
to serve women who find it strange that priests and a few ruling
priestesses should be allowed several mates, and no one else. And
why should my spirit blackrobe not love me as he does and keep
his power, when you kept yours, as you say?"

Frostflower shivered again. The dreams for which Windbourne punished himself overseverely . . . The power for free-travel, being the same power used for time and weather manipulation and to a lesser extent for all the functions of life, was latent in every child, of the farmers' folk as well as of the sorceri. Was there indeed some instinctive form of free-travel that took the shape of dreams, that sorceri and farmers' folk alike practiced without recognizing it? Was Windbourne unknowingly so proficient in this form as to seek out the same priestess time and again, although in trained free-travel he was still like a baby trying to take its first steps? But Windbourne was no older than Eleva, perhaps a year or two younger—he could not have visited her as a "tall young man" when she was still a young girl.

"Lady, do you wish me to stand guard over your dreams?"

The priestess laughed. "The only bedmate I've had since my husband's death? No, Frostflower, he does not force me—god, demon, sorcerer, or heresy, he is welcome. So you *can* leave your body, then? Where had you been this afternoon when you left your body in a trance in the townmasters' cellar?"

I have trapped myself, thought Frostflower. "Not far away, Lady Reverence."

"But you can go farther?"

"Not quickly."

"You cannot fly like thoughts? Nor even like birds?"

Frostflower shook her head. "No faster than our physical bodies. That is another reason I believe your young man in a black robe must be a simple dream."

Eleva sighed. "Unfortunate. I had hoped to send you tonight, but if you must go at a walk . . . and then, no doubt you'll need a chance to sleep first. Well, tomorrow may do as well—or as ill, depending on how guarded they keep their talk even when alone. And I can promise you plenty of time undisturbed. I'll guard your body myself." She paused, twisting left fist in right palm. "We had best go to the Truth Grove. My sibs and other priests have the right to enter this alcove-hall at any time, but once a ruling priestess has begun a private ritual in the Truth Grove, not even a ruling priest may intrude against her command."

Chapter 8

Thorn did not like sleeping in rooms above stables. She was used to the smells of warriors' barracks, but not to those of animals' stalls. The stink whuffled up through the cracks in the floor and hit her nose through the smudge-incense when she woke in the night.

What had waked her this time? One of the fly-ridden cows or donkeys below stamping and snuffling again? Or Windbourne's damn cat, which now sat on the window ledge licking its paws?

With a full moon shining in through the window screen and two pots of cheap smudge-incense sending out their heavy smoke, the room was not so much dark as murky-gray, as if the smells had become visible. The cat had the right idea—get to the window for a breath of fresh air. Thorn got off her straw mattress and joined Coyclaws at the window screen, which was thin, old, badly carved and splintery. The cat was splintery, too, hissing and turning with paw raised and spread, but Thorn put out one hand to rub its head and muttered, "Quiet, Azkor gut you." Coyclaws dropped the angry front and went back to licking her paws. Pretending not to recognize her comrades was a favorite game of the cat's, prob-

ably to show how different she was from Dowl, who regarded
every damn bugger that came along as a bosom friend. "Go down
below and catch a boggy rat," said Thorn. Coyclaws went on
washing her face. At least cats kept themselves clean.

The warrior studied the moon—a raider's moon, according to
the old tried-and-best theory—full, bright, and unclouded. Said
to give raiders the best chance of invading unfamiliar territory,
while the defenders, who were supposed to know their farm blind-
folded, would have the best chance on a moonless night. Thorn
was not so sure, but—

Just as she had begun to think about dousing the smudge-pots
and letting the night air come in unchoked, the breeze, which had
been blowing parallel to the window, died down and a bunch of
mosquitoes danced through the air towards her face. Waving,
slapping, and cursing, she backed away into the smudge-protected
interior. A warrior learned to put up with insects without moving
when she had to, as during a raid, but Thorn had no reason to
leave herself open to their stings, buzzing, and feathery little wings
and legs now. Besides, on a raid she would be dressed.

Sorceri slept fully clothed or in their undergarments, but Thorn
did not want to wake to the instant need of fighting or escaping
and trip over a long, tangled skirt as soon as she jumped up. And
she needed whatever little luxuries she could find as tokens to
herself that she was not really a blackrobe. Most nights she stripped
completely as soon as Windbourne, worn out with his penances,
had fallen asleep on his side of the room.

She looked at Windbourne. He lay trance-stiff. If he were free-
traveling already, his entity, as they called it, might be sitting up
trying not to look at her. Resisting the temptation to spread her
arms and spin around a few times to torment him, she got her robe
from the chair and put it on. Windbourne's entity might not be
alone.

Thorn shivered, shrugged, went back to her mattress, sat on
it, fished Stabber up from beneath its edge, and began polishing
him with her robe in order to be doing something. Maybe it had
been Frostflower's entity, free-traveling up to this room, that woke
her. Frost claimed that no one, probably not even a dog or mos-
quito, could sense a free-traveler except another disembodied free-
traveler. But Thorn found that hard to believe. Surely there must

be some hint—a breath on the eyelids, a whisper in the brain, a slight stirring of the smudge-incense smoke. . . . Maybe a sense of Frostflower's presence had called Coyclaws up to the window ledge?

Still, the cat was washing itself as if totally unaware of any unusual tension. Thorn shifted on her mattress.

She wished she had slept through. Waiting was always the worst part of warrioring, but waiting like this, completely excluded from whatever was going on—not even sure anything *was* going on—no action to look forward to except hearing a report of what was happening a quarter of a day's walk away . . . She glanced at the moon again. It was higher than it should have been according to the plan. If Frostflower had started from Five Roads at full dark, she should have been here before now. So either something had happened—she was late, not coming until tomorrow . . . or not able to come at all? Or she had come and gone and the bloody sorcerer had fallen asleep again without waking Thorn to report. Or maybe she was here, telling Windbourne half a damn night's worth, and Thorn unable to glimpse her or hear her.

She should not have let Frostflower go into Five Roads alone. And she felt too damn useless sitting here like a . . .

Windbourne stirred, groaned, sat up. The cat jumped down from the window and strolled over to him, tail up.

"Was she here?" Thorn demanded.

He sighed and shuddered. "She was here. God, and us not there!"

The swordswoman stood. "Tell it straight and clear, sorcerer!"

He began stroking Coyclaws as if to help steady himself. "Her message to us is . . . that we should turn back northward. They seem tolerant enough of other sorceri in Five Roads Crossing, but the watch is still strict for one of my description, and the warriors would surely recognize you if they saw your face. And after to-day . . . The priests held ceremonies in the town today . . ."

"She wants us to start out right away? Without waiting for her?"

"At first she said we should go at once, leave her to follow as soon as she could. I persuaded her to let us wait three nights in South Edgewaste, but—"

"What's gone wrong? Where is she?"

"She . . . did not want you to . . ."

"Didn't want me to know? Didn't want you to tell me? By the gods, sorcerer, if—"

"Rosethorn, she didn't want to tell me, either! I made her tell—"

"You made *her?"*

The cat snarled and leaped away from Windbourne as if he had jerked her fur. "She could not lie," he said, "and she saw that if she continued to say nothing, I would think it worse than it is."

"And? Bloody Hellbog, sorcerer, you can't lie either, and if you don't tell me what this situation is that could be worse, I'll go back to that stinking town and find out for myself!"

"She is . . . she's a prisoner, Rosethorn. In the priests' town alcove-hall."

"Gods! And it could be worse?"

"She is being treated very mildly, almost like a guest. She was arrested for a small thing, coming too near a holy hall and listening to the ceremony. Her Reverence . . . the priestess Eleva . . . seems to mean her no harm. Nor do the Townmaster and First Wallkeeper. Indeed, Lady Eleva insisted on guarding her alone—there is no one else in the priestly house with them, she is not bolted in nor chained in any way. . . . They seem to have given one another their trust, Rosethorn. As you and I did that night. They're even sleeping in the same alcove. No one would harm her body; it'd mean desecrating a priestess' bedchamber."

They were clever with their words, these sorceri. No outright falsehoods, but a careful selection of facts to give whatever impression they wanted you to get. Allow for a double filtering through sorcerous prudence by the time it reached Thorn, and it sounded pretty damn bad. "No one can harm her except Lady Eleva. If they don't intend to hurt her, why not purify her right away and let her go?"

"The other ruling priest—Rondasu—seemed angered out of measure, ready to punish her severely. Her Lady Reverence crowded him out somehow, demanding that Frostflower be left to her and the Townmaster. As if between them, they would protect her from Rondasu's anger, perhaps guard her until she could safely travel north again past his farm."

Thorn snorted. "Master Youngwise polishes the dice for whichever Reverence he thinks he can get the most out of. And Eleva's as likely as any other priest to have poisoned her husband, maybe a little more likely."

"No! This proves she did not! Why kill him and then show kindness to—?"

"Why not? If it is kindness. Damn your guts, sorcerer, you're ready to trust a priestess you've never even seen? Hellbog, I've lived with them, worked for them, been brought up all my life to reverence them, and you're readier to trust 'em than I am! All right," she went on, as he moved forward into the moonlight and she glimpsed the shock in his face, "I know what you want to think about Her Lady Reverence, but which one's more important—a sorceress you *know,* one of your own kind, who's risking her guts for you like a selfless idiot—or a priestess who may have poisoned her husband and tried to get you stoned and swung for it?"

"We cannot go north again, Rosethorn," he said.

"I'm glad you're finally letting your bloody brain do a little of your thinking." The warrior glanced around. "She's not still here, is she?"

He shook his head. "She left before I came back into my body. She hopes to return to hers in time for almost half a night's sleep."

Thorn nodded. "Better let her get back to her body as soon as she can." The way she understood it, it was a kind of Hellbog for sorceri whose bodies got destroyed while they were out free-traveling. "Bloodrastor! We'd better not risk letting her see us on our way—we'll have to give her plenty of time to get back, and by the time we get started . . . We can't very well get to Five Roads, find a way in, find her, and get her out and have anything like a decent chance to escape without a full night for the whole job!"

"I can go to Five Roads Crossing tomorrow and give myself in exchange for Frostflower," Windbourne said proudly.

"You're thinking with your blasted farthole again. They'd gut you and keep her. And know she's our friend into the bargain." Thorn began to pace, almost stepping on the cat, which hissed and jumped back up to the window and from there to Windbourne's shoulders. "Either we're too late already," Thorn went on, "or there's some chance tomorrow night will still be in time."

"We might be able to reach Crinkpetal's house tonight," the

sorcerer suggested, "if we could get through the towngates somehow."

"Unh. Yes, there're ways inside the walls besides through the
gates. Thief-holes, thief-tunnels, thief-notches and rope hooks for
climbing—a town the size of Five Roads, the bloody robbers
make new ways in and out before you can find all the old ones.
With a few hours to prowl around on the outside where townwarriors don't patrol that much . . . yes, we might find one, if the
gods are feeling very generous. . . . What were both ruling priests
doing in the town holy halls today?" she asked suddenly. "What
the Glorious Harvest kind of ritual was it? Frostflower listened in,
you say? Did she tell you anything about it?"

Windbourne was silent.

"Stirring up the fire again, weren't they?" Thorn went on.
"Scolding the townsfolk for letting us go—promising them Hellbog and demons' claws for minding their own business and letting
priest-killers slip out of town behind their backs? Well? Speak up
or I'll know I'm right!" This was how he must have gotten the
details out of Frostflower that she had not wanted to tell him.

"How . . . did you guess, Rosethorn?"

"I'm a priests' woman, remember? A few lifetimes ago, I'd
have been a priestess myself—warriors were, in the bloody old
times. And I'm not sure I like the idea of trusting that flowerbreeder
again."

"If Crinkpetal were a man who took priests' threats seriously,
he would not have helped us the first time."

"Everybody changes, sorcerer. And don't shut off Hellbog
threats because you don't believe in the place."

"I have no need to believe in the place," Windbourne replied
in a low voice. "I carry Hellbog in my mind—a more hellish bog
than your simple, unthinking conception—surely no one who
spends life in such a state can hope for the happy afterdeath. But
Crinkpetal believes in nothing, warrior. If he did, I would have
converted him long before now. Since he does not, he chooses to
remain among the farmers' folk, where he has his wealth; but
secretly he laughs at their lies."

"Azkor's teeth! And outwardly, he's not very likely to risk his
position, is he?"

"He believes in friendship. He risked everything for us the first time, Rosethorn."

"I've had experience with the kind of friendship these farmers' cattle have for sorceri."

"So have I." Windbourne looked at her steadily in the moonlight. "And I have had to put my trust in a priests' woman whom I did not even know."

"Hellbog!" For a moment, Thorn's anger seemed about to burst. Then she laughed. The bastard was right. But if Thorn believed in all the gods and all the demons, she also believed in all the flips and bounces of a good set of dice—she had always been a gambler. Besides, it would give them a better way to spend the rest of the night than sitting here scratching each other's nerves. "All right. I'll tell our landlady we've just had word . . . a dream, enough farmers' folk believe in dreams, she'll accept that . . . of trouble back in our retreat so we've got to leave right away. We'll go out the north gate. I'll tell the gatewarrior the same story; she wouldn't let a sorceron inside at night, but she should be willing to let a pair of us out any time. We'll double back where the road curves out of sight around that bulge of forest, find the Wendwater Wheelpath, and take that to Five Roads—we should miss Frost that way even if she's not far enough ahead of us by then. If we find a thief's hole through the wall in time, we'll spend the day with your friend Crinkpetal. If not, we'll spend it hiding in the woods outside town."

"We must lie to innkeeper and townwarriors here?" said Windbourne. "Would it not be the lesser falsehood to creep out of this town, as we must creep into Five Roads Crossing?"

Thorn sighed. "Wedgepopper, they saw us come in, and if they find us gone and haven't seen us go, they'll assume the worst and start the hunt from here. If they see us go north openly—we'll leave a message for our companion to follow us—they're not so likely to worry about where we are. It's a bloody bad gamble whatever we do, but I'm not going to shave the damn dice against myself!"

Coyclaws arched up on Windbourne's shoulders, spat, jumped down and began chasing something in a corner of the room.

Chapter 9

Every bed Frostflower had ever seen in a priestly alcove was large enough for two. Eleva had decided they would both use the bed in one of the alcoves on the west side of the hall.

"Is it not against your customs?" the sorceress asked, aware that even Elvannon had had her sheets removed and washed after the night she spent in his farm.

"Your minds may be very different from ours," the priestess replied, "but I suspect that your bodies are not." The only precaution she took was to sprinkle a thin line of perfumed powder down the center of the mattress sheet—if this was a special precaution. She told Frostflower it was standard practice when two farmers shared a bed for the single purpose of sleep; when they shared it with the additional purpose of coupling, two more lines of powder were sprinkled across the first; when one slept alone, the powder was sprinkled in a circle beneath the pillow. Perhaps all this was true. Eleva certainly chanted the incantation that accompanied the sprinkling with the quickness of long familiarity; it was in the old priestly language, and Frostflower caught a few phrases dealing with "protection," but protection from what she

could not tell. "If it's not against your customs?" Eleva had asked
when the powder was sprinkled.

"If it will not contaminate you to sleep beside me, Lady Reverence, it will not contaminate me to be protected from your demons
by your prayers."

Eleva laughed and snuffed out the lamp.

The decision to free-travel that night had cost the sorceress
considerable uneasiness. But any immediate danger to the priestess
and herself seemed much less than that to her friends in String-of-
Beads. She could not be sure that her warning would keep them
away; but if she did not free-travel to them, they would be even
more likely to come to Five Roads, and if she emphasized their
danger, at least they would come forewarned.

She did not leave her body until sure that Eleva was well asleep.
On her return, she noted with relief that Eleva still slumbered
safely and peacefully. Then she slipped back into her body and
fell into the sleep of exhaustion.

Free-traveling always created some imbalance, for the body
rested while the entity was absent, but the consciousness still
required its full measure of sleep on its return. And Frostflower
had many emotions to sort out in her dreams that night. She did
not awaken until about midday, her body aching from too much
rest but her mind clear and calm, at least for the moment.

She heard voices in the long hall, and the other side of the bed
was empty. She rose, put her black robe on over her smock,
smoothed the sheets, folded the blankets and puffed the pillows.
The voices were conversing softly, unhurriedly, with no audible
tension or urgency.

Dared she intrude on the conversation, or did the priestess
expect her to wait concealed? But in that case Eleva could have
tied the silk door cords across the curtain as a signal to her prisoner-
guest to stay in the alcove. And Dowl, too, was gone from the
bedchamber—perhaps sitting with the priestess and her visitor.

Frostflower left the alcove, crossed the corridor, and looked
into the long hall through one of the archways. She made no
attempt to conceal herself, but neither did she do anything to call
attention to her presence.

Eleva sat in a cushioned chair with armrests and a low back, turned at a three-quarters angle from the archway. She had a bit of candied fruit in one hand and stroked Dowl with the other. Her visitor sat in a similar chair, facing her. A man in early middle age, his body showed the love of good food and his green silk robe, lavishly embroidered with flower designs, showed the wealth to buy it, but his face showed the traces of more worry and sorrow than, by his expression, he had deserved. A table stood between them, arranged with food and drink, and the back of a third chair was visible beyond the table.

"You'll cause talk, Reverence," the newcomer was saying. "It's never been done."

Eleva waved her piece of fruit. "By 'never,' you mean never as far back as living memory reaches. My late husband's grandmother could remember a fashion folk once had of braiding their donkeys' tails with colored ribbon. It's the sort of thing we keep no records of, and in a few more generations it may fall into your kind of 'never.'"

Dowl looked at Frostflower and whined, but returned his attention to the candied fruit in Eleva's hand.

"Each trade keeps some record of matters that most concern itself," the visitor began, "and I can assure Your Reverence . . ." Belatedly, his glance followed Dowl's to the sorceress in the archway. His eyebrow rose and he seemed to shake his head very slightly, but almost at once he went on. "Your . . . guest . . . seems ready to join us, Lady."

Eleva turned and smiled. "Welcome to the day, Frostflower. I thought it best to allow you as much sleep as you cared to take. So I sent Eaglesight's barracks-girl to good Crinkpetal with an invitation to come here and talk over a matter of trade while I waited. Will you eat your breakfast now? Crinkpetal has been so kind as to bring us food."

The merchant smiled nervously. Crinkpetal the flowerbreeder —did Eleva know he was a sorceri-lover?

Frostflower smiled and inclined her head, hoping no sign of recognition showed in her face. "Thank you, Lady Reverence. Thank you . . . Merchant Crinkpetal? My hunger's not yet fully awake."

"Then come and sit with us until it is." At last Eleva fed Dowl the piece of candied fruit. "Don't worry—I instructed him to bring us plenty of such food as requires no death but that of plants."

Frostflower nodded and took her place in the waiting chair. Crinkpetal had not brought milk and vegetable food exclusively— there was cold fowl on the table as well and a boiled cow's tongue, partly sliced away. But there were also crusty, braided buns, soft spice cakes and yeast bread with new greens baked into it, an egg-and-vegetable loaf, several kinds of candied fruits and a piece of honeycomb. No firm cheese, but soft white curds, and there were both onion-sauce and thin strawberry jam, depending on which flavor one preferred to mix with the curds.

"Crinkpetal's sons carried the baskets," said Eleva. "They've returned home, since we'll be keeping the food. You won't need to cook today, Frostflower. Not unless I prove unable to so much as boil water."

"Mint, bay, or apple-mix?" said Crinkpetal, opening a triple-compartment tea box. Frostflower put a few pinches of dried mint leaves into her cup and the flowerbreeder poured steaming water over them from the small silver kettle that had been keeping hot on a tripod set in the brazier. "Lady Eleva's payment," he went on, "is more generous than the food. I must hope the food sellers never learn of my meddling in their market."

"I calculated your payment on the theory that you had bought it prepared from the food sellers," said Eleva. "But you won't find me so over-generous in your customary trade. You need to make a good profit on what you do sell, since you balk at selling more. Would you believe, Frostflower, that this merchant has actually been trying to persuade me *not* to buy his goods?"

"Hardly that, Lady Eleva." Crinkpetal began to study the tray of candied fruit. "I've only tried to point out that what you plan has never been done before. At least, as you say, never within memory, nor within our own family records, and my great-grandmother was flowerbreeder to your great-great-grandfather."

"And you fear to be implicated in my heresy if you sell me my flowers now, eh?"

"It's not for a merchant to judge questions of heresy among priests, Lady Reverence," Crinkpetal replied, reminding the sorceress of Master Youngwise. "But it was only in my grandfather's time that the lesser sort of townsfolk began planting their own flowers, and there was some question as to the orthodoxy of that. The High Gathering took several years to decide it."

"And meanwhile, as I recall from *our* family records, your grandfather Astereye moved from our farm to Five Roads Crossing and made his wealth from the new fashion."

"Nor has the wealth decayed in my mother's dealings nor mine, Lady Eleva." The merchant seemed to be arguing that he did not need a new, questionable source of income. "Not even that profligate middle son of mine was able to drain us beyond recovery."

Eleva tsked. "You may have wealth for your children and grandchildren, and enough business among the townsfolk to keep your money-cellar replenished—but have you no spirit of adventure, Crinkpetal?"

He finally made his selection from the tray of fruit—a cluster of honeyed raisins. "I've had adventure enough, and little of it pleasant. Surety and safety, ten or twenty more goldens a year going into my cellar than come out, and a peaceful old age to watch new colors develop in my gardens, that's all the adventure I ask."

"Cows' breath! Ten or twenty goldens' profit a year, old pretender! A hundred would be nearer the truth. And the time's long overdue when honest farmworkers should be allowed to enjoy the color townsfolk enjoy around their own cots."

"Your farmworkers live in the midst of growing things, with more fields and trees than buildings within the farmwalls. At this season especially, they live surrounded with the blossoms that promise food. Many of our townsfolk have nothing but a short strip of earth between dwelling and pavement and the Truth Grove garden—they could not even walk in that in my grandfather's time. When the High Priestly decision came from Center-of-Everywhere, it spoke of the danger that townsfolk might forget the mystery of Aomu and Voma with so little example of it before their eyes." The raisins held halfway to his lips, Crinkpetal spread his free hand. "I don't try to contradict you, Lady. I only point out what was argued before, and what may be argued again if you—"

"Then let it be argued again!" The tabletop being covered, Eleva slapped the armrest of her chair, causing Dowl to lift his ears and look at her. "Sweet Raellis! My brother has more serious

matter than this for that charge of heresy he makes his favorite
threat against me! Or do you side with *him*, Crinkpetal? Is my
power so obviously brittle that you choose to lean toward his?"

"Reverence, Reverence!" The merchant put his raisins down
untasted. "I side with no one—I try to live my life and breed my
flowers in peace with all. And will your folk think my flowers a
good trade for their small savings? Will they not prefer to continue
using all the land around their cottages for the embellishment of
their suppers?"

"I think not. I'm going to try a new plan of sharing out the
field crops to my workers this harvest. And do you know what
they grow the most of, in their cottage gardens? Those food plants
that give the showiest blossoms in the spring. I tell you, Crinkpetal,
I am giving my people the chance for flowers if they wish them.
I would prefer giving them a chance at the best flowers, yours,
but if you fear my brother's alarms of 'heresy,' I'll deal with
Pollenfinger or I'll distribute seeds and cuttings from my own
plants."

"I did not say that I would refuse you, Lady Eleva." He spread
his fingers again. "Far from me to scorn a large new market. Did
I not help you a few hatchings ago with your plan for 'steam-
gardens'?"

There followed a long trade discussion of the various flowers
and decorative leafy plants Eleva wished to buy.

Frostflower could hardly believe that Eleva had summoned the
flowerbreeder here simply to arrange the purchase of flowers for
her workers. Outrageous as the plan might be to priestly custom,
she must have a far more pressing business today. If she suspected
Crinkpetal to be a friend of sorceri, even the same one who had
helped Thorn and Windbourne, was she probing him for confir-
mation of her suspicions?

Crinkpetal seemed at times to be trying to communicate some
secret message to the sorceress. Once, when Eleva asked the ad-
visability of using a certain strain of roses he had developed, of
such a deep gray color that some eyes saw them as blue, he replied,
"Aside from the expense, Lady, and the fact that even the townmasters shy from owning so obviously priestworthy a flower, my
Gray Silver Rose has a particularly long thorn—a thorn I've not
yet succeeded in breeding out, which makes the bush undesirable

in gardens where small children play. Because of its thorn, even your fellow priests wait to plant the Gray Silver until their children are ten or twelve years old. Intassa herself refused it, you remember, because of the children."

"Intassa is overly timorous," said Eleva. "Blowingbud and Coddlemeasure have taught the children very well how not to meddle with the flowers. Well, now she's taken her own Vari to my brother's farm with her, I'll buy two of your Gray Silver bushes for my own garden, at least. You may be right about the workers' gardens, however. The gods know workers' children tumble up in the middle of worse dangers than rosethorns, but they may prefer brighter colors, anyway."

"The Deepwine would be a better rose for them, Lady Eleva. Its thorn is very small, for all that the blossom is almost the color of blood."

Another time, he said of a variety of longstem lilies, "In breeding for their brilliant color, I unhappily developed a very frail stem. Within a few more seasons, I should be able to correct this fault, but the present generation of plants should be placed where they'll have shelter from the wind—away from the edge of the wind, they do well enough, but a sudden, sharp-edged wind can reduce a row of orange blooms to an ugly wreck." He seemed to give a very slight emphasis to such words as "rose," "thorn," "wind," and "edge," and frequently to direct a glance at Frostflower shortly before or after pronouncing such words. Had the warrior and sorcerer already come back into Five Roads despite her warning, as she feared they might? Had they been captured? Here, sequestered with Eleva, Frostflower had no more way of learning what happened in the town around her than if she were three days' journey distant. Only when she free-traveled again could she learn anything else but what the priestess chose to tell her. Or perhaps they were hiding with Crinkpetal again, and he hoped for some secret message from her to take back to them. What message could she give him? And how could she convey it?

Or might he simply be trying to warn her, through the mere fact of cloaking their names in Eleva's presence, that the priestess was not to be trusted?

Was all this mistrust justified, or was it as foolish as Thorn's

early mistrust of Frostflower had been? Could there be no mutual
trust and frankness anywhere in the middle Tanglelands without
a mutual initiation of suffering to open the minds to one another?

"Well, my old friend and favorite flower-merchant," Eleva said
at last, with a smile that looked open and honest, "I hope to make
it well worth your time to have spent this morning with me, and
if your cook were not your own son, I'd try to hire him away from
you. But for now, no doubt you have your plans for the afternoon,
as we have ours."

"If I had more than the two children left and could depend on
one of them to carry on my business without the other's help,
Lady Eleva, I would most certainly hire him to you for a cook."
Crinkpetal rose and touched palm to lips. "All gods and goddesses
prosper your plans, Reverence."

"And turn your frustrations to benefits." Eleva lifted her hand
in a priestly blessing—without, however, rising from her chair.
But then, as if suddenly remembering an errand, she laughed and
stood. "I'd almost forgotten. I must walk with you to the door—
I want to retie the thongs inside the curtain and summerscreen
after you've gone."

While she was absent, a yellow cat appeared from somewhere
behind the dais and leaped up onto one of the empty chairs. Frostflower caught him before he could proceed to the tabletop, held
him in her lap and fed him a piece of the egg-and-vegetable loaf,
all of which brought Dowl whining to her side, so that she had
to feed him as well.

Eleva returned and sat again, still laughing. "The good old
hypocrite," she remarked, not unkindly. "Wishes for the gods'
blessings come no more sincerely from Crinkpetal's mouth than
they would from yours, sorceress! Ah, so Yop's returned, has he?
Well, Gris is probably around somewhere, too, and I did my sibs
an injustice last night, thinking they took them to avoid my feeding
them poison."

"Have you spoken of your gods with Crinkpetal, Lady?"

Eleva chose a piece of candied fruit at random. "He'd hardly
report his skepticism to me, Frostflower. No doubt he thinks himself very clever in concealing it. But one cannot grow up a priest
and fail to learn the signs—a certain glassiness in the eyes during

ceremonies, a visible lack of fervor in singing hymns, a studied reluctance to speak of the gods lest one speak of them too flippantly, and so on. At least, one cannot grow up the child of suspicious parents and sibs ever anxious to mark down such evidence for use against their enemies without learning such signs." She popped the fruit into her mouth and snapped her fingers stickily. "But as long as there are so few like Crinkpetal, and as long as he keeps his opinions to himself and obeys his townmasters and priests in all other matters, I see no harm in it. Better a good-hearted, hard-working hypocrite like Crinkpetal than a pious, plotting priest like my brother. What? Have I shocked you, sorceress?"

"Lady Reverence," said Frostflower, "you yourself believe in your gods?"

Eleva stopped in the act of lifting a small cluster of raisins and stared at the sorceress. "Would the gods permit a priest to rule who did not believe in them? If I had not had such difficulty getting you into my own keeping, Frostflower..." She shook her head, separated one raisin from the cluster, and ate it. "No, of course not—Rondasu would never dare risk using a sorceron. He leaves that to his half-heretic younger sister. In any event, Frostflower, it's not what we believe or disbelieve that creates the gods' existence!"

If Eleva was sincere... "Lady, if I might talk with you about these things—sincerely, keeping back nothing?"

"You're not trying to convert a priestess, Frostflower?"

The sorceress shook her head. "Perhaps to convert myself."

Eleva slapped the arm of her chair. "Cows' breath! Well, not now. Certainly not now! You'll not give up your sorcerous powers for a while yet, Frostflower—oh yes, I know you practiced them again last night. Have you any idea what it's like to awaken in the middle of the dark hours and find the person beside you motionless as a newly dead corpse?" She leaned forward. "Where did you go, Frostflower? Did you go to my brother's farm already last night?"

The sorceress shook her head. "Had I known you wished it at once, Lady..."

"I would have wished it, yes, had I known you still had the vigor. I thought you'd need to rest. Well, they should all have been asleep, with little enough for you to learn from them . . . though if I'd sent you after them at once, while they were still on their way from Five Roads back to his farm—well, the past is settled!" She sighed and sat back. "And wherever you did go, was it on my concerns or your own?"

Frostflower took a moment to phrase her reply. "Our concerns are closely intertwined, Lady. But I learned nothing likely to help you."

Eleva gazed at her for several heartbeats, then shrugged. "No doubt Rondasu and Shara would press you for a more detailed answer. Perhaps Intassa would, too, although I cannot see her wielding whip and knife herself. But I will not press you. You're ready to go where I direct you now?"

The sorceresss nodded. Anxious as Eleva seemed to prove her trust, Frostflower could do no less than assume her sincerity and respond in kind. "Even to set out from your Truth Grove, Lady Reverence."

"I'd hope so, seeing that will be to both our greater safety! Have you guessed why I summoned the flowerbreeder here?"

"To have him bring food we can trust? To fill your time while you allowed me to sleep?"

"In part. And why I kept him sitting with us so long to speak of a trade matter that could wait?"

"It should probably not wait overlong, Reverence. Already the season's past to give your people the earlier blooming flowers."

Eleva tempted Dowl over to her side with a bit of sliced cow's tongue. "But I wanted one witness to see us here together, to know that I had neither cowed you nor had you spellcast me before I took you into the Grove. Remember him, Frostflower. His secret sorceri-love may be older than my lifetime. If the worst happens, if you should need a refuge, seek out Crinkpetal, in Wiltdown Street, in the northeast part of town."

"What do you fear may endanger us, Lady?"

Eleva rose. "Very little, if we act soon enough and if the gods' design favors us so far as to arrange something for you to learn at once." She fed Dowl a last bit of fruit. "Are you ready?"

"Now, Lady? But you have no acolytes yet."

"I've decided not to use any. There's a branch of the tunnel

that leads from this building to the rear alcove of the old temple—
we'll use that. I'll raise a chant from time to time, loud enough
for anyone near the temple to hear a little something—they'll
know I'm inside, but they won't know you're with me. There will
probably be rumors, but all anyone will *know* is that I'm conducting
some private ceremony in the Grove and must not be disturbed
or intruded upon."

Frostflower nodded and rose, first lifting the cat down from
her lap before he could take the excuse to leap up to the table.
"What of this food, Lady?"

Turning her fist in her palm, Eleva studied the remains of the
meal. "Best gather it up and carry it with us. Will you do that,
Frostflower? I'll fetch the candles and incense."

If I could have met this woman in different circumstances,
thought the sorceress . . . If we could have discussed matters of
eternal importance, rather than this devouring concern of a few
people's lives in a small area of the Tanglelands . . . and yet it is
such concerns, small as all of us are in ourselves—the life and
death of a few priests and sorceri, the destruction of a few anthills,
the bees of a single hive collecting drops of nectar and spreading
grains of pollen from individual flower to flower—that weave the
very fabric of all nature.

And so it was important to learn the truth of what had happened
here, important for an even greater reason than the safety of Thorn
and Windbourne, important even though within a hundred years
all of them would be dead and forgotten. Perhaps it was even more
important to learn the truth of Deveron's death than to learn the
truth of which gods ruled nature. Deveron had been no less important than the first cloud signaling the lines of ferment between
warm air and cold—he, and those whom his life and death had
drawn together, were also part of the pattern, though whether it
was a fixed pattern or a fluid one . . .

Eleva had referred to the design of the gods as if she believed
the priestly assumption of a future already fixed and settled. But
she had also referred to the changelessness of the past, as if she
considered the past fixed in a way the future was not. She apparently remained undisturbed by Crinkpetal's presumed skepticism,
and she did not fear to break custom by her own actions. And even

if all this were a mere pose, and Eleva herself wicked and treacherous, she had said one thing that Frosflower would nurture in her mind—an idea she herself had often thought but never expressed, not even to her brother Puffball, so that when the priestess threw it off boldly, almost casually, it had thrilled through the sorceress like an echo that seemed somehow to corroborate the original voice: Truth existed somewhere beyond mortals' conception of truth.

Chapter 10

Thorn and Windbourne had reached Five Roads about the time that sudden storm clouds covered the westering moon. Taking advantage of the darkness, they had groped their way around the townwalls, the sorcerer twisting the breeze—and sharpening it when necessary—to keep hitting the masonry at an angle, while the warrior listened for suspicious whistles. Thus, they had finally found a thief's tunnel, blocked with stones fitting not quite closely enough to keep out a whistle when the current was directed at just the right angle. A sorceron, Thorn thought, would make a handy assistant to a patrol of townwarriors out looking for robbers' tunnels; as things were, the honest patrols had to wait for natural telltale winds.

By the time they had gotten into town, dawn was on the way, orange through the storm clouds, leaving them only enough margin to reach Crinkpetal's house and get in through the hidden door in the garden wall.

The flowerbreeder had not been delighted to see Thorn and Windbourne again, but at least he had stayed their friend, and the warrior trusted his peevish complaints about their return more than she would have trusted vows of undying good faith.

All the same, when Eaglesight's favorite barracks-brat showed up, a few ballad-lengths after the last spit of rain, to request Crinkpetal's attendance on Lady Reverence Eleva that morning, Thorn had not been slow to voice her own suspicions. At first she had tried to insist that she and Windbourne should go along disguised as servants to carry the baskets of food that were part of Eleva's request. But the flowerbreeder had been as stubborn as the swordswoman.

"You're here and I won't betray you," he had stated, "but you'll repay the favor by not betraying me. You'll not be seen leaving my house by daylight, especially not with me."

Thorn's morning's wait had not been helped by the need to keep her voice low when she felt like raging. "If you can get out of your stinking body," she had remarked to the sorcerer—the "stinking" was inaccurate since the rain had washed them both and Crinkpetal's trusted servant Speckless had brought them hot rosewater and linen towels to wipe off the rain—"why the Hell can't you travel around? What's the extra trick? Azkor's tail! if I were as competent a warrior as you are a sorceron, I'd have been killed in my second raid!" She must have said something like this a few times too often, because at last he responded by lying down and going into the deathlike trance that could signify free-travel. Then, having no one else left to grumble at, she grumbled at the ants and bees, and wondered whether she would try to drag Wedgepopper along or leave him in his silly trance if the townwarriors came.

The sorcerer did not return to his body until Crinkpetal was back in the garden and walking toward the cottage.

"How far did you get?" Thorn said.

"I was almost able to disengage completely."

"Hellstink! You didn't even get quite out of your blasted skin? Why the demons' farts bother?"

"It spared my having to listen to those of your comments aimed directly at me, Rosethorn. And you still wear the black robe. Your language does not fit it."

Before Thorn could reply that her language had been mincing sweet and pure when they were out in the open, the flowerbreeder entered the cottage. "Her Reverence did in fact, it seems, summon me for no more sinister reason than to bring her breakfast and to discuss trade matters. Your friend is well and, to all apeparances, reasonably safe for the time being. Probably safer than we are."

"So she *is* with the priestess in that bloody town alcove-hall?" Thorn began.

"And you, Crinkpetal," Windbourne said in almost the same moment, "you are safe? Her Reverence does not suspect you?"

The merchant grunted. "I think she suspects me of heresy and of befriending your people in general. As far as I could tell, she seems not to suspect me of harboring any sorceri at present. Nor does she seem to suspect that her sorceress is your friend."

"Then why is she keeping her?" Thorn demanded. "Don't tell me any of this bloody nonsense about overhearing the ceremonies—she could have purified her of that in less time than an egg-boiling last night."

Crinkpetal spread his hands. "If it were not incredible, I would say that Her Reverence, like myself, may incline to befriend sorceri—that she fears Frostflower may be in some danger from His Reverence Rondasu, and is guarding her to keep her safe from his authority. Eleva told me—before your friend woke and joined us—that no doubt I would hear rumors today, since folk can hardly hear chanting in a town Truth Grove without starting rumors, but that no matter what tales might reach me, she and the sorceress would be acting together in all good feeling and spirit of cooperation."

Windbourne relaxed visibly. "Then it seems we should have followed her instructions, Rosethorn, and—"

"Stinking Hellbog! Because you people can't lie doesn't mean the bloody farmers can't. Just what the Seven Names are they going to cooperate on in a Truth Grove? She's taking Frost into the blasted Grove with her? Alone?"

Crinkpetal shrugged. "I've known her since she was a child— she was always one of my best customers, and I would have called her as sincerely pious as a priest should be, for all her whimsical talk of the gods and doctrines—but she seems to have changed since His Reverence died—grown more sure of herself, bolder, more outspoken—but also more suspicious of everyone around her. She seems convinced her brother and sister are trying to poison her, or at the least seeking to charge her with hard heresy and take away the rule of her farm from her. As they may be—I wouldn't trust that pair myself, though I'd be more careful not to give them evidence on an inscribed parchment, so to speak. But if her fear of them has gone deep enough, yes, she may have decided it worth the risk to persuade a strange sorceress to do some kind of spell-casting against them."

"Spying, more likely," said Thorn. "But Frostflower wouldn't even spy for her without a damn good reason."

Windbourne had begun shaking his head. "Have you been our friend so long, Crinkpetal, and never learned that we injure no one except in the last extremity—we do not drop hornets' nests in folks' stomachs. Much as they may deserve it, some of them."

Crinkpetal carelessly made the circle gesture that more pious folk used to ward off sorcery. "I've seen you people grow plants and gather little rain clouds out of the air to water them. Aside from that, I neither know, nor wish to know, nor greatly believe anything of your powers, whether I hear it from you or from your enemies. But I think Frostflower herself is in little danger for the rest of today."

Unless Eleva's gone mad, thought Thorn. Frost will be as much at the mercy of one farmer as of a score of them, in a Truth Grove. Especially if the one farmer's crazed enough to act without aco-lytes—"ritual levity," they call that sort of thing. Aloud, the war-rior said, "Well, at least she won't be in any danger tomorrow, because we're getting her out of there tonight."

Chapter 11

"And suppose they *do* go to Eleva instead of coming to us?" said the priestess Shara, pulling the legs from a roasted grasshopper.

"It's hardly likely, sweet sister." Rondasu motioned the young servant who stood near the table to refill his wine cup. "Not after what I said to them yesterday."

"She'll be the handier to them, as long as she remains in Five Roads. And there's been no sign yet that last night convinced even our younger sister of the malice of sorceri."

Rondasu drank deeply. "Aye. It seems the sorceress was more cautious than we . . . feared. Or Master Youngwise is slow in sending us the news."

"I pray all is well," murmured Intassa. "But I had never seen it in her, husband . . . the vindictiveness you hinted at. Not in two hatchings of living with her after his death."

The priest smiled. "You only knew her as an elder wife, my dovelet. You did not grow up with her as a sister, to learn all her little signs of temper. A tiny wrinkle at the corner of sweet Eleva's pretty mouth, a small crease half-hidden by the brown mole at the inner tip of her eyebrow."

"Oh, aye, brother," said Shara. "You watched her face closely enough, did you not, all those years she was ripening? And the rest of her body as well?"

He made a fist, thumb wrapped inside fingers, and smiled at it. "No more closely, dear Shara, than I watched yours."

"Aa! I was five years older, sweet sib—you never watched me ripening; you could only admire me ripened."

"Do not think, dove Shara," he replied, with a sliding glance at her, "that you taught me everything."

Intassa stirred uneasily in her cushioned chair and opened her mouth as if to speak, but Shara spoke first.

"A great pity, younger brother, that we could not have traded private parts."

Intassa blushed. "Shara, this is for Raes and Aeronu to decide in their godly wisdom. You cannot question—"

"Oh, but I can. From the time I was six years old and they told me that this red-faced squalling baby brother of mine would inherit everything—even my own little garden of stalk-lilies and herbs— and I must marry someday and leave this farm. Do you know, I remember very clearly looking down at you one day, Rondasu, while you slept between feedings, with the nurse dozing and Silk-hands gone on some errand, and that day I thought, All I need do is reach down and cover his mouth and pinch his little nostrils."

Intassa shuddered.

"But you mustn't let her words trouble you, dovelet. Here, try the sweetherb sauce." Rondasu leaned across the table and spooned reddish sauce onto the small squares of crust-fried chicken on Intassa's plate. "How long must we wait before lighting more candles, Shara? We are not poor edgelands or Center priests. We can afford to waste. I can hardly tell the sweet sauce from the peppery."

Shara smiled and glanced around at the sunset twilight reflecting faintly from the white, mosaic-covered walls and floor. "Is any color important to you, brother, except the color of wine? As for our wealth, I am the one who inspects the storerooms. You merely strut about the fields showing off your holy authority. Two candles give us sufficient light to finish our meal."

Rondasu took another drink of wine, laughed, and turned back to his wife. "As you can feel, dovelet, they're only her words. She did not pinch her baby brother's nose, and she lived to rejoice in her virtue."

"No, I did not follow my impulse that day, but I prayed every morning and night to Raes and Aeronu, Voma, Aomu, Raellis, Meactira, Maejira and every other god and goddess to correct the old mistake and give me my brother's sex."

Rondasu motioned again for wine. When his cup was full once more, he lifted it a little unsteadily, drank, and tried to hold it out to his sister. It tilted in his hand, spilling a dollop. He put it down and shoved it across the polished tabletop to her. "Share my wine, sweet sister. Celebrate our mutual joy that the gods were right after all."

Shara lifted the cup and drank. Lowering it, she said, "Turtle-foot, wipe up that spill of your priest's. Gods, must I tell you everything?"

The young servant blushed, compressed his lips, and bunched up the towel he carried across one arm.

"His name is Swiftcurrent, Shara," murmured Intassa.

The older priestess shrugged. "It was Turtlefoot when he was a child, and he should not have been allowed to change it. Swift-current! It should still be Turtlefoot, Turtlehand, Turtlelimbs, Turtletrunk! —Of course you'll share our cup also, dear Intassa, our new little dovelet?"

Intassa nodded, meanwhile trying to give the young servant a furtive, reassuring touch as he bent and wiped up the spilled wine. Shara waited until he had finished before attempting to pass the cup.

"We must train new houseservants for table as soon as the old ones take their adult names," she remarked.

"The expense, Shara dove," Rondasu murmured sarcastically, choosing which saucebowl to dip a grasshopper into. "And when you're finished there, boy, pour me another cup."

"Not only is he still as graceless as when he was Turtlefoot," Shara went on, "but now the whole meal must stop when he bends over the table. At least when he was a child we could still see one another over him."

"As well as we can see anything by two candles." Rondasu coughed. "I'd aimed for the sweet sauce!"

"Likely your hand was more at fault than your eye," said Shara.

"And yet Swiftcurrent is very slender," said Intassa. "And very quick on the road."

"I don't deny he has his uses." Shara ran her gaze over the

youth's body. "But they are not at the tableside. Ah!" she went on as he straightened. "Finished at last, Swift-turtle? Here, Intassa, celebrate our joy in the places we hold here in Rondasu's hall."

Intassa drank and began to return the cup to her husband. He waved his hand. "I don't take back the wine I give my women."

"Very true, once you've decided where to give it," said Shara. "Turtlehand, didn't you hear His Reverence ask for another cup?"

The young man put his left arm across his chest in sign of obedience and left the hall, running as if to disprove his name.

Shara gathered several grasshopper legs between her thumb and forefinger, dipped them into a bowl of sauce, and ate them daintily. "Meanwhile, brother, suppose some guilty townsman does decide to unburden himself to the nearest priest, rather than the mildest? When you planned yesterday's preachment, you hadn't planned on leaving Eleva in Five Roads, had you?"

He waved his hand and smiled. "Chastising a sorceress. She put herself in grave danger there, of a spellcasting like her husband's."

"We lighted candles and offered prayers for her safety, of course," said Shara.

He glanced at her and licked his lips as if to taste the film of wine. "Aye. In any case, she's proved her severity—rumor will take care of that, if Eleva does not. What townsman would go to her now?"

Shara half-turned to Intassa. "Hear the wisdom of Rondasu drunk. Even more awesome than the wisdom of Rondasu sober, is it not?"

"Slustru was always my chosen god, sweet sister," the priest replied. "His wine clears my thoughts. Eleva promised to share the judgment with Youngwise."

"You can still trust Master Youngwise after his stupidity in allowing that sorcerer's escape?" said Shara.

"Master Youngwise should be all the more anxious to prove his severity, dove, to keep our favor."

"Unless he prefers Eleva's favor."

"Not prefer us, with his own former Second Wallkeeper for our raidleader, and Eleva with no one but Splitgut?" Rondasu licked his lips again. "Oh, no, Youngwise may try to keep one foot in each farm as long as he can, but when the crisis comes, he'll set both feet firmly inside our walls."

"It . . . seemed a gentle enough sorceress," said Intassa. Then, as if abashed at having spoken, she plunged her silver pick into a piece of chicken and made a desperate effort to eat.

"Poor, trusting dovelet Intassa," said Shara. "How fortunate you are to have found a haven with us, who can guide your thoughts. If you had lived much longer with our heretic sister, she might have pulled you down into Hellbog along with herself."

Rondasu drummed his fingers on the table. "Hellbog or Glorious Harvest, it's still far off for all of us." He glanced around in the direction from which Swiftcurrent should return with another cup for his wine.

"Deveron thought it was still far off for him," said Shara. "We would all do well to keep our actions as clean as our dovelet Intassa does, would we not, brother? But, of course, you've been studying very closely with her of late. Why do you not come more often to pass her instruction on to me, Rondasu?"

He slapped the table lightly in a gesture of annoyance. "Because you've always insisted on making yourself the instructress, older sister! By the Seven Names, Intassa could teach you much if you were truly eager to learn!" The priest rose and strode halfway across the hall, not quite in a straight line. "Swiftcurrent! Turtlefoot! Do you have toes or roots on your feet?"

Shara, having finished her own chicken, speared and ate a piece of Intassa's. "It's a pity, dovelet, you had no better material than that to instruct. I wonder if you *could* have taught me the meek and gentle way to the Harvest Gates?"

Intassa looked nervously towards her husband in the darkening hall. "Shara, if you would marry—it's not too late—you're not old, many priests would—"

Shara laughed. "Many old priests would be glad enough of a helper drudge with my ability for a second or third wife, to help them run a farm I could hardly hope ever to rule. As for the priestlings still in need of a first wife, where would I find one beside whom even our Rondasu did not look mature? Here I am in my own farm, the place I have loved since my memory began, the place that should have been mine . . ."

"But you have not the joy of husband, you can never bear babes—"

"You found bearing your son a joy, did you? As for the joys of a mate to come to my bed . . ." Shara laughed again. "Oh, no, dovelet, I know very well what I am lacking there!"

"Turtlefoot!" Rondasu shouted again, going a few steps further. "Demons' droppings, boy, I'll take a strip off your ankle!"

Intassa rose and hurried across the hall to him. "Rondasu, you must not—must not be too stern with the boy. Here—come back to us, take my cup if you won't have your own back again . . ."

"That tiny cup of yours, dovelet?" He laughed. "Two mouthfuls at a time, it holds—more pouring than drinking! Well, let it do until that rootfoot comes. Intassa, little lovelet, my little guide to the Glorious Harvest . . ."

"Aye," said Shara. "She'll guide us both to the Harvest Gates. You've left one of your carrots, Rondasu." She leaned over and poised her pick above his dish. "Hurry back or I'll eat this little carrot of yours!"

They returned to the table. Shara waited until they were seated again before she skewered the carrot and ate it, still leaning toward her brother. "And one thing I've learned, Rondasu, is that you should not have prodded the townsfolk's consciences up again yesterday. But you would not listen to me, so now we've reminded all of Five Roads—aye, and Eleva as well—of what they would have gently forgotten without your prodding."

"What do you mean?" Intassa seemed about to sway forward, but supported herself with one arm against the table. "Could any of us—Eleva, you, I—especially Eleva—have ever forgotten Deveron and how—he died?"

"In your opinion, probably not," Shara replied. "But your opinion, dovelet Intassa, is worth very little now." She turned back to Rondasu. "And why, wise Reverence, did you think it advisable to rouse them up for a sorcerer who, if he is wise, will never come near this area again? Was his absence not serving us as well as his death?"

"But we should have hunted him down!" cried Intassa. "Why did we wait so long? The gods will punish—"

Her voice had grown loud, and perhaps that was what woke the child in an alcove to the right. "Little Vari!" Intassa went on, trying to rise. But she gasped slightly and fell back into her chair.

"Silkhands will lull your little bratling back to sleep soon enough," said Shara. "Rest easy, dovelet, she knows how to rear children. Did she not raise me, Rondasu, and Eleva, all three, after the old nurse died? And did she not raise us without your foolish Coddlemeasure's help? Ah, here is our Turtlecurrent back at last!"

The young servant had paused, panting, at the edge of the hall. Besides the cup, he carried another jar of wine. "Forgive me, Reverence," he apologized, coming forward and putting the cup down on the table with as much respect as he could manage, his arm being unsteady through haste and nervousness. "Spicefingers said you would likely want more wine to help fill it, too."

"How presumptuously clever of Spicefingers," said Shara. "And was it because of Intassa's scruples, sweet brother, that you decided to make yesterday's pretty gesture?"

"Intassa's not far from right. They must have been gossiping, wondering why we had done nothing all this time."

Shara twitched one corner of her mouth. "Does Intassa need a salve for conscience to soothe her for marrying again so quickly? Or did she marry you so that she could stir up your lazy scruples?"

"Seven Names, Shara!" Rondasu waved his cup at the servant. "This will die down like the first alarm, and meanwhile we'll get a better place in the gossip because we made the motion and Eleva didn't."

"Husband!" said Intassa.

Even allowing for the natural whiteness of her skin and the uncertain light of two candles, she appeared to have grown deathly pale, and the expression on her face heightened the effect. Pushing down hard on the armrests of her chair, she rose to her feet, leaned heavily against the table. "I did not . . . you did not marry me to . . ." She gasped, clutched her midriff, and fell sideways to the floor.

"Intassa!" The priest rose, overturning his newly filled cup.

She was already writhing and twitching. She began to scream.

"More sorcery," said Shara, standing and looking down at her. "Swiftcurrent, you know whom to summon. His Reverence and I will get her to her bed."

The young servant was still holding the wine jug. In his haste, he dropped it while turning and ran out without seeming to notice the breakage.

"But I fear Herbwise will not be able to help her," Shara went on. "No more than Eleva could help Deveron." She looked at her brother and smiled.

"Gods, Shara!" Tipsiness shaken off, he pushed past her and

gathered Intassa up in his arms. She made an effort to lie quiet there, but already her mind seemed beginning to wander. From the nursery alcove, her child's screams were mingling with hers.

"You taught me, brother!" said Shara in a low voice. "You instructed me to devise ways of getting poison into one person's wine beneath the very eyes of everyone else around the table. Should I have let the skill rust away after using it only the once?"

"Gods!" he repeated, turning to her, speaking over his wife's constantly moving head. "She knew nothing—she suspected nothing—"

"There's another sorceron prisoner in Five Roads and a chance to purge out the townsfolks' consciences on her. Would you rather have died yourself to give them that chance, Rondasu?"

"It was not necessary, Shara!" His voice shook with anger, and there seemed to be tears in his eyes. "Great Jehandru! I loved her!"

The nurse Silkhands appeared in one of the archways, holding the child in her arms and staring into the hall. "Lady Intassa? How shall I quiet your son if—"

"Sorcery is at work here," said Shara, turning to the nurse. "More such foul sorcery as killed Reverence Deveron. Light herb candles over the child's cradle and pray! We've already sent for our physician, and we must begin our own prayers, to guard ourselves—if we live, we'll make the sorceress pay for this, Reverence Rondasu and I!"

Horrified, the nurse nodded and disappeared.

Shara turned back to her brother. "You've got the heir you needed—her son, the heir you couldn't have from me. We have the sorceress to blame, and she sent out her spell against our household while in Eleva's keeping—what further evidence do you need of our sister's heresy? And you'll forget you thought you loved your dovelet, brother, once you come back to my bed at night!"

Chapter 12

The moon would be just past full. Not that bright moons mattered so much inside a good-sized town. In the warm seasons, when thieves could come out without freezing their fingers, Master Youngwise kept most of the street lamps kindled all night.

"I don't suppose you can do anything to get us a little more cover?" Thorn asked Windbourne. "A good wind and rain to douse the lamps? Or a nice heavy fog?"

He shook his head. "The conditions passed with last night's storm. I might be able to wrap a small fog around us, maybe a little wider than the street."

"Unh. Nice and inconspicuous." Thorn shook her head. "Well, better trust the common robbers' way. We had one in All Roads West who used to make it a big game, never went out except when there was a full moon. Lasted three bloody years before we finally caught her, too! Called herself Moonchild. Gods, I wish I'd taken a few lessons from her before the scaffolding!"

The flowerbreeder had refused to give Thorn any garments that might be traced back to him, but he did provide her with plain flax-twine. She used it to garter her loose buff underbreeches and the top of the light smock that sorceri wore under their robes. The

skirt of that smock she cut off. It left her hardly decent—Windbourne, turning to make some comment, blushed and quickly
turned around again until she had put on her black robe. But all
she had to do now was shed the outer robe and she would be ready
for action, with no hindrance from loose cloth.

The black robes themselves, though they announced "sorceri"
to anyone who happened to see them, would also help make them
harder to see. "Funny," Thorn remarked. "I never thought of it
before, but when they insist you people wear black, they make
it easier for you to sneak around at night."

"We do not sneak around," said Windbourne. "We live openly
and honestly. What I am doing tonight is extraordinary and strains
my vow of Truth to the uttermost."

"But the priests and everyone else in the Tanglelands *think* you
sneak around at night, so why do they make it easier for you? Why
not make it the law that you wear some other color? Light gray,
maybe. Or orange."

"Light gray would be too close to the farmers' sacred white.
Any other color would cut into the choice honest commoners
enjoy. Besides, the priests could never agree on one single color
for us, not nowadays. Black is standard throughout the Tanglelands
only because it's ancient tradition."

"Um," said Thorn, examining the idea of black clothes for
warriors to wear on raids. Despite everything, she felt almost
happy. Bloodrastor-First-of-Warriors! it was good to be going into
some kind of action that more or less resembled warriors' work!

"What about this damn cat of yours?" Thorn went on, as Coyclaws took one of her recurrent notions to rub against the warrior's
leg as if determined to make Thorn appreciate her catly grace.
"We'll let the flowerbreeder keep her for us," she answered her
own question.

"No," said Windbourne. "Coyclaws must choose."

Thorn stared at him. "What?"

"You know we always allow our animals to decide."

"Demons' turds! You don't leave your cows and goats to wander away into the mountains if they choose to. And how do you
keep your damn eggs safe to eat if you let your cocks go wherever
they please?"

"Have you ever seen a cock among our fowl, even in such a retreat as Frostflower's? We either buy all our pullets from the farmer-priests before they reach maturity, or do without eggs. And our very cows and goats have more freedom than farmers' cattle. Yes, we cajole them, teach them to follow the herder; but we do not pen them in pasture, and the pens and shelters we build for them near our own houses are for their protection, not their confinement. And our cats and dogs have as much freedom as we ourselves."

"Maybe a Hell of a lot more," said Thorn. "Anyway, we can't have her side-stepping along with us tonight and maybe tripping us up or calling attention to us. She stays here with Crinkpetal."

"If she chooses," said Windbourne.

Thorn glared at the white cat, which had started washing itself again. The warrior searched around quietly until she found a box of ink paste that the flowerbreeder used for marking the names and prices of his plants on the jars he sold them in—for his own convenience, of course; most of his common customers could not read and had to depend upon his word anyway. She carried the box to the washstand and went to work. She did not explain what she was doing, and maybe Windbourne assumed she was washing her hands, since she kept her back to him and he seemed to be busy with some kind of muscle-flexing exercises sorceri used to stay calm.

When Thorn had two-thirds a basinful of inky water that stained her elbow at a dip, she tied the sleeves of her robe down around her wrists, put on a pair of gardener's gloves, picked up Coyclaws, and plunged her into the ink-bath.

"What are you doing?" cried Windbourne, jumping to his feet and starting across the room. The cat was yowling, spitting, twisting its body and lashing out with extended claws and snakelike tail, but Thorn held it down with one gloved hand around the ribcage while she used the other hand to rub the liquid wrong-way into the fur.

"Go on yowling and you'll get a black tongue, too, cat," said the warrior, as she pushed its face down into the dye. "Take off your robe and spread it out on the floor, Wedgepopper—we'll need to dry this bugger out a little so she won't leave her futtering footprints all over Crinkpetal's cottage."

He had sense enough to obey and help dry the cat. By the time they started out, Coyclaws had so far forgotten the indignity that she rode on Windbourne's shoulders. But she continued to keep her distance from Thorn.

The folk of large towns not only slept late in the mornings, they stayed up late in the evenings. Thorn and Windbourne had to wait until about midway between full dark and midnight, long after everyone would have been asleep in a farm. Even at the hour they finally set off, they had to watch for groups going home from inns and taverns; but drunkards were loud and easy to avoid. The streetwarriors were fairly easy to dodge, too, since Thorn remembered their routes from her time as Third Wallkeeper. Coyclaws seemed to be on fairly good behavior, but Thorn did not trust her. Three or four times the cat streaked silently away from Windbourne. Thorn assumed it was most often to chase down some rodent, but once she glimpsed another form the size of a cat or small dog in the side street where Coyclaws darted. Windbourne hesitated a little, but made no comment as Thorn wordlessly prodded him on. Caterwauling came from the side street behind them, joined after a moment by a man's angry shouts and a few plops— most townsfolk kept a small stack of fist-sized bags filled with pebbles, cinders, or sand near their windows to throw at cats, noisy drunkards, and suspicious shadows. Then a woman started shouting at the man to the effect that he was a bigger disturbance than the cats. Thorn and Windbourne cut through the first pissing-alley that would bring them out a street away from the commotion. Such vocal brawls sometimes went on until the townwarriors arrived to scold the awakened sleepers back to bed. The noise was still audible in the distance when Coyclaws caught up with her human companions again.

At last, with no further incident, they neared town-center and circled around to approach the yard through the public garden between the ancient temple and the priests' alcove-hall.

The temple seemed the best place to begin, unguarded as the door was by anything but a silk curtain and sanctity.

Coyclaws struck out on her own again, disappeared in some bushes, and reappeared briefly, a blot of movement slightly darker than the surrounding grass, before she jumped onto a tree that grew near the wall of the priests' private garden and vanished from sight against the black trunk. Her own muscles aching for strenuous action, Thorn did not blame the cat for taking the chance to climb.

Thorn and Windbourne reached the edge of the garden. He started to step into the paved yard. She caught his arm and held him back. She had glimpsed a shadow that shouldn't have been there.

Giving his shoulders a short downward push to indicate he should stay where he was, she untied her rope belt and edged forward. She held the belt in both hands, ready to use as a stranglecord, and kept her black robe closed and overlapped in front with her elbows—that way, she still kept the buff undergarments from showing, but was ready to drop the stranglecord, shake off the robe and have Slicer and Stabber in her hands in a moment.

A swordswoman, an axewoman, and two spearwomen stood guard in front of the temple door. Their discipline was perfect. The only sound they made was their breathing. The swordswoman looked like Eaglesight, though it was hard for even a warrior, trained to night action, to be sure.

If there had been only one, Thorn could have crept up from behind and choked her into unconsciousness. Even two, and she might have risked taking them on. Not four. Even if she could defeat them all, the noise would alert the priestess, the townmaster, and the whole bloody barracks as well.

Damn! thought Thorn. She returned to the sorcerer and pulled him back into the garden. He had the sense to follow silently, without questions. When they got almost to the tree Coyclaws had climbed, back where the rustles of wind and night-prowling creatures would help cover their whispers, Thorn explained. "Townwarriors. Four."

"Should I . . . Thorn . . . do you want me to help you . . . knock them unconscious?"

"A sorcerer? Offering to help batter people? Lose you your powers, wouldn't it?"

"If . . . If it's needed . . . to save her . . ."

The night atmosphere must have gotten to him—that morning he had been ready to believe Frostflower safe and happy in the care of his idealized priestess. "Think Frost would want you to save her that way? Besides, we can't take on four, not here in earshot of the whole damn town-center."

He couldn't have been too eager to fight. He made another suggestion at once. "A back way into the temple?"

"None. If there were, it'd be guarded, too. At least we know they must still be in the damn Truth Grove."

"A thief's tunnel through the wall?"

"Thieves don't rob holy halls! May be a tunnel from the priests' house, though."

"From the . . . priests' dungeons?"

"There must've been one once, if it's not blocked off now."

"And the priests' house?"

Thorn pointed to the wall that divided the public garden from the priests' private grounds. "Can't go in through the front door—damn townwarriors would see us. Have to go over the wall back here."

They both looked at the tree Coyclaws had climbed, a huge old walnut with a deep crotch. It grew closer to the wall than Thorn had first noticed. She could see two thick limbs, each as big around as a ten-year-old oak, branching over the wall. "Your bloody cat's probably there already," said Thorn, taking off her robe, twisting it into a bulky strand and tying it around her waist.

She was nettled when the sorcerer followed her up the tree without first taking off his robe and skirted undersmock. "I suppose you'd be as clumsy in trousers as I am in skirts," she remarked when he reached the limbs overhanging the wall.

"We don't fight, warrior. That doesn't mean we avoid athletics."

"All right, come on," she said, unable to tell from his whisper whether he had retorted or apologized.

The wall was about half again as high as a man's reach. Once beyond its top, Thorn hung from the branch by her arms, let go, and landed lightly. Very simple, but the sorcerer held back.

"Come on down. Or isn't jumping part of your athletics?"

"I'll stay here in case you're wrong about the tunnel—I can reach down and pull you back up."

"And if there is a tunnel, I'm not losing any more time to come back and tell you! Either you can come with me now, or you can sit up there and wonder until sunrise."

That brought him down beside her. He landed as easily as she had, but said at once, "And if there's no tunnel?"

"Then I'll climb back up on your shoulders, you fishbrain." Untying the robe from her waist and draping it over her left arm, Thorn peered around. She had never been in a priests' town garden before. She had known by the size of the walls that it was smaller than the priestly garden behind a farm hall; she should also have guessed it would be cluttered with several small cottages, replacing the hallside cottages of a farm. Instead of a Grove, it had a central fountain—that was good evidence of a tunnel to the temple Truth Grove next door.

Windbourne was shivering as he had not shivered, to give him due credit, when they were in the streets where the danger was more immediate. "Well," he whispered, "where shall we look for this tunnel of yours? Must we . . . go inside the dwelling?"

Thorn squinted at the back wall of the main building, which looked like several unbroken curves of masonry. Then she gestured around at the cottages. "Take your choice. One of those has to be the kitchen, and there's usually a tunnel that comes up in the kitchen so the cooks can get to the storerooms underground. Or you can check the main hall for doors on the garden side. I'm checking the fountain."

"The fountain?"

"Usually all the tunnels connect. Sometimes they don't. If they don't, chances are the one that leads to the temple next door will start near that fountain—I'm guessing it's the seasondial, and they'd probably want to tie it with the Truth Grove."

"I don't want to hear any of that," he said.

"Unh. Frost would've been interested. I forgot you wouldn't pay a fishscale. Main hall might be your likeliest place to look."

He glanced toward the hall, then started for the nearest cottage.

"You're that shy of the priests' damn dwelling, Wedgepopper," Thorn muttered to herself, "and you think you can follow me up into their holy hall?"

As she had guessed, the fountain did indeed form a seasondial, with its tall, pointed stem, pierced bronze disk through which the water dripped, and ancient stone basin with grooved rim. If these dials were put out where everyone could see them, anyone with a good memory and sufficient time and interest could probably figure out the rudiments with three or five years of observation.

Had Frost had a chance to see it? There was a surprisingly similar one in her own retreat, but without the fountain.

Three arbors flanked it like the points of a triangle. The stone benches and pedestal table in the first were unmovable. Thorn had gone on to the second arbor and begun twisting the table when she heard approaching footsteps, broken by a sneeze.

She turned and looked up. Windbourne was hurrying towards her, wearing his blasted cat around his shoulders once more like a white shawl. White? The sorcerer sneezed a second time.

"You think you're imitating a damn nightingale?" said Thorn.

"The tunnel—it's there, in the kitchen."

"Unh. And how did that rutty animal get the ink off?"

Windbourne's face was in the shadow, but he sounded as if he was grinning sheepishly. "She covered it. She got into a broken crock of sifted flour in the kitchen."

"Probably broke it herself. Well, dust her off before you sneeze the town down around us, and let's get to your tunnel in the kitchen." Thorn might well have been close to finding another and possibly more direct tunnel to the Truth Grove; but the tunnels would be too dark for even a warrior's eyes, and the kitchen would have lamps or candles.

Trying, overgently, to brush the flour out of his cat's fur, Windbourne led the way back toward the kitchen.

"We've got to be quiet," Thorn muttered, "but not so damn quiet you can't give that beast a couple of solid whacks."

"It was Coyclaws who showed me the tunnel, Thorn."

When they got inside, Thorn saw what he meant. Windbourne had left the door to the tunnel ajar, but it would have been closed when he first entered the kitchen, and while not designed for secrecy, it was not designed to be especially obvious either. It was the same as any other section of wall: lime-washed plaster with a wooden gridwork that formed hand-high, finger-deep cubicles from the floor (except where stoves, cupboards, and other kitchen furniture stood) to an arm's reach above the cooks' heads. While the little cubicles against the solid walls held various spices and small implements, the gridwork attached to the moving door was equipped with hooks for towels and longer pieces of equipment like ladles and tongs; but the sorcerer would hardly know that.

Thorn herself had not been in farmers' kitchens very often, in a sorcerous kitchen only once, only long enough to notice some of the differences. The door was cut away at its bottom to help keep the tunnel aired out and to give the priests' cats free passage; but the opening was only about as high as the dark boxes of wood and charcoal that stood along the base of the wall, forming one shadow with the black stone floor. Enough moonlight came into the window, however, to show the smear of flour from the broken crock on the floor, and the line of white pawprints from the mess where Coyclaws had rolled in the stuff to the tunnel door, where it ended abruptly. After jumping down into the tunnel, Coyclaws must have walked the rest of the flour off her pads before springing up into the kitchen again.

Thorn pulled the door open. "Get your wickstick lighted and I'll find us a couple of lamps."

Though not allowed near an open flame in most towns, sorceri secretly carried their own compact boxes with iron, flint, and wickstick—the need for fire between towns outweighed the danger of being searched. As his bits of fire-gear clicked on a stone-topped work surface, Windbourne asked, "Thorn . . . why those guards at the entrance to the Holy Hall?"

"I don't know. One or two I could understand—guards of honor to signal a ceremony going on. Four . . ." Thorn located a couple of lamps. She did not tell Windbourne what bothered her still more: the holy hall had seemed too quiet—not a sound from inside it all the time they had approached it through the outer garden. If it were not for the warriors, she might have thought her friend and the priestess were not in there now. She thought she would feel a little less unsure what the Hell was going on if she had heard even one strophe coming from the temple.

The lamps filled, newly wicked and kindled, Thorn led the way into the tunnel. Unlikely as they were to hear anything very soon that might guide them, she strained her ears as tautly as her eyes. Windbourne began, "What if—" and Thorn cut him off with, "Quiet, damn you!" He did not speak again during the time they spent in the underground passageways, not even when Thorn paused at a branching.

The first such division was at the bottom of the stairs down from the kitchen, where one tunnel would lead back to the main

hall, no doubt to the ablution chamber and storerooms. The other—
Thorn hoped—led to the old temple. She was surprised on coming
to a second and third place where two tunnels met. The town
dwelling lacked the aboveground storage of a farm, but the priests
should not need to store so much here. She remembered barracks
tales she had heard, while growing up in All Roads West, about
midlands priests who still kept the ancient underground prison cells
in use. In all her years of working in the midlands, Thorn had yet
to meet a warrior who admitted to helping priests get their prisoners
down to those underground cells . . . but many edgelands warriors
believed such tales and ballads almost as gullibly as did commoners
and sorceri; and at the first groanlike sound from one of the side
passages here, she was ready to turn and investigate it. However,
she heard only her own footsteps, Windbourne's, and the cat's.

One of the first skills young warriors learned was how to keep
a sense of distance and direction. After just about the right number
of paces, Thorn brought her party to deeply footworn marble stairs
leading up. They should lead into the ancient temple, and this was
borne out by the dark-blue temple curtain that hung in the doorway
at the top of the stairs.

Thorn stopped to listen, Windbourne obediently halting behind
her and, for once, holding Coyclaws back.

The curtain was somewhere between the thickness of summer
cloth and winter cloth, and it moved slightly with the air currents,
despite the fact that it trailed on the floor. There was just enough
light in the temple's interior to lend the curtain a faint sheen.

There! Was that a sigh? Frostflower's?

Thorn climbed a few stairs, until the top one was within arm's
reach, stopped and listened again. She heard another distant sigh,
followed by footsteps that sounded soft but not guarded. They
stopped almost directly overhead, and then came the glur of liquid
being poured, a little splashing, and some squishes as of a wet
cloth being wrung out. The footsteps retreated again.

Thorn handed her lamp to Windbourne, who had followed her
up. She bunched her black robe together and laid it on one end
of the top stair. Then, very gently so as not to hiss them against
their sheaths, she drew Slicer and Stabber.

She turned back and leaned toward Windbourne's ear to whisper
that he should stay in the tunnel—he couldn't fight anyway—and

at that moment Coyclaws made a sudden decision to streak past them up the stairs and beneath the curtain.

"Damn bloody cat!" Thorn swore under her breath. She thrust the curtain aside with her left arm and sprang into the temple before the advantage of surprise was completely lost.

As she had guessed, she came up in a semichamber—a scallop in the back of the temple's circular inner wall. To her left was a cupboard; to her right a ledge with basin, ewer, towels, and lighted lamp; straight ahead another doorway, its curtain about two-thirds of the way open. The Grove itself began seven or eight paces from where she stood. Its several rows of artificial trees blocked her view—all she could see was one candle flame, the light of several more, a few corners of altar topped with unmoving black shadow, and a glimpse of moving white above the shadow. But the same trees would also be blocking the view of that figure in white.

The cat was already trying to climb one of the carved trees. The priestess, clearly alerted to the intruder's presence, started between the trees toward the rear alcove.

Windbourne crowded up behind Thorn. She gave him a light backward jab with her elbow. Sword at the wary position, knife held ready to throw, she strode forward.

The priestess reached the outmost row of trees, and they stood in full view of each other.

Thorn had seen Eleva often enough to recognize her—short, thin, cocky smile, ready frown. She was frowning now. She carried a candle in her right hand and she lifted it higher, so that it caused grotesque shadows on her face.

"Lady . . . Reverence—" stammered Windbourne. "We don't— we mean no—"

"Quiet!" said Thorn, and took another step forward, raising her sword slightly. "You've got a sorceress here, Lady Reverence."

"You are forbidden to enter this Grove without my permission," the priestess replied. "I do not give it."

Thorn dared not voice a threat—she might have to carry it out. Wordlessly, she raised Slicer to downthrust position, the blade hovering above Eleva's left collarbone.

Maybe the priestess sensed that, for all her bold front, Thorn had not quite shaken off religious dread. She gazed back at the warrior steadily. "You cannot cut a new mouth anywhere in my flesh that will give you my permission to enter the sacred Grove."

"But if we beg you, Lady?" said Windbourne. "If we swear to you that we mean no harm?"

Eleva stared over Thorn's shoulder and squinted—the light was excellent for a warrior, but no doubt very bad for anyone else.

A scream came from inside the Grove. The priestess turned her head, and Thorn seized the moment to swing her sword arm out of range and bump Eleva aside with her left shoulder. The priestess fell against the nearest artificial tree. Thorn pushed past her.

The warrior felt a spot of pain on her back and a thin arm around her waist. Eleva was trying to hold her back. Thorn could have pulled free from the arm—maybe breaking it—but the spreading spot of pain meant the priestess had set fire to her flimsy undertunic.

Dropping sword and knife, she half fell, half rolled backwards. The trees were well anchored, but the one they fell against cracked as they rebounded from it to the floor. The cat jumped down spitting, landed briefly on Thorn and sprang to safety.

Rolling and wrestling, Thorn got the fire out and was about to pin Eleva beneath her—the priestess had good fighting instincts but no training or weight—when she felt arms around her neck, trying to pull her away.

"Wedgepopper!" she choked, striking upward with one arm, trying to hold Eleva down with the other, and feeling a beat like approaching footsteps echoing with the pulse of her blood. "Damn your—"

"Stop this!"

Windbourne's grip loosened and Thorn glanced round. Frostflower stood leaning against a tree in the middle row, trembling violently, one hand stroking Dowl's head in rapid, unconscious strokes, the other twisting a damp towel until its last moisture dripped to the floor.

"Stop it!" Frostflower screamed again. "Lady Intassa's dying!"

"Or don't stop it," said yet another voice, "and I'll save you a bad scaffolding."

Thorn looked around and up. Eaglesight was joining the party.

"Thorn?" the wallkeeper went on. "Young idiot, you were free and clear! All right, roll off Her Reverence and lie flat. Don't go for your sword—I've got three more women outside and it was hard enough to keep two of them from following me in right away."

"Oh, God!" Frostflower gave a sob. "To come from *that* and find *this!*"

"You are her friends?" said Eleva.

"They are my friends, Lady," the sorceress replied with another sob, more controlled. "As Her Reverence is my friend, Thorn!" she added.

Thorn rolled away, stood, and looked at Eaglesight. "Then I want a bloody good explanation before I die!"

Eaglesight squinted at Windbourne, who was standing by, staring at Eleva, with his hands twitching as if he would help her up but didn't dare offer to touch her. "Lady," said the wallkeeper, "I think that's the bastard we caught last winter for causing His Reverence's death. Should I—?"

"No!" The priestesss rose, rubbing her arms. "I take them under my protection, all three of them. Intassa, sorceress—what have they done to Intassa?"

Dowl whined and looked up at Frostflower. "Poison, Lady," said the sorceress. "Oh, God!" she repeated, burying her face in her hands. "To stand there—to see it all—not even to be able to warn her!"

"The same poison they used for my husband?"

Frostflower shook her head. In helplessness, not in negation. "I did not see His Reverence's death. But I think . . . I think it was the same."

"Gods!" said Eleva. "I thought she'd at least be safe from *that!* At least until Rondasu had a son of her—Gods forgive me! What happened? Did she learn? Did she come to suspect?"

"There's nothing we can do, Lady?" said Frostflower. "No way, no hope?"

Eleva struck her small fist against one of the trees. "She may be dead already—pray the gods she is, and out of her pain! If there were any way to help, I could have saved Deveron—"

"But you thought it was sorcery?" said Frostflower.

"*I* did not! No—perhaps I did—but I also suspected . . . Gods, I'm not sure how much I already suspected that night, but I nursed my husband as if it might have been anything and everything. Oh, gods, Shara was nursing him, too! Frostflower, was it both of them, or—"

"It was Shara, Lady. I think Rondasu did not know, did not plan it for Intassa—but he had planned it for your husband! Lady, I hurried back as if running. If you have horses—"

"None closer than my farm."

"A few fast donkeys, then," Thorn suggested.

"We'll try it! Sweet Raellis, we'll try it!" Eleva ground fist furiously in palm. "We may be too late to save her, but, by the Seven Names, we can get her son and her old nurse out of that Hellbog farm—we can do that much for her! Eaglesight, have my wagon . . ." Her tone changed. "Wallkeeper, whose notion was it to set four warriors outside this building?"

"Master Youngwise's, Lady," said the old warrior.

"At whose command? Not at mine! Gods!" the priestess screamed suddenly, "Are you *all* in my brother's pay?"

"I wish to Hell I was in *somebody's* pay," muttered Thorn.

"It's my guess and Master Youngwise's, Lady," said the wallkeeper, "that Reverence Rondasu could find some reason for breaking in on you, even here. Pretending he didn't know, or—"

"Or charging me with heretical ceremonies." Calming herself with visible effort, Eleva picked up one of the lamps Windbourne had left on the floor near the wall. "Don't bother with my wagon. I think Youngwise keeps mules for certain messengers? Have his best mules saddled and haltered at once."

"Listen!" said Windbourne.

Footsteps in the yard, approaching the temple—a group of four, Thorn guessed, at least two of them warriors, and one of them . . .

"That's Master Youngwise," said Eaglesight, her head slightly cocked.

"My sibs!" Eleva struck the tree again. "They've sent their message to seize the first sorceron as a blamecatch for Intassa's death—as they did for Deveron's! And they already know which sorceress they'll charge, and where to find her!"

Eaglesight waved her sword at Thorn's where it still lay on the floor. "Get your weapons, warrior. I won't ask you to die empty handed."

"You're not my commander now," said Thorn, recovering Slicer and Stabber. "I'd have gotten them without your bloody permission."

"You will not squabble, and when they come, you will remain quiet until I give the command," said Eleva. "Wallkeeper, you're Youngwise's warrior; I cannot command your allegiance, but if you will stand by me—even should he command you otherwise—you may claim your place as my chief and most honored raidleader. Thorn—"

"I'm content to be chief townwarrior," said Eaglesight. "But I'd say Youngwise is still on your side."

Eleva sighed. "We'll hope so—as nearly as he can be called on anyone's side but the town's. Thorn?"

Thorn gave the full-armed salute, touching the garnet in Stabber's pommel to her forehead. "Promise me a pardon, Lady Reverence, and I'll fight Azkor for you." *I'll fight anyway, to save the sorceress,* she added to herself.

"You have my pardon at this moment. You are also in my pay. If Jehandru is kind, my pardon will still be honored by most of my fellow priests."

The townmaster's party was at the door; they could hear him mumbling with the three guards Eaglesight had left there. The wallkeeper took an uncommitted position near the wall. Eleva glanced at Frostflower. "It seems our tunnel is hardly a secret, but it might still give you a way to elude the search."

Frostflower shook her head. "I would rather stay here and trust to your protection, Lady."

Eleva smiled and turned to Windbourne. "And you, sorcerer? They won't know of your presence, and none of us will tell them."

He went down on one knee. "Lady Reverence, if my presence will endanger you further—"

"Go or stay!" said Thorn. "Here they come." She got in front of the sorceri. Her back and shoulderblade throbbed where a draft hit the bare, burned skin; she wished there were time for Frostflower to heal it.

New points of light, flickering in and out of sight behind the artificial trees, cast additional, moving shadows that marked the progress of Master Youngwise and his group. Piously keeping to the clear space between Grove and wall, they appeared in a few

moments and stopped, facing the priestess across the last few
strides of aisleway. A long-legged youth in the short tunic of a
runner stood beside Youngwise. Both the men carried lamps, and
the one in the runner's hand was shaking uncontrollably—it must
be almost out of oil, or it'd be slopping. Five warriors waited in
the rear—Eaglesight's three and two more that the townmaster
had brought. They looked uncomfortable.

"It is sacrilege to intrude on a priest in the Truth Grove," said
Eleva.

Youngwise glanced at the people around her. "Mine is not the
night's first sacrilege, Lady Reverence, or I would have waited
outside, despite my news. Lady, your brother's wife is dead."

"As my husband died?" said Eleva.

Youngwise nodded. "His Reverence directs that the sorceress
be speared at once."

Thorn changed her grip on Stabber, ready to throw him at the
first spearwoman who lifted her weapon. She heard Frost move
and hoped the sorceress was getting into place behind one of the
trees.

"Does he also direct you to seize me?" said Eleva.

The townmaster spread his hands. "Do not insult us, Lady.
Your brother is aware that she has deceived Your Reverence as
well as the rest of us, and in his wisdom and concern for you, he
deems it safest to spear her at once. And as we see two sorceri
here," Youngwise went on, looking at Windbourne, "and as we
have two women with copper-headed spears and two more with
iron-headed, it might be safest and most comfortable for all of us
if we disposed of them both at the same time."

Thorn lofted Stabber and Slicer to catch the light. "The first
woman who raises her spear, Master Youngwise, you get a knife
in your fat belly, male or no male."

One of the women with an iron-headed spear began to raise
it and took a step to the left to give her throwing arm more freedom,
but a glance at Thorn made her lower the weapon and step back.
The other four huddled a little closer together.

Master Youngwise, however, only looked down at his small
potbelly. "Fat? Rather less so, I think, than most other men of my
age and prosperity. As for the rest of it, Thorn—that *is* Thorn,
I think?—since you seem to be one of the obstacles between my

spearwomen and the sorceri, the first spear will undoubtedly be aimed at you."

"No one but a priest or priestess may command blood to be shed in a Grove," said Eleva.

Youngwise put the tips of his fingers together and bowed slightly. "Nor have I given such a command, Lady Reverence. I have merely conveyed to you the directions of your brother."

And given us time to take cover, you old wall-straddler, thought Thorn. She glanced around, saw that Frost had gotten herself and Dowl behind one of the trees and Windbourne had gotten in back of the priestess. The swordswoman stepped behind the nearest tree, easing into a position from which she could spring out at the warriors behind the townmaster.

"Rondasu may have commanded a slaughter," said Eleva, "but he is not here present, and so my command is the holier. I take both these sorceri under my protection. Whoever harms them commits as great a sacrilege as if the blow were aimed at me!"

Youngwise cocked one gray eyebrow. "I had never heard a priest's sanctity could be extended quite that far, Reverence, though it hardly befits a simple townmaster to question these things. Your brother may question it, of course."

The runner put down his lamp and lay on the floor, arms extended. "Lady, I was sent—His Reverence directed—if you should not wish her speared at once, I was to serve as—as—stripper—"

Eleva looked down at him. "Turtlefoot, is it not?"

"I was Turtlefoot, Lady . . . my child name. . . . Now I'm Swift-current and . . ."

"And anxious to prove you're adult enough for such a task?" said Eleva. "Tell Reverence Rondasu I refuse that kind of spearing as firmly as the other. Or if you fear returning to him with your hair still brown, leave off serving him and serve me instead."

"Seeing that we have two sorceri here," said the townmaster, "and the second, if I'm not mistaken, the young male we've been searching for since midwinter, we might try forcing them to strip each other."

"Leave this temple!" said Eleva. "I've endured your defiling presence too long."

Youngwise bowed once more. "I made the suggestion, Lady

Reverence, so that I could tell your brother, with my hand in his, that I did everything in my poor power to see his directions carried out. From this moment, the quarrel must be between you and him. Unfortunately, were you both to stand before Their High Reverences in Center-of-Everywhere tonight, I fear I would wager my goldens on him." Youngwise touched fingers to forehead. "Before I go, may I ask if you'll permit us to arrest this outlaw warrior, once our own Third Wallkeeper? Or is she also under your holy protection?"

"Thorn is under my protection equally with the others," said the priestess.

Windbourne stepped out from behind her and lifted one arm. "How long does a townmaster take to obey a priestess? Remember, Master Youngwise, I have never been stripped!"

Well, well, well! thought Thorn. Has he finally decided he's got something in him, or does he just think it's safe to pretend?

"All gods guide you and bless your people," said Master Youngwise. After a glance at his First Wallkeeper, he turned and herded the other warriors out. None of them acted sorry to go.

"Well, Eaglesight," said Eleva, breathing deeply and rapidly, "will you continue to serve such a doubletongued scoundrel?"

Eaglesight pushed herself away from the wall, where she had been leaning at ease as if to enjoy a ballad. "Lady Eleva, if Master Youngwise had wanted to serve your brother, he could have ordered his spearwomen to throw as soon as they saw the blackrobes, and claimed he was only acting as Rondasu's voice. As for me, I wouldn't leave my post for anything less than First Raidleader, but I'm old enough that leading raids doesn't sound all that pleasurable anymore." Sheathing her sword, she held out the lamp in her left hand to Thorn, who put Stabber away in order to take it.

"We can hardly ask for the townmaster's mules now," said Eleva. "But I can still claim my own wagon and donkeys. Have them readied at once and brought here to the holy hall. And I will still trouble you to find clothes for my warrior."

Eaglesight nodded, saluted the priestess, and strode away after Youngwise, leaving only the runner, who still lay on the floor.

"She's right," said Thorn. "The old bastard will stay on the wall as long as he can, Lady, but if we don't push him off ourselves to your brother's side, he'll sit on the wall with one leg dangling on our side and the other tucked up beneath his own behind."

Eleva shrugged. "Those who will not choose a side put themselves above the gods. And you, Turtlefoot—Swiftcurrent?"

"Lady Reverence," said the runner without lifting his head, "I was raised in your family's farm. . . . I do not know any other, whether other halls are better or worse. . . ."

"Lady," said Frostflower, "this was the young man who served them tonight at dinner."

Eleva stepped close to Frostflower and spoke so low that Thorn, who stood with her back to them and kept watch on the servant, could only hear enough to gather that the priestess was asking whether Swiftcurrent had had any part in the murder and the sorceress was replying that she thought he had not. After a moment, Eleva stepped forward again. "If you come into my service, Swiftcurrent, you will live behind a bolted door until this trouble with His Reverence Rondasu is finished. If I win, you may be taken to Center-of-Everywhere and made to tell all your story and, if need be, submit yourself to the judgment of the High Gathering. If Rondasu defeats me, he may well hang you for changing your loyalty. But if I win and if you prove your good faith, then I promise your life will be very much better in my farm than in Rondasu's."

Swiftcurrent raised his head and lowered it again at once. "Lady . . . you've—befriended sorceri . . . the same ones who sorcered and killed . . ."

Frostflower went to the young man and knelt beside him. It was hard to see which of them trembled more, but she laid one hand on his shoulder, and, though he jerked at first, he did not pull away.

"If you so completely believed that we killed them," said the sorceress, "would you not have left this place with the townmaster and his warriors?"

"Good," said Eleva, "but say no more to him."

"His Reverence ordered me not to return without . . . seeing that Lady Eleva was safe. . . . Lady!" cried the servant, "If I could leave here, run away to Glantregion or Nearmidnorth and never trouble—"

"No!" said Eleva. "You must choose now: Reverence Rondasu or Reverence Eleva."

Swiftcurrent pushed himself up from the floor, felt his face as if searching for wrinkles, took two shaky steps forward, knelt before the priestess, and lifted his hands to her.

"Then take off my brother's token," she said.

Still trembling, he lifted the chain with Rondasu's symbol from around his neck and held it up to her. She snatched it from his hand and hurled it to the floor. The noise brought a yelp from Dowl and a scurry and hissing from Coyclaws, who had been crouching forgotten in the shadows.

"Pick it up, Thorn," said the priestess. "My anger threw it down, not my sense. Better to melt it and rework the metal than to leave it here in foolish scorn. Swiftcurrent, you will have my token to wear when we are back in my own farm. Thorn, take him in charge and go watch for my wagon."

Thorn saluted. "With all respect, Lady Reverence, I'm still an outlaw in everybody else's opinion. I'd rather not go out in plain sight without you."

"I did not accept you into my service for your caution."

"Call it skin-sense," Thorn replied. "Besides, you gave me a pretty damn nippy burn, and I'd like a little sorcerous healing on it."

The priestess smiled, pulled a golden from the small white purse at her belt, and edged the coin into Thorn's left hand, between fingers and lamp. "I have not forgotten your wish to be in somebody's pay."

"Swiftcurrent," said Frostflower, "was Lady Intassa already dead when you left?"

"Yes . . . dead. I—saw it myself." He stared at the floor. Frostflower covered her face with her hands.

"She was not as strong as her first husband," said Eleva. "And perhaps she had less will to live. But the child, Swiftcurrent? What of her son, Invaron?"

Swiftcurrent looked up and blinked. "Invaron, Lady? Who would harm the child?" He glanced at Windbourne as if not quite sure, even now, that sorcery was not behind the deaths.

"Lady," said the sorceress, "I think your brother wants Vari for his heir. I think . . . oh, God! I think he is never likely to beget his own child."

Eleva gazed at her. "Say no more of this. Not here. Some truths

might defile even a Truth Grove. Yes . . . Vari is safe. If they have
the time to raise him, they will try to twist his mind, but for now
he is safe. That will give us some time to plan—though we must
plan quickly. Well, Thorn, does your skin-sense prefer to lead us,
or to guard our rear?"

"If I lead," said Thorn, "I want to give the orders until we're
back in your farm, Reverence."

Eleva hesitated. Thorn's request was as custom-breaking as
anything else that night. No warrior ever gave commands to a
priest or priestess, because no priest or priestess ever joined a
raiding party or was otherwise entrapped in such a situation. But
Thorn guessed that Eleva's use for her required just this kind of
boldness toward priests, and Thorn's guess seemed to be well
founded, for Eleva said at last, "Well, then, command us, and let
me see what kind of raidleader you'll make."

So Thorn became "raidleader" of four non-fighters and two
animals: looking back, she saw that the cat had rejoined them, this
time curling herself in Eleva's arm. The priestess was stroking
Coyclaws absentmindedly, not noticing or caring that some of the
white flour and black dye was rubbing off onto her white robe.

While they waited in the doorway, Frostflower finally had her
chance to heal Thorn's burned back. She had just about finished
when Eleva's small wagon arrived, Eaglesight leading the pair of
donkeys with one stableman to help her.

Thorn considered the situation as she pulled on the warrior's
trousers and tunic Eaglesight had brought her—poor practice-
session stuff, but more serviceable than sorcerous underclothes.
"Only two can ride," she announced, buckling the leather belt. As
she noticed Eleva glancing at Windbourne appraisingly, the
swordswoman went on, "Your Reverence and Frostflower will
ride. These two scoundrels and I are just getting our legs stretched
out."

Eleva frowned at Thorn. "I had thought the two sorceri should
perhaps ride. Surely one of them can rein my gentle donkeys as
well as I."

"We depend on your priestly sanctity," the warrior replied.
"Priestly sanctity doesn't walk beside a wagon."

Eleva smiled, shrugged, and obeyed orders.

Not quite trusting the runner Swiftcurrent, Thorn secured his right knee to the lead donkey's neck by a four-pace length of rope. This brought another slight frown from Eleva—although she must not quite trust him either if she planned to keep him in a bolted alcove—but no protest from either Swiftcurrent or the donkey. None of them spoke again until they reached the Northwest Gate, where Eaglesight directed the gatewarriors to let the party through and then returned with the stableman to town-center.

Thorn had begun by walking on Eleva's side of the wagon, tacitly intending Windbourne to walk on Frostflower's side. But once out on the Mirrelroad, he worked his way around to Eleva's side and Thorn let him stay there. If Wedgepopper wanted to itch, let him itch. At least he was showing initiative in something besides thinking up penances for himself and telling Frostflower what sorceri should and should not eat. Besides, Thorn was just as happy to work her own way around to Frostflower's side of the wagon.

When they were well away from town, Frostflower asked, "Lady Reverence . . . you said that those who will not take part in a struggle put themselves above the gods?"

She spoke so low that if Thorn had still been on the other side of the wagon she might not have overheard all the words.

"If the gods love truth and justice," the priestess replied, "it seems clear they must favor the mortals who are most nearly truthful and just. At least to rejoice when they win."

"But we are not gods, Lady," said Frostflower, "we do not see everything clearly at once, and if we do not choose one side or the other, may it not be from ignorance—humility—rather than pride?"

Eleva *tsk*ed to the donkeys before she replied. "You think I was hasty in condemning Youngwise, Frostflower? Or are we speaking of Master Youngwise?"

"No, Lady, I . . . Lady, forgive me!" the sorceress exclaimed. "I feared that *you* had poisoned your husband!"

"Ah?" said Eleva. For several moments she seemed to concentrate on driving the mules. Dowl whined and bumped his way between Thorn's leg and the wagon. Thorn reached up and rubbed Frostflower's shoulder. The runner glanced back, stumbled a little for the first time, caught himself and walked on, timing his pace with the donkey's. In the light of the wagon lanterns Thorn could see Windbourne gazing at Eleva almost the way Dowl sometimes gazed at Frostflower. Only the cat acted unconcerned, sitting on the back of the wagon trying to wash her fur white again.

"In a way," Eleva said at last, "I am complimented. There's a proverb in the second or third scroll of Eltern, 'Those who are incapable of great sin are rarely capable of great good.' We'll ignore the notion that according to that proverb my sibs should have it in them to become the greatest benefactors of our generation."

"They are your sibs, Lady Reverence," said Windbourne.

She turned her head to look at him.

"I meant—" he hurried to explain "—their capability, your capability—but where they've turned it to evil, you've turned it to good."

Eleva faced forward again. "We've not yet heard all that Frostflower witnessed. But I suspect you're putting too great a burden on me, sorcerer, if you want me to do good in proportion to their evil."

Chapter 13

"Would you prefer to take the children to one of the cottages for the rest of the night, Blowingbud?" Eleva asked in a low voice.

The young nurse glanced again at the sorceri. "No, Lady, best not interrupt the children's night."

Eleva had chosen her new nurse well. She nodded and touched the young woman's arm. (Comfort and reassurance for everyone but herself!) "Yes, best to let them sleep undisturbed; we were fortunate not to wake them when we came." Blowingbud was a good, faithful servant and deserved to know more of the situation, but the truth had so deeply disturbed Frostflower, a stranger. Eleva needed time to decide how much the nurse might assimilate without passing on her grief and horror to little Evron and Evra.

Thorn came back from hanging the winter door at the alcove assigned to Swiftcurrent. Blowingbud had plainly been baffled that the runner was to be bolted into his chamber and the sorceri were not, but she seemed to accept it as a move not to anger the black-robes. Eleva watched her move past them, nodding respectfully but careful not to come within arm's reach, and disappear through the arch to ready their beds. Then Eleva beckoned to Thorn.

There would be no rest for either priestess or warrior yet, but there was a tray of cold food and drink waiting in Eleva's office;

the nurse had prepared it at the same time as the meals for the sorceri and runner. Except for Blowingbud, only the two gate-warriors and the night watchgirl knew of their arrival. Eleva poured a cup of wine for herself and began to pour one for Thorn, but the warrior shook her head and filled her own cup with water from the second flask.

"We must strike quickly, before they strike," said Eleva. "But there's not enough of this night left, and by tomorrow night..."

Thorn sat, putting one elbow on the table. "If we don't make our move before tomorrow night, what do you expect your sibs to do?"

Eleva also sat. "When Rondasu learns that I've taken you, the sorceri, and Swiftcurrent under my protection, he will probably demand that I accompany him to Center-of-Everywhere on a charge of heresy. When I refuse, he'll have the excuse I suspect he's been wanting to raid my farm. He may even send his warriors into this hall to spear the sorceri." Eleva swallowed a mouthful of wine. If Rondasu had a warrior as daring as Thorn, the priestess might expect to be murdered in her own hall during the raid and her death blamed on Frostflower and Windbourne.

"If he has a traditional-minded raidleader," said Thorn, "she'll want to raid while the moon's still bright. That'll be within the next two or three nights."

"His raidleader is Strongneck, once Second Wallkeeper of Five Roads. I believe you know her, Thorn."

"Hellbog! Yes, that bitch would love the chance to spear sorceri in a priests' hall."

"We'll have a few hours between dark and moonrise tomorrow night," said Eleva. "I know you don't like to raid without the moon, but if we could take them by surprise, in the early part of the night..."

Thorn grinned and shook her head. "Reverence, I'd love to try leading a raid in the dark of the moon. But we'd be shaving things too fine." She took a cold leg of roasted spring chicken from the tray, but did not begin to eat it. "Gods know I'd rather fight than dither around . . . but suppose, when your brother demands you go to Center with him, you agree? Your whole aim's to get him and Shara there anyway, isn't it? Why not let them do the work and turn the edge against them once we're there?"

"Because if they arrange the journey with us under their . . . charge and keeping, none of us are likely to arrive. He'll demand both sorceri be stripped. You'd not want Frostflower to suffer that a second time?" (Nor do I wish to see that sorcerer inside any other woman! He is so like the blackrobe of my dreams.) "He'll also demand you go in bars and chains, Thorn, if he does not demand your immediate scaffolding and hanging. Once on the road, all of us, Swiftcurrent as well, will probably be dead of some strange malady or sorcerous mischief or gods' revenge within three or four days. No. I prefer to take my sibs under my charge and keeping, and bring my witnesses alive to Center-of-Everywhere."

"Then turn the edge against him right away. Go to him tomorrow morning and demand he accompany you to Center."

"He will refuse. And he has the visible charges against me. And I can hardly let knowledge of his crime and my sister's spread among the common folk—little as we priests may deserve our reputation for sanctity."

"Don't give him the choice," said Thorn. "Hellbog, I've had enough of this giving suggestions—it's what the sorceri do; they never order each other around, just give each other suggestions. How many of your women do you think we could depend on to follow me right away?"

"They will all follow you."

Thorn took another drink of water. "You've already got a raidleader. She's not going to like giving up her place overnight to an outlawed sorceri-lover. And if she's any good, she'll have the other women's loyalty and they won't want me."

"They will give you their loyalty because I command it."

"Lady Reverence," said the swordswoman, "maybe when you took over this farm, you could dip right in. Maybe you got loyalty right away, and you're so used to being obeyed without question that you think all you've got to do is give your command. But it doesn't work that way in warriors' barracks. If I had a couple of hatchings and a chance to fight a few of your women one-to-one, yes, I think I'd get their respect. But I couldn't be comfortable leading them today, on the strength of your command, any more than I'd be comfortable going into a raid with an untempered sword."

Or than I would be riding a colt not yet trained to obey the directions of knees and reins, thought Eleva. Yes, Thorn was probably right. Warriors were a class apart; they would accept the knowledge of priests' guilt and help to keep the secret from common folk, but that did not necessarily mean they could bring themselves, between one sunrise and the next, to lay their own hands on a priest. Nor, as she looked back, had her own assumption of command been perfectly smooth. A few of her most traditionally-minded people had even left to find work in other farms when she built her steamgardens. "Well, warrior, do you have a plan?"

"We should be able to find one or two women in your barracks whose minds are old-fashioned enough I can talk them into helping catch priests. We'll go openly in daylight so there'll be no chance of its being mistaken for a raid. Demand he accompany you to Center-of-Everywhere on a charge of poisoning, and when he refuses, I'll seize him and our one or two others can seize Lady Shara."

"And when he summons his own warriors, or when they see us sacrilegiously leading their priests back through their own farm and gates?"

"I've attacked a priestess and threatened a townmaster tonight," said Thorn. "The sacrilege won't be that much worse if I hold a priest with my knife at his neck."

"And suppose they try to stop us for all that?"

Thorn seemed to flush slightly in the lamplight. "Then they'll think again before attacking us when I move Stabber to Lady Shara's neck."

"And if she dies as well? My sister would not surprise me if, in such a trap, she ran herself upon your blade."

"Then . . . Well, when they're both dead, it'll save the High Gathering some debate. You're still a priestess, so his warriors probably won't dare touch you—you can say I acted without your foreknowledge and approval, let 'em hack me apart, then claim Rondasu's Farm as his only surviving sib."

"On behalf of Intassa's son," Eleva murmured, partly to remind herself. Two farms to rule for the next . . . almost twenty years, until Invaron was old enough to claim rule of his . . .

"We can take the rest of your women along, too," said Thorn. "Leave them at the farmgates or outside the hall. You could even command them to seize me, if I have to kill your sibs."

The thought of Shara and Rondasu actually dead helped drive out the temptation of so much power. But Deveron and Intassa—that thought hardened her again.

"Thorn," said the priestess, "I cannot determine whether you are incredibly unselfish or incredibly desperate, whether you are devoted totally to the Great Giver of Justice or to Azkor and his demons."

The warrior looked mildly surprised, as if it had never occurred to her to probe into her own character and motives. She had begun to eat the leg of chicken while waiting for Eleva to speak, and now she finished chewing and swallowing a bite before she replied. "I'm a simple gambler, Lady Reverence. I think we'll be able to seize them and bring them to Center alive, if we act soon enough and if you have at least one other good warrior who'll follow my lead. As for unselfish—" She grinned and shook her head. "I'm bargaining with you for Frostflower's safety. And Windbourne's. And a brand of pardon for me if I survive, or, if I don't, a posthumous pardon, with the burial of an honest warrior and a full round of prayers and ceremonies to get me past the bloody demons."

"You shall have all you ask." Eleva extended her right hand across the table. Thorn glanced around, put down the chicken leg and hastily wiped her hand on her tunic as if disliking to soil one of the linen napkins, and linked fingers with the priestess.

"Now," Eleva went on, "at what hour should we strike tomorrow morning?"

"Best be at Rondasu's gates by dawn, before he has a chance to start out for town or here. But . . ."

"But we would need to leave here at once. And there is still our other warrior to choose—I think you will have to make the final choice there, Thorn."

"So we can't very well get there before . . . say, halfway to midmorning. Well, which is your brother more likely to do first, bury his poor wife or come for you?"

Which *would* he do first? In his place, thought Eleva, I would come for my runner and the sorceri. Yet Rondasu cannot know that Frostflower was in his hall, unseen, to watch the poisoning of Intassa. He will not know—unless Youngwise sends him a messenger—that Thorn and his first blamecatch are with us. So he will think himself safe. Unless Swiftcurrent's failure to return alerts him . . . and he may well assume that the runner lost his youth stripping the sorceress. As Rondasu planned, perhaps.

"If he had any feeling for Intassa," Eleva said aloud, "he may decide to bury her first. And by what Frostflower has told us, I think he did love her, as nearly as he could ever love anything beyond his land and his rule."

"That'll give us a little time to play with, even if he uses the short burial. Maybe we could confront them in the field."

"Oh, gods!" Eleva bent forward and put her face in her hands for a moment.

"Lady?"

"Nothing. I just realized . . . to break in upon her last honors . . . and then I realized I can hardly bear the thought of her body cut by *their* hands, scattered in one of *their* fields! Yes—sooner than allow that, we will break in upon their rites as early as we can arrive. I'll begin by claiming her body for burial in her first husband's farm!"

"Rondasu's Farm should be yours soon enough, Lady, if things work out according to our plans and the gods' justice. I'd been wondering if it wouldn't be better to make him come to you, seize him here in your own hall? If Shara doesn't come with him, it should be fairly easy to demand her person once we've got his."

"I doubt it. My sister might see it as her chance to seize the farm for herself and hold it against us." Even as I myself might do, thought Eleva, were I in her place, with so many sins already in my past. "But perhaps we can have the best of both plans. I'll send a runner to my brother's farm at once, to demand that Intassa's body be returned for burial here. We may be able to save her body and force my sibs to come here to us, all in the same move."

Chapter 14

"Thorn . . ." Eleva's face suddenly grew eager. "Suppose *I* served as your second warrior?"

Thorn studied her. "How does your size compare with your sibs'?"

"I am the smallest, by a head. Shara the tallest, thanks to her mother. But I believe I am also the quickest."

"How about the strongest?"

The priestess hesitated. "We wrestled only a few times, in childhood. I always lost to Shara but she was almost seven years older! We never wrestled after we both had our full growth. I never again dared wrestle with Rondasu, not after the first time."

The swordswoman thought back over her few moments' grappling with Eleva and shook her head. "You've got pluck, Lady Reverence, and you're not weak for your size. With the proper training from childhood, you could've made a bloody good spearwoman. But we don't have time to train you tonight. And then," she added, trying to choose her words carefully, as she saw the eagerness drain out of Eleva's face, "when it came to the point, do you really hate your own sibs enough to hold a knife steady at one of their throats?"

The priestess smiled wanly and shook her head. "No. Not steady. Probably enough to plunge the knife through, but not . . . so, it must be another warrior."

"Better check the gatewarriors first," said Thorn. "If one of them will do, we don't even have to wake anyone else in the barracks. The fewer women who suspect what we're planning, the better."

The priestess left Thorn alone in the office to question the warriors with a free tongue. The swordswoman moved around to Eleva's chair in token of the fact that she was in full command for the time being.

The first gatewarrior began by pulling the doorcurtain back about halfway and looking in with a good balance of confidence and respect. At Thorn's nod, she came all the way in, letting the curtain swing into place behind her. She touched fist to lips and then stood at attention with her hands lightly on her hips, a tall, thin young woman with pale skin, hair that looked silvery in the lamplight, and a large knob of new but well-carved and highly polished golden pinewood as a pommel decoration on her sword. She was maybe seventeen or eighteen, old enough to be trustworthy now, if ever.

"Why did you salute me, warrior?" said Thorn.

"I saluted the occupant of the priestly chair," the younger woman replied.

Thorn nodded again and gestured to the empty chair. The other sat.

"Your name?" said Thorn.

"Starstroke."

It had a near-sorcerous ring. You found that sometimes, especially in warriors with high ideas and an infatuation with the knowledge that several lifetimes ago they would have been priestesses. Not that the warriors were trying to imitate sorcerous names; often they were among the fiercest sorceri-haters of all. They were trying to imitate what people usually supposed were the meanings of priestly names in the old language, and it came out sounding sorcerous. (Thorn wondered if Frost had ever thought much about that.) And then, Starstroke—Silverstroke, that one warrior Thorn had liked so well last summer. Starstroke—Starwind, Frostflower's name for Thorn's own son. Starwind—Windbourne . . .

Thorn was not one of those women who searched for omens in the way a leaf fell across her weapon, but with another warrior to find in a hurry and nothing else to guide her, all these name links certainly had the look of an omen.

Thorn filled a cup with wine and pushed it across the table. Starstroke shook her head and pushed the cup back to the center. Her wrist already showed the sinews that indicated good strength in a thin body. "Starstroke," Thorn asked, "who's most likely to murder a priest?"

"Another priest."

"Who else?"

". . . A warrior, I suppose . . . maybe a sorceron."

"Unh," said Thorn, more pleased than she let show. Most folk, even among warriors, would have put the sorceron first. "All right, Starstroke, suppose you see one priest on the point of murdering another. What do you do?"

The younger woman hesitated. "How is the first priest attacking?"

"Say you see him pouring poison into the wine."

"I could not be sure it was poison. But . . . I would upset the wine as if by accident."

"Say the first priest is about to use a pillow and smother the second?"

"I would . . . Which priest are we supposing to be my Reverence, my employer?"

"Neither of them. You just happen to be around."

"Then I would make a noise and wake the sleeping one. Warrior, I cannot see how I could be present in the bedchamber with two strange priests, and I fail to see the purpose of—"

Thorn slapped the table. "Maybe you think we're just playing some silly game at this time of night for the demons' sport of it? You make a noise, the sleeping priest wakes up, and the attacking priest pulls out his little dagger and goes for his neck."

"I . . . think I would use the circle-hold from behind. Then I . . . would obey whatever commands the other priest gave me."

Thorn nodded. Starstroke had given answers close enough to the kind Thorn had been hoping for to indicate she was a good risk. Thorn's final choice would be a gamble no matter how many women she questioned, and she had always gone into play with the idea that the gods preferred a bold gambler to a shilly-shallying one.

She reached across the table for Starstroke's hand. "Are you willing to swear secrecy?"

The younger woman stared at the extended hand. "Who will be in the most danger if I refuse your secret?"

"Probably your own Lady Reverence."

Starstroke looked up at Thorn's face, down again at the table. After a moment, she stretched out her hand and linked fingers with the older woman.

"They thought to get Deveron's Farm?" Starstroke asked after Thorn had explained her plan and part of its motive. "But why Intassa?"

"Shara was jealous of her," Thorn said tightly. The mere fact of two sibs humping together did not horrify her as it probably should have—never having known her own parentage, she had gone through a year or so of adolescent nausea at the idea that every male she milked *could* be an unknown brother, and then finally decided it was not worth the fear. But in this case she did not need to fake her disgust. No prick was worth committing murder for so you could keep him all to yourself, everyone knew they were sharper when they could get a little variety anyway.

"Then," said Starstroke, "Shara alone was responsible for Intassa's death, but Rondasu was the more responsible for Deveron's? Then I would like to ask the favor of seizing Rondasu!"

"You would? Why?"

"It was His Reverence Deveron who hired me."

"You may find it hard enough just to grab a priestly body without that body also being male," Thorn pointed out, remembering the scruples she had had to overcome in order to fight back against a couple of outlaws despite their maleness.

Starstroke leaned across the table and gripped Thorn's arm. "Lady Intassa was nothing to me—even Lady Eleva isn't that much! My allegiance is to His Reverence! Let me seize Rondasu— it'll be easier for me to take the one most to blame for murdering Deveron."

The sudden display of temper rather pleased Thorn. If anything had been unsatisfactory about Starstroke, it had been her seemingly perpetual caution, almost too calculating for a youth her age. Thorn nodded. "All right. You take Rondasu, I'll take Shara, if she comes. Now let's get some sleep. Her Reverence is giving us a couple of alcoves here in the hall."

Chapter 15

Eleva's young runner Dart arrived back in her hall soon after dawn. He brought only a vocal message: Rondasu would come at once. He had not sent back Eleva's wax tablet with his own reply; he might well be keeping her message as new evidence of her madness.

"How did His Reverence look when he read my message?" she asked Dart. "Enraged? Amused?"

Dart looked at the floor. "Lady Shara took the tablet, Reverence. She said His Reverence was mourning in the Truth Grove, and she'd give it to him. Then she sent me to one of the cottages and had the Second Nurse give me wine and fruitloaf. When His Reverence sent for me, he . . . he didn't frown or smile, he only told me to say he would come at once."

Eleva sighed. "You've done as well as any messenger could have done. Go to the farmgates now so that as soon as the watchgirl sees how many he's bringing with him, you can run back and tell me."

She summoned Blowingbud and instructed her to take the children to the arbor-house in the northwest orchard for the day. She thought they would be in no danger, but she preferred them and

their nurse to be far out of hearing lest the events in the hall
engrave an ugly memory in their young minds.

And the sorceri? Eleva woke Thorn and told her to bring Frostflower and Starstroke. No doubt she should have delegated the
task of rousing Windbourne to the sorceress, but she reserved it
for herself.

Dawnlight was beginning to filter into his alcove, but Eleva's
lamp was still useful. She stood there a moment gazing down at
Windbourne as he slept, thinking where best to touch him—on
the cheek, the brow, the cleft in his chin, now covered with one
or two days' bristle of light golden beard.... Had her dream-lover
always had that cleft chin, or only since she heard the description
of the sorcerer who had been seized in Five Roads and escaped,
the one whose innocence Maejira the Merciful had shown her in
another dream?

As Eleva's hand hovered above the sheet, Windbourne's cat
suddenly bounded up, brushing the priestess' arm and landing half
on the sorcerer's chest and half on the bed. Eleva withdrew her
hand and stood back immediately as Windbourne sat up, grappling
lightly with the cat even before he opened his eyes, as if used to
such an awakening.

"Sorcerer," said Eleva.

He opened his eyes and looked up at her. She thought he started
a little. "Lady Reverence? Has something...?"

"Come to the dais end of the long hall at once," she said, then
turned and left the alcove. Although he had been sleeping in his
robe, he might still be shy of coming out from beneath the sheet
in her presence.

The cat was shrewder than I, Eleva scolded herself—we needed
dispatch, not dreaming.

Within a few moments they were gathered, Eleva sitting in her
ruling priest's chair, Thorn half sprawled on the edge of the dais,
the others standing respectfully. The dog stood near Frostflower
wagging his tail; the cat lay at Eleva's feet. They could hear
Blowingbud in one of the far eastern alcoves dressing the children
for their day's excursion.

"My brother is on his way here," said Eleva. "We do not know
how many warriors he may bring with him, whether in an hour
or two this hall will hold a few people struggling, or many. The

more women in the fight, the greater chance Rondasu has of defeating me, and if he wins, there will be suffering and death for you sorceri. You may be wisest to leave my farm now."

"Bloodshed in a priestly hall?" whispered Frostflower.

"There has been poisoning in this hall," the priestess replied. "Why not bladework? It's honest in comparison."

"There will be suffering for us if you are defeated, Lady Reverence, whether we are safe or not," said Windbourne. "And can we not help you afterwards...even in your success?"

Eleva smiled at him. "I'd thought you would hide in the forest until this morning's work is done. If I win, you can return—if my sibs win, you can find the Mirrel River, follow its course north to the northern Wendwoods, and so, with luck and skill, avoid pursuit."

"I will not leave you, Lady Reverence," said Windbourne.

"It is your choice, sorcerer," she replied. "I will not attempt to command any one of your people. Frostflower? Will you escape now?"

The sorceress was trembling, but she shook her head. "To be caught and trapped alone in the woods? I would rather trust in your protection, Lady, and be caught with all the rest if it comes to that."

Thorn shook her head. "Take to the woods, Frost. That's your best chance."

Eleva had never explored the old tunnels as far as she would have liked. But in every farm the warriors had long used ancient priestly escape routes to slip out of the farm and enjoy nights in the nearest taverns.

"Starstroke," the priestess demanded, "you warriors have a tunnel that comes out beyond the walls?"

The young warrior flushed. "Lady Reverence, I have never—"

"I did not ask whether you had ever used it yourself."

Starstroke touched fist to lips. "Yes, Lady, there are some tunnels that come up outside the walls."

"Good. Explain to Frostflower how she can find these tunnels and where they will bring her up. They can be reached from the ones immediately below this hall?"

Starstroke nodded.

Eleva turned to the sorceress. "You can wait in the tunnel behind the dais. If you hear the conflict going against us, follow Starstroke's instructions and find your way out of the farm through the tunnels. If we lose, we may still manage to join you and escape together. Now, Windbourne, if you will not leave me, where will you stay?"

He hesitated. "It has long been my intention, Lady Reverence, to purge myself by proclaiming my innocence openly, in the face of my accusers."

"I admire that. Unfortunately, if you stand in plain sight beside my dais and help me confront your chief accusers, you may complicate my work."

"I . . . have no wish to do that, Lady Reverence. Let me wait in the tunnel with Frostflower. I can at least block pursuit if the need arises."

Chapter 16

From her position just inside the arch, Thorn could see Eleva
seated in her chair on the dais, Starstroke waiting behind the arch
directly across from Thorn's, and part of this end of the long hall.
The priestess had no weapon except her thin, ceremonial silver
dagger, which she held in her lap, its tip just visible above her
knee. She was breathing deeply, but her profile was calm and she
sat motionless. She looked as if she had been trained for years to
know when to give a battle call. Bloodrastor! Thorn thought, What
a warrior she would have made . . . if only she'd been a little larger
boned! She should have lived in the ancient days when ruling
priests and priestesses sometimes did lead their warrior-priestesses
in raid and defense!

Starstroke had retreated too far into the shadow of her arch for
Thorn to see her expression, but the lines of her body looked a
little too tense to please the older swordswoman. A warrior could
take the edge off her strength and agility by waiting too long at
too great a tension. Well, you could hardly expect a youth like
Starstroke, who had probably never even lost a length of skin in
a Truth Grove, to await the moment of daring sacrilege as coolly
as an old hand at priestess-mauling like Thorn.

Frostflower was down in the tunnel, as safe as possible and presumably hugging Dowl. Windbourne would be nearer the top of the stairs, maybe just far enough behind the doorcurtain to see a little without being seen—so long as he didn't cause the linen to move, or let go of his blasted cat. (Thorn had insisted that for once the sorceri hold their animals in the tunnel, by force if necessary.) The runner Swiftcurrent was still bolted safe and snug in his alcove. They should have the long hall to themselves.

The day must be bright outside. Though the sun could not be very high yet, the skyshine coming through the roof vents already gave the hall plenty of light. Eleva had lit incense-candles at either side of the dais only for priestly effect.

Eleva's runner Dart had brought word about three balladlengths ago that Rondasu's party was in sight: two in priests' white, one in warrior's tunic and trousers, and one in worker's garb. The priests and warrior rode horses, the worker rode a fast mule, and they were coming at a good pace. Thorn guessed that Youngwise had not sent Rondasu full details of last night's events—If Rondasu and Shara knew that Eleva had both sorceri and a desperate outlaw with her, they would surely have brought more than a single warrior of their own. But why that single warrior? Maybe they intended to seize Eleva as she intended to seize them.

Thorn and Starstroke had made a quick decision that one warrior in Rondasu's party was not enough to merit summoning another woman to help them. Starstroke proposed that she attack Rondasu's warrior while Thorn seized both priest and priestess. It might have been a good scheme, but Thorn had no idea how good Starstroke was with her weapons, and no time to test her. She considered taking on Rondasu's warrior herself, but she did not quite trust Starstroke to seize two farmer-priests at once. "We'll keep to our original plan," Thorn had said at last. "If Rondasu's warrior is stupid enough to attack us when we've got both Their Reverences in our arms with our blades ready to stick into them they'll command her otherwise pretty damn quickly."

As for the worker on the mule, he or she must have been brought to hold the riding beasts when Their Reverences dismounted—a sign of disrespect to Eleva's servants, but no fighter to worry about. Eleva had sent Dart back to the gates by a roundabout path with instructions to run and rouse the warriors' barracks if any more of Rondasu's women should appear, following at a distance.

Eleva's sibs might have reached the farmgates by the time Dart had reached the hall. They might be passing through the east orchard by the time the sorceri were safely in the tunnel with their dog and cat. And then there was nothing to do but wait.

The incense-candle had burned down about a knuckle's-length when Rondasu and his party finally entered the hall. Eleva's only visible reaction was a further straightening of her back and a slight twitching in the muscles of her neck and her lower right arm beneath the elbow-length sleeve. Thorn moved farther from the archway and counted the footsteps that fell on the floor tiles—two sets of stiff-soled priestly sandals and one set of soft leather boots that came down with a heavy, warrior's stride. As expected, Rondasu's worker must have stayed outside with the mounts.

One sandal and the hem of a white robe came into Thorn's view and she prepared to move yet farther back, but the priests stopped there, about seven strides from the dais. The warrior also stopped. She would be some paces behind the priests.

Eleva rose, crossing her silver dagger aslant her small chest and covering its tip lightly with her left hand so that she looked like a statue of Maejira the Merciful.

"Well, sister?" said a man's voice—Rondasu's, obviously, and he spoke with a quiver of suppressed rage. "Explain your message."

"My message—which you must prize, since you did not return my tablet—was very clear. I demanded the immediate custody of my husband's son Invaron, his nurse Coddlemeasure, and the body of his mother Intassa, and I advised your immediate preparation for a journey to Center-of-Everywhere."

"She's mad!" said a woman's voice—must be Shara's—and the sandal and white hem in Thorn's line of vision moved half a step forward.

Eleva turned her head very slightly. "Did you bring me Shara as a pledge for the safety of the child and his nurse, Rondasu? Or did you bring her because you feared she might defile your wife's body if you left her alone with it?"

Shara took a full step toward the dais (coming into view so

that Thorn had to shift farther back). "Can we continue to ignore her madness, brother?"

"If I am mad," said Eleva, still without raising her voice, "come with me to Center and prove it to the High Gathering. But I will bury Intassa in the field with her first husband before we go."

This time Rondasu stepped forward—Thorn got a glimpse of his pointing arm. "You will return with us and live bolted inside your old alcove until you recover your reason! I will not expose my sister's madness to the High Gathering."

Eleva turned her head towards him again. Her eyes seemed to narrow and glitter slightly. "*I* summon *you* to the Gathering, brother and sister. You do not ask why?" She moved her left fist to her side and turned her right hand to point the dagger at them— Maejira the Merciful changing into Meactira the Threatening. "I charge you with the murders of my husband Deveron and his wife Intassa."

Someone coughed—it must be Rondasu's warrior. The others were silent for a few heartbeats.

Then Shara laughed. "We need not prove her madness, brother! She will prove it herself!"

Eleva seemed to point her dagger at Shara. "Yesterday at dinner, Rondasu, you offered your wine to our sister. Since you had already drunk too much, you spilled some of it on the table. Sister, you drank from the cup first, then commanded your attending servant, Swiftcurrent, to wipe up the spilled wine. While the others naturally watched him, you poisoned the cup, then passed it on to your brother's wife."

"Mad!" screamed Shara.

"I suppose you had the poison always with you," Eleva went on, "waiting your chance. What better chance than when you had a sorceress ready for blamecatch, in the keeping of your unorthodox sister Eleva? But the High Priests in Center-of-Everywhere know there are poisons which produce deaths like those of Intassa and Deveron."

"Swiftcurrent?" said Rondasu. "Swiftcurrent could not have told you—he could not have seen—"

"But you feared he might guess, did you not? And perhaps even speak, despite his timid youth and lifelong loyalty. So you sent him, of all your messengers—the same lad who had already given you his day's service, rather than a rested servant—you sent him with directions that he offer his body for a power-stripping. Do you not fear to send so many witnesses to the dais of Jehandru, Who listens to all folk alike?—you who love to charge *me* with heresy and impiety!"

"Crazy!" said Rondasu's warrior. (Gods, he had brought that bitch Strongneck!) "Why would Lady Shara kill her own brother's wife?"

Thorn tightened her grip on Slicer. If things were at the point where Rondasu's new raidleader dared break into a priestly interview . . .

But Eleva lowered her arms as if to signal that she was purposely avoiding the battlecall. A few moments more and Eleva might hope to confuse her brother's warrior into neutrality or even make her change sides.

"I doubt your priest and priestess want me to answer that," said Eleva, "but I do not like the thought of what my brother might do in my own bedchamber and bed if he were to bring me back into his hall as he desires. How do I know all this? Perhaps from those true dreams the gods send me, that you always mocked. As for my husband's death, Shara was visiting us at that time. She accomplished his poisoning much as she accomplished Intassa's. But she had poisoned Deveron on your own instructions, Rondasu!"

"Seize her!" cried Rondasu. "Didn't I tell you a mad priestess loses her sanctity? Seize her!"

Maybe Strongneck would have held off by now with confused loyalties. But before they could find out, Starstroke had jumped into sight, waving her sword and screaming at the priest.

Thorn cursed and rushed out to join her. Strongneck was raising her spear. "The priest!" Thorn shouted, seizing Shara. "Damn you, grab the priest!"

Starstroke reached out her left hand—hesitated—jerked it back and just stood pointing her sword at Rondasu. Strongneck threw her spear. Starstroke screamed and fell back with the weapon sticking through her sword arm.

"Damn!" shouted Thorn. Getting a grapplehold on Shara's neck with her left arm and trying to ignore her struggles, Thorn rushed toward Strongneck.

Strongneck had more brains in her arms than in her head—she was spearwoman and swordswoman both, and she already had sword and knife in her hands.

Eleva screamed. Thorn glanced round to see Rondasu on the dais, his own ceremonial dagger in his hand. Each sib was trying to hold back the other's blade. Starstroke was babbling and trying to pull the spear out of her arm.

By body weight alone, Rondasu would finally overpower Eleva. The only hope was to slice Strongneck right away—and not let go of Shara to do it! Thorn whirled back, hauling the priestess round with her.

And caught Shara on Strongneck's sword.

The priestess went on struggling, like a warrior who got a wound and didn't realize it in the heat of battle. In fact, at first Thorn wasn't quite sure whether the sword had thunked into her own flesh or Shara's. But Strongneck drew back with a cry of horror at the blood spurting from a tear in the priestess' white robe, and Thorn used that moment to thrust Slicer into Strongneck's midgut.

She yanked Slicer out again, let Strongneck crumple, and turned back toward the dais, still dragging Shara.

Windbourne had appeared in the doorway to the tunnel. Rondasu had Eleva down now, her back pressed to the overturned chair, his blade almost at her neck. Windbourne jumped onto the dais, reached down, and seized Rondasu's neck.

There weren't any flashes, noises or wasps. But Eleva gave a gasp that wasn't for her own sake. And Rondasu let the knife slip from his fingers, looked down at his hand, uttered a shrill scream, and slumped forward, burying his head in his arms.

Within a few heartbeats, his hair had gone white and he had shriveled like a raisin.

Chapter 17

Windbourne pulled his hands from the earth at last, sat back against one of the orchard trees, and shook his head. "It is gone."

Frostflower released her breath slowly, wondering if the attempt had cost her more effort than him. They sat alone on the edge of a footpath between the orchard and a field of barley. "Perhaps if we tried outside the farmwalls?" she suggested.

He opened his eyes, looked at her, and began to brush the soil from his hands. "The where makes no difference. My last burst of power came within the priests' very hall, did it not?"

"In moments of great emotion, much is possible—even folk never trained in our skills sometimes find unguessed strength. But now, in your calm mind...Windbourne, you've often said the skills never came easily to you?"

"Frostflower, Frostflower!" He sighed, put his head back against the peach tree, and smiled a little. "Do you find it so hard to believe that God's rules for the world still hold true in other cases than yours? I harmed a man. None of us may keep the power after using it to harm another."

The sorceress felt a tear in her left eye. "But your purpose was not so much to harm the priest as to save Eleva—it was an unselfish use of power."

"Was my first purpose to save Her Reverence? Or rage against the priest who would harm her?" Windbourne rubbed Dowl's head. (Coyclaws had apparently chosen to accompany Eleva and Thorn to the burial of Lady Intassa's body in the same field with her first husband.) "Frostflower," Windbourne went on, "I'm tired of constantly pricking at my soul. I don't regret what I have done. . . . It's almost as if a great weight had fallen from me along with my power."

She wiped her eyes. "Perhaps if it ever comes again to saving a life . . ."

"I pray it does not." Again he shook his head. "Frostflower, I think the skills never meant to me what they mean to you. To you, they seem to be a pleasure and consolation in themselves. To me they were always somehow . . . a test, duties I must practice to prove my innocence, my worth." He smiled. "And in that last moment . . . I'd never thought the power could come so easily to me, so unthinkingly—that *I* should be able to wither a man to such an age in a few heartbeats! It was as if the efforts of my entire life had all been preparation for that one instant. No, I do not think I could ever again have found so much satisfaction in the power." He glanced at her, lowered his gaze again, and fondled Dowl with especial gentleness. "So perhaps it's best that my power is gone." He looked at her once more. "Believe me, this present rest . . . peace, almost . . . is a fair purchase for the price I paid."

This time Frostflower looked away. If Windbourne had retained his power, might his faith not have been shattered like hers? Perhaps God—or the gods—are more gentle than we imagine, thought the sorceress; perhaps I survived the loss of my certitude more easily than I would have the loss of my power, and perhaps Windbourne has the greater need of his faith.

"It has its own kind of comfort, this burial practice of the farmers," Windbourne remarked. "To be returned to the earth . . . in a way, this soil god and goddess of the farmer-priests seem not too different from the Father and Mother aspects of our God, ever producing their offspring. So buried priests are taken into their own godhead."

Frostflower glanced at him and shivered. What he said might be a holy insight, a pick to unravel one of the knots in her own doubt and confusion . . . but that Windbourne should be the one to give it to her seemed ominous. She herself had explained the priestly doctrine of Aomu and Voma to him—had her doubt planted doubt in him?

Coyclaws suddenly sprang from the tree onto Dowl's back, beginning one of their mock spats. The funeral was over—Eleva had come through the orchard with the cat, and the sorceress had not heard them.

"Is it truly gone?" said the priestess.

Frostflower nodded. "It seems to be, Lady."

Eleva sat on her knees beside Frostflower and looked at Windbourne. "What will happen to him now? Thorn says that when you lose your power, you must either marry, or grow stale and embittered. Can he find . . . a sorceress to marry him?"

Windbourne shook his head. "I will not look for one, Lady. I would not ask one of my own kind to give up her own power out of pity for me."

"And yet we farmers and our folk live very comfortably without power, at least without your species of power," she said. "Windbourne . . . on the way to Center-of-Everywhere we'll talk of how best I can repay you."

Perhaps Eleva wished to begin talking of it now, alone with him. Frostflower rose quietly and left. Only Dowl followed her back to the hall.

Thorn, who had assisted at the burial, found her some time later in Eleva's study alcove, staring at a scroll-case door marked with the Self-Lighting Candle, the sign of a forbidden scroll within its cubicle.

Quickly as Frostflower had followed Windbourne up out of the tunnel, Rondasu's raidleader, Strongneck, had already been dead. Shara refused to let a sorceron touch her, so Eleva had bound up her wound, pronouncing it superficial. Windbourne had bolted Rondasu in the alcove readied for him, and Frostflower set the bone in Starstroke's upper arm, which had been broken by the spear, and sped the healing. The young warrior had accepted Frostflower's help passively, continuing to weep after she was healed, even as Frostflower tried to assure her that with practice and exercises she would be able to use her sword again.

"Don't waste your effort, Frost," Thorn had said when she

approached them after bolting Shara into another alcove. Then, looking down at Starstroke, "You lousy, rotten set of dice!"

"Thorn," the sorceress had protested softly.

"You didn't see it, Frost. If this young idiot had done what she was supposed to instead of snapping on me like a brat's damn toy sword . . ." The older swordswoman shrugged and moderated her tone. "Well, I guess it's my fault, too. I must've been tired, I made a bad gamble. Not the first in my life, probably won't be the last. Just get the sniveling bitch out of my sight for awhile."

At Eleva's direction, Frostflower had taken Starstroke to one of the hallside cottages and put her into trance to compensate for speeding her body's time to heal the wound.

Eleva had put Rondasu's stableman in another cottage. He was confused and uninformed, but he seemed glad enough of luxury to rest in while he tried to work things through his obviously slow mind.

Then the priestess had sent a request to Youngwise and Eagle-sight that they meet her on Mideastroad Straight at the Farmfork and accompany her into Rondasu's Farm. She had not taken Thorn or the sorceri on this errand, for their appearance might rouse opposition, and they deserved to rest. They later learned that on reaching Rondasu's Farm Eleva had gathered his houseservants, principal workers, and Second Raidleader to inform them her brother and sister had suffered grievous injury in an accident and might not recover, even though she was taking them south to the priestly town for their treatment. She made her brother's folk accountable to Master Youngwise until she or their own priest returned. Shaken by the news, none of Rondasu's people protested when Eleva claimed Intassa's body and brought it, along with Invaron and the nurse, back to her own farm—the child weeping with confusion and infant sense of loss, alternately clinging to Coddlemeasure and to Eleva.

Vari's wounds, at least, seemed likely to scar over quickly; little more than two years old, most of his life had been spent with his nurses, and he showed delight in returning to his former play-mates Evron and Evra. "Indeed," said Eleva, "for all of poor Intassa's love and the greater part Deveron allowed her in her child's rearing, the difference might not yet have grown quite clear to Vari between his natural mother and the other priestess in his first home. And Coddlemeasure suckled Vari—Intassa could not. I suspect old Silkhands reduced Coddlemeasure to a breechcloth-washer in Rondasu's Hall, but now she can take the chief part of Invaron's daily care again. That may help console her, too . . . Rondasu's Farm will be named as Invaron's as soon as possible, for the sake of his mother and lest the Demon-Goddess of Greed clutch me as tightly as she clutched my brother. With Master Youngwise visiting the farm once or twice a hatching to receive the reports of the chief workers, and Silkhands in the hall to direct them between his visits—she was a fearsome nurse, but I think she may prove a passable administrator—with Crinkpetal sending them word when the Marker Days come, and with no neighbors powerful enough to dare attempt a raid, at least Ron-dasu's folk—Invaron's folk—should be able to store their winter supply of food and fuel without a priest in the hall."

She left her own farm in the charge of Crinkpetal, even in-stalling him in her hall. He grumbled at having to leave his own business under his sons' management for most of the summer, but finally confessed it would be good experience for the lads; and more than half his selling for the year had been done earlier in the spring. "Besides," Eleva confided to Frostflower and Windbourne with a chuckle, "whether he admits it or not, he'd much rather be left here to guide my farm than be taken along to Center as a witness. Oh, yes, looking back, I think I understand what all his talk about rose thorns and edges of the wind meant that morning, but I'm not going to inquire into it. If we ask you to keep our secrets, Frostflower, we must be ready to keep yours."

The priestess transferred her raidleader Splitgut to Rondasu's Farm and persuaded Youngwise to lend her Eaglesight to get her own barracks in order and find her a better permanent raidleader. "I no more fear an attack on my farm than on Invaron's during my absence," she said, "but no farm will remain secure forever without a good, strong barracks. Eaglesight has promised to inspect my smith Rediron's work and buy a sword from him; that should encourage my own warriors to buy their weapons at home."

The priestess spoke of all this to both sorceri, but she looked oftener at Windbourne. That was the night Thorn spent resting after receiving her second brand of pardon, which she had insisted Eleva give her before they set out on the journey to Center-of-Everywhere.

They left on the second morning after Intassa's burial. All the party rode. The priestess took one tent-wagon for the sorceri, Swiftcurrent, Dowl and Coyclaws, a second tent-wagon for Rondasu and Shara, mules for Starstroke, two servants, and another pair of chosen warriors—brought more for honor than for protection, since Eleva's priesthood was enough to keep away outlaws, and as yet only Thorn dared handle Shara and Rondasu, with a little help from Starstroke, who seemed trying plaintively to make up for her failure during the crisis. Eleva and Thorn rode horses, Eleva's a rust-red mare named Rastar. Horses being the privileged mounts of priests, Eleva honored Thorn highly by mounting her on one. The first few evenings, Thorn grumbled to Frostflower that the honor was damned uncomfortable by the end of a full day.

The journey would have required nearer two hen's-hatchings than one on foot, but with all riding they shortened the time considerably. Most nights they spent in a farm or a town, lodging in the priestly alcove-hall if the town were large enough to have one, otherwise in the house of townmaster or prosperous merchant. Thus, Frostflower reflected, they left a trail of spreading rumors about two blackrobes traveling in all apparent friendship with a priestess and entering farms without fear. On the few nights they spent in woods or wildfield, one of Eleva's servants cared for the animals and the other helped the warriors make camp and cook the meat while Frostflower and Windbourne prepared the rest of the meal.

Eleva clothed Rondasu and Shara in blue silk robes such as might be worn by wealthy merchants and explained them in towns as cousins of her nurse. They had been crazed, she said, by the loss of the rest of their family in a fire and must be bound in their wagon by day and put behind bolted doors at night lest they injure themselves. How she explained them in farms Frostflower did not know, for Eleva always spoke privately with the other priests, who remained silent on the matter afterwards.

One skeptical townmaster tried questioning the sorceri about the crazed old man and surly woman. Windbourne answered, sternly and sharply, according to Eleva's tale. "After withering Rondasu to save Her Reverence," he explained to Frostflower next day, flushing slightly, "shall I hesitate to tell a small lie for her sake?"

Midway to Center-of-Everywhere, on the second night they had to camp in the wilds, Shara somehow managed to free herself, crawl from the wagon, and get the pointed iron spit which the warriors had used to roast their meat.

For some reason—either because Shara had disturbed her or because she was pursuing some nocturnal creature, Coyclaws leaped onto Thorn's chest and off again, waking the swordswoman in time to see Shara in the fireglow, moving toward the sleeping Eleva. Thorn had shouted and thrown her knife, striking Shara in the leg. With the wakened camp closing in around her, Shara plunged the spit into her own stomach.

Reaching the wagon's tent-door at that moment, Frostflower had seen the end of Shara's arm movement and the first dark spurt of blood.

Frostflower hurried down but Eleva held her back. "Lady," the sorceress had said, "wounds that must be fatal in the body's natural time, we can sometimes heal quickly enough to—"

"She's pulled Thorn's knife out of her leg," Eleva replied, pointing. "Keep back! She'll stab whoever comes near enough."

Starstroke had come forward, taken a spear from one of the other warriors, and finished it, while Frostflower turned away, able to avoid the sight, if not the sound—a last scream that seemed less of fear or pain than of rage. Windbourne half carried the sorceress back into the wagon, where she lay listening to the burial chants that Eleva began at once.

So they had left Shara cut and buried in a field of wild grasses. "In her place," Eleva said the next morning, "I would have done the same as she did. She would never have confessed willingly; the most she could have hoped was to demand my Groving also, with a counter-charge against me. And I think my Groving would have been gentler, for the witnesses are all mine, even to Young-wise's written parchment." She looked at the sorceress, whose shock must have shown in her face, and went on. "Yes, Frost-flower, even we priests may be submitted to such questioning, but

only in the Truth Grove in Center-of-Everywhere, and only by
priests of the High Gathering. And I would not have allowed you
to be Groved. I would have demanded to answer all questions,
myself alone, on behalf of all my witnesses, as would have been
my right. And I would have outlasted Shara, if there's any truth
in the doctrine that the gods prefer justice to evil."

"Why go on to Center now?" Thorn had said. "Rondasu
shouldn't be any danger to you. He might've been if he'd reached
that age naturally, but if he's still got any spirit left, he sure as
stink hasn't shown it."

Frostflower had nodded. Rondasu was still a young man with
all a young man's greeds, lusts and ambitions, but now he was
hopelessly trapped in an old man's body with no chance to have
acquired an old man's wisdom and serenity. He appeared to be
sinking into the senility that came of ceasing to expand one's
wisdom and knowledge.

Nevertheless, Eleva had covered her left hand with her right.
"If judgment on my sibs had been our only purpose in journeying
to Center, then I think I would now return home. But we have a
better purpose. We must go on."

Nothing but apprehension—which Frostflower could not help
but feel now and again despite Eleva's reassurances—disturbed
the rest of their journey.

Where edgelands farmers like Elvannon tended to be the most
tolerant of sorceri—perhaps because they knew more of them as
neighbors, perhaps because very few intolerant priests chose to
live so near them—hatred of blackrobes seemed to grow harder
as one went deeper into the midlands. So it was a surprise, even
to Eleva, when they neared Center and found the suspicious glances
decreasing again and more and more folk inclining to treat Frostflower and Windbourne with tolerance, courtesy, sometimes even
tentative acquaintanceship beyond what Eleva demanded for them.

Priests and priestesses seemed to make up at least a quarter of
the crowd in Center-of-Everywhere, and they had no reason save
example to the commoners for extending courtesy to sorceri because a rather young priestess demanded it. Yet when their curiosity was satisfied, most of them accepted the situation more easily
than had common folk in towns ten or fifteen days to the northeast.

The widowed Lady Ena, who lodged Eleva's party, had heard nothing of them until their arrival, but she instructed her cook to prepare food according to the restrictions of sorcerous diet and then proceeded to show more interest in discovering whether she and Eleva might be distant cousins than in any other aspect of the case.

Eleva went at once to claim her place in the High Gathering, but returned to announce that she had found the Great Hall empty, the few priests who had met there that day having left early. "Small wonder the nearedgelands priests have such a poor opinion of the Gathering!" she remarked to their hostess as they sat at supper.

"The meetings are larger and longer in the winter," replied Lady Ena. "At this season, they've all gone to see to their farms and crops—those who still have farms. I think your mother's Aunt Weldra was a daughter of my father's Grand-uncle Imron."

"I do not think my mother had an aunt named Weldra, Lady." Eleva still seemed annoyed. "Who is First High Priest this year?"

Every priest at least twenty-five years of age, every ruling priestess, and every eldest wife of a ruling priest had the right to sit in the Gathering and vote on any matter for decision. All other members of the priestly class, high-ranking warriors with at least twenty-five years of experience in their profession, and townmasters could also sit in the Great Hall when there was room for them (it seemed there was rarely lack of room) and give their opinions in discussion; sometimes one of those who showed special wisdom might be granted the right to vote. Each Midsummer Hatching-Day, the Gathering elected one of its members First High Priest to preside over it for the year and make any decisions that must be made between meeting and meeting. This year, as the year before, Lady Ennealdis was presiding as First High Priestess.

Eleva went to visit her in the First Priest's Alcove-Hall that same evening and came back in a more cheerful mood to say that Lady Ennealdis was a wise and venerable woman, very likely worth the rest of the Gathering put together. She advised them to present their case the day after tomorrow.

Next morning Eleva went to the Great Hall early to take her place and stir up sympathy. Windbourne also left Lady Ena's hall, with no companions except Coyclaws and the messenger Swiftcurrent. Frostflower had planned to spend the day in Lady Ena's study alcove, but at last, about midday, she forced herself to venture out with Thorn.

"You can't just sit here and let your mind swelter the whole silly day," said the warrior. Besides, Thorn had received generous payment from Eleva for her services and was eager to visit the shops. "And if you're not with me, Frost," she added, "I'm likely to dice all my money away before I can get myself a new pair of trouser-lacings."

Center-of-Everywhere, or what she saw of it, seemed a clean and lovely town . . . and surprisingly quiet, almost as if the center of the Tanglelands was like the center of a storm. The heart of priestly government was also a refuge for priests who had lost their farms to their raiding neighbors. Those who knew enough of the past said that this town's inviolate sanctity was more ancient than the sanctity of priestly flesh; and if Center had ever been walled, no trace of the walls remained. Even the small and modest dwellings of the most impoverished priests were surrounded by gardens, and most of the gardens were unwalled, save for the small, private area behind the hall. The town had a score of temples, and many of their yards were planted with herbs, grasses, clover, and flowers rather than paved with stones. The noisier and more odorous crafts, like smithing, tanning, the making of candles, soaps, salves, and many kinds of foods, were banished to the edges of the town, as were the inns with stables; and instead of large neighborhoods of shops crowded together on long streets, the shopkeepers' buildings tended to cluster in groups of four or five, each group with its own gardens. Where other towns had pissing-alleys, Center had a scattering of small, enclosed buildings and passageways to underground tunnels. Perhaps a third of the commoners who lived in Center worked as priests' servants rather than as merchants and artisans, and a kind of semipriestly dignity and cleanliness appeared to have worked its way through most of the population.

To Frostflower's relief, she and Thorn continued to meet far more simple curiosity than open hostility, even though rumors of strange sins connected with their reason for coming had spread by now through the town. The common folk of Center had seen other cases of priests bringing priests here to charge them with crimes, such cases often ending in the quiet disappearance of one of the priests. Fortunately, whatever the folk of Center suspected, they did not seem to blame the sorceri for corrupting anyone's faith. Perhaps they understood that no sorceron guilty of that would have been allowed to roam the streets. At the same time, they seemed much less timid of sorcerous power than their counterparts in the midlands. More than once, small children, many of them in priestly white, gathered around Dowl to pet him with a touching carelessness of whether or not they brushed against the sorceress while doing so.

Thorn bought a warrior's tunic of heavy crimson silk with a few gold threads in the weave, trousers of light, unbleached wool lined with linen, brown velvet trouser-lacings, a new belt of black leather with a large buckle of carved oakwood, new boots of plain dun hide (her purse was growing light by now), and a knee-length blue wool cloak. All this before she saw a leather sheath crossed with silver and studded with a flawless piece of blue sheen-amber. Frostflower thought the sheath rather ugly except for its gemstone, but it fit Thorn's knife exactly, and the warrior remarked with a shrug that did not quite hide her disappointment that had she seen this at the beginning of the afternoon, the rest of her new clothes could have gone to spiked tails.

Eleva had offered Frostflower pay commensurate with Thorn's, but she had always refused it, and now she had only two dreamberries and a few small coins left. She had already made three purchases that afternoon: a wooden rattle with chips of marble for Starwind, and, for herself, a small jar of rose-scented lotion and a thumb-sized applewood statue of Maejira the Merciful (the rules against sorceri coming near statues of gods were made by individual priests and townmasters, and no one had ever judged it necessary to make them in the priestly town itself). She now calculated that, by asking Eleva for some of that proffered payment after all, she could afford the sheath. While Thorn was looking at perfumes in the next shop, the sorceress bargained with the weapons-merchant, paying him one dreamberry to hold it from all other buyers for three days. She could not help wondering if, in a way, she were putting a pledge on her own future—hoping for a kind of omen?—and if the weapons-merchant, for all his polite smiles, were expecting that she would never return.

Late in the afternoon they met Windbourne and Swiftcurrent.

The sorcerer was carrying his purchases in a long bag, but he did not offer to show his friends what he had bought. Frostflower returned with the two men to Lady Ena's home while Thorn stayed at a neat, smallish tavern to risk her last few coppers in a game with three or four priests and priestesses who threw the dice quietly, gracefully, and for very small wagers.

The swordswoman returned late and happy. She had won, building her coppers into a silver and a half; she said they might have been several goldens had the priests rolled for higher stakes, and it was a good sign for their luck in the Great Hall tomorrow.

But if good luck with dice is an omen, thought Frostflower, what of the name of the First High Priestess? Ennealdis—it was so similar to Enneald, the name of that priestess who had been so hard and unpleasant last summer.

The Great Hall was surrounded, not by adjoining alcoves, but by small cottages, arbors, and garden houses, separated from the main building so that those who sat in them could not hear the discussions of the High Priestly Gathering. Since the day was cloudy and intermittently stormy, the two sorceri, Dowl, Coyclaws, and Swiftcurrent waited in a cottage rather than an arbor.

Eleva left them there shortly after dawn when she went into the Great Hall, accompanied by Thorn and Starstroke, who carried Rondasu in a curtained litter. A pair of priests in their very early twenties and two servants sat in the cottage with the sorceri and Swiftcurrent, ostensibly to escort them when word came from the Gathering. The window lattices had been covered with parchment against the weather, so Frostflower kept the door open a little and watched the priests and a few white-haired, silver-tunicked warriors go into the Great Hall, trying to keep count of them and wondering how nearly they would fill the long chamber.

Swiftcurrent was summoned to the Great Hall almost as soon as its heavy, permanent doors had been closed to signal the beginning of debate. A longish ballad's-length later, Windbourne was summoned; he left the cottage nervously, with Coyclaws riding on his shoulders. The priests returned after escorting them. One of the servants made a fire in the small fireplace and heated gingerwater for those still in the cottage, including the sorceress.

At midday, a large number of priests emerged from the building and dispersed into the nearest houses and small taverns. Shortly after this, a young priestess came to escort Frostflower from the cottage and tell the others they were dismissed for the midday meal.

She led the sorceress and Dowl to another cottage. Here a small fire burned in a raised central hearth, and beside it an old priestess, wearing a wreath that was no more than a simple gold band around her white hair, sat alone at a table laid with a meal for two.

After nodding to the young priestess, who bowed slightly and left, the old one opened her palm to the sorceress. "Come, Frostflower. It's somewhat past the usual hour—you must be hungry. Your dog, too. Eleva's told me what you may and may not eat, and I am following that diet with you today."

Frostflower sat in the chair across from her. Dowl stood beside the hearth and began to eat eagerly from a bowl of food set ready for him.

On the gold chain about her neck the old priestess wore a large gold disk, a finger's-length in diameter, engraved with what appeared to be a version of the Self-Lighting Candle. It was the first such disk Frostflower had ever seen. "Lady Reverence Ennealdis?" she asked.

Ennealdis nodded and poured wine for each of them. "You must not be apprehensive. I imagine I would be, in your place. So perhaps we'd best have the questions first and our meal afterwards." She held up her right hand, palm out and fingers up. "Not about the deaths of Deveron, Intassa, and Shara. All that was settled well before midmorning. You won't need to tell the Gathering what you know, nor how you came to know it. Rondasu confessed at once, when he saw the runner Swiftcurrent. . . . I think sight of the boy actually confounded him less than it jogged his memory."

"Oh." The sorceress took a sip of wine—Southvines Foaming. "What . . . will happen to him, Lady?"

"Rondasu has already died. It was a quick death. The Gathering judged that your fellow sorceron had administered justice enough to satisfy Jehandru. We will let those outside the Gathering believe he died for heresy; we leave it to Lady Eleva to give out whatever she wishes remembered in Rondasu's own area, consistent with priestly honor."

Frostflower put the cup to her lips again, but her stomach seemed to contract and she set the wine down without drinking. "Then what justice have you left to deal out, Lady?"

Ennealdis sighed. "A delicate matter. No one in the Gathering could remember a similar case, and they decided at last to follow the proposal of Pendoru and his faction and leave the final decision to my own poor wisdom. Can you swear, Frostflower, that your companion Windbourne has lost his power for sorcering?"

Frostflower shook her head. "I cannot swear it, Lady. I believe it is so, and I think he believes it even more firmly."

Ennealdis rubbed her pendant. "I feel better satisfied than if you had told me positively. I've found there is very little certain knowledge on this side of the Harvest Gates. Well, so it's possible that someday in a moment of danger he may suddenly find he has his sorcerous power again. I hardly think that need worry us. More serious is the possibility that it may suddenly return to him in a moment of anger in his wife's bed. But if Eleva has no fear of that, I think it overzealous of us to fear on her behalf."

Frostflower started so noticeably that Dowl lifted his head from his food and whined.

"You did not suspect?" said Ennealdis. "They did not speak of it to you because Eleva guessed she would need your answers in this matter, and she felt we were likelier to trust you if we thought you'd had no chance to prepare the answers she wished you to give. But you really did not suspect?"

Frostflower thought back. "Yes," she murmured, "I think I would have suspected, had they been anyone else but a priestess and a sorcerer. But—would you allow it, Lady?"

"Would *your* people allow it?" said Ennealdis.

Frostflower shrugged helplessly. "I suppose, if the priestess or priest came to the sorceron's retreat. But I have never heard of any farmer-priests who wished it before."

"Oh, they would remain in Eleva's Farm," the priestess replied. "There seems to be little question of that. She would not give up her rule. And you may be aware that priests and priestesses do marry faithful commoners from time to time. The commoners remain commoners, though with the special privileges of permanently consecrated acolytes. Windbourne has asked to convert and become one of our 'farmers' folk,' as you call them. But this is the question I must ask: Is it possible that any of you would sincerely choose to worship all our gods?"

Frostflower looked at the old priestess for a moment and dropped her gaze. "If I were to become convinced that your creed is the true one, Lady, I could not remain in my own. Yes, it is possible."

"Is this an abstract example, or a decision you might actually make?"

The sorceress turned her cup, watching the liquid fail to swerve with the vessel, so that a speck of dust on the wine's surface remained at the right side. "Lady, I experienced something that should not have happened according to my own creed, and I've seen other things that should, perhaps, have happened as they did according to yours. Yes ... someday I may ask to be admitted into your holy halls as a sincere worshiper. As for Windbourne ... I cannot see his mind, Lady. I have difficulty enough trying to see my own."

"Windbourne took off his black robe this morning to make his request," said Ennealdis with something like a small chuckle. "Beneath it, he was wearing a pale yellow tunic and brown trousers."

The clothes must have been the purchases he had bundled yesterday with so much care.

"But can he even know enough of our doctrine," said the priestess, "to make the choice?"

Frostflower used her food-pick to remove the speck of dust from her wine. "I have told him something of it, Lady. Something of your teachings about afterdeath and the Glorious Harvest, something of the mystery of Aomu and Voma. Lady Eleva may well have told him more."

Ennealdis ate a raspberry. "Well, he must answer a number of questions before he can be initiated as an acolyte, but if he still asks for initiation when he's learned all the answers ... You welcome converts into your retreats, do you not? I see no reason why we should be more possessive with our truth than you with yours. So. This afternoon we shall question him and teach him whatever we find still necessary, tonight we shall initiate him as an acolyte and let Her Reverence Eleva marry him, and tomorrow we shall announce the fact to the Gathering. Yes, we'll make a very happy pair of them, at least for a hen's-hatching or two, which is perhaps as much as any mates can expect." She held out a dish of roasted nut kernels wrapped in honeyed rose petals. "Now, Frostflower, we'd best eat."

Frostflower took the dish and scooped a handful of kernels into her plate. She wondered if Windbourne were trying a first taste of meat—or at least cheese—this midday, whether he had bought a silk tunic or kept to wool and linen. But the question she asked was, "Lady, we have met such gentleness here in Center-of-Everywhere?"

"And you can't understand that, here in the heart of all priestly custom? This is quite safe for you—" Ennealdis indicated a bowl of green sauce with fine lumps, into which she was dipping a twist of bread. "Entirely vegetable—mainly peas and parsley, I think—with a little crumbled egg. As for your question. I did not come here as a failure myself, Frostflower; I chose to claim my place in the Gathering when I released my farm to my oldest son, almost thirty years ago. But at least three-quarters of the priests who remain in the Center throughout the year either came because their neighboring priests raided them from their farms and they were unable to acquire new land for themselves, or else they are the children and descendants of such. They remember more clearly the actual, proven threat to their personal power from others of their own kind than the seemingly fanciful threat from your people. We all know that in theory you threaten our power, but I've yet to meet a farmer—except Ronadsu—who can tell of experiencing sorcerous danger at first hand, discounting servants and commoners commanded to the work of stripping. Besides, most of us have very little left to lose—our lands gone to other priestly families; many farmers of the midlands and edgelands scoffing at us as a dithering, doddering crowd of incompetents—not, perhaps, without reason—and sometimes defying our rule outright; the very commoners of Center living with us in a close familiarity unlike the awe we remember from our old homes. . . . It sometimes seems as if you sorceri must be the only folk remaining who fear and fully respect us. And then, we see so few blackrobes here—I believe you are the first that our Center-born children under the age of ten or twelve have ever seen, and their parents have probably neglected to warn them against you from their cradles." She fed a piece of bread and sauce to Dowl, who had left his own bowl and padded over to her.

"But," the priestess continued, "don't think all feeling against sorceri is gone from here. Pendoru and Entrun are not my friends in the Gathering, and I suspect they threw the present decision to me in hopes of using my decision to prevent my reelection to the First Office next Hatching-Day." The priestess shrugged and smiled. "I've played into their design, but perhaps they have played into mine, too. Of what use is the High Office if it cannot be spent to purchase what its holder considers best in the sight of Jehandru and Maejira?"

Frostflower nodded and ate for some moments in silence. (Ennealdis' name had proved to be no omen after all. Did that mean the sorceress should stop suspecting the truth of the priestly idea of omens, or was she now searching for an omen that denied omens?) At last she said, "Lady Reverence . . . your medallion, is that the Self-Lighting Candle?"

Ennealdis lifted the golden disk and looked down at the engraved circle quartered with four points like stylized flames extending inward toward a lightburst pattern in the center. "Yes, it's a form of the Candle, though it's said to have other significances as well."

"I would not ask to learn anything in your secret writings, Lady," said Frostflower, "but if you could tell me a little that is not? Reverence Rondasu's and Lady Shara's poisonings of Reverence Deveron and Lady Intassa—if you could assure me that such things as this are not . . . described in the forbidden scrolls?"

Ennealdis' smile formed slowly and lasted while she spoke. "You have a great desire to learn what is in those writings, have you not? Eleva told me of it."

Frostflower glanced up. "I hadn't realized—"

"No, perhaps you did not tell her in words, but there are other ways of reading folks' desires. Such as glimpsing a timid finger brushing wistfully over a scroll-case door marked with the Candle. Well, Frostflower, I myself have often thought those scrolls are set apart as secret and privileged principally to stir up the interest of those of us who are supposed to read them. But we must ask you to guard our secret of Rondasu's and Shara's sins as carefully as you've guarded the identity of those other people in the ballad with you. And you deserve some payment in return." Ennealdis reached into a pocket of her long white sleeve, brought out a copper disk, and put it down near Frostflower's plate.

The sorceress picked up the disk and examined it. On one side, engraved into the copper with gold, were her own name in priestly letters and three strawberry leaves surrounding a blossom—apparently the emblem of the farm that Ennealdis had once ruled. On the other side was a Self-Lighting Candle like that on the First High Priest's medallion, with a single strawberry blossom in the center instead of a lightburst, and the name Ennealdis beneath it, a small lightburst in front of the first letter and a tiny, stylized seven-branched tree after the last.

"The one side is an ordinary safe-passage token," said the priestess. "The other side shares with you my own privilege of reading the secret scrolls. Although my High Priesthood may only last a few more days, the privilege will last as long as my life. But be careful to whom you show it. No doubt there are priests who would not only refuse to honor it, but might treat you more harshly because of it. And don't wait too long before using it, either. I am seventy-eight years old already."

Frostflower blinked, swallowed, and extended her hands. The priestess accepted them, pressing them for a few moments in her own.

"What a great show of gratitude," Ennealdis said at last, "for a privilege that many of us think more nearly a burden! Well, let's finish our meal." Then, just before releasing the younger woman's hand, she added, "Have you never thought, Frostflower, that it may be the use of your sorcerous power for harm, and not the forcing of your bodies, that destroys your innocence?"

"I have thought . . . something like that, Lady, though not in such clear words. But it does not end the problem."

The young warrior Starstroke left Center-of-Everywhere the next day to find work in the southern Tanglelands. Swiftcurrent entered Eleva's service. With two farms to administer until Invaron's maturity, she planned to train Windbourne in the daily management of the one that had been her brother's, and to make Swiftcurrent his principal assistant. "The priestly authority," she said, "will still come from me, in Invaron's name. And they say that those marriages in which wife and husband share visits rather than constant daily life are among the happiest."

"Your folk will accept Windbourne?" said Frostflower.

"They may continue to believe that sorcery killed Deveron and Intassa," Eleva replied, "but not your sorcery or Windbourne's. We'll make sure of that, with some help from Master Youngwise and Eaglesight. And who will question the innocence and conversion of a sorcerer purified in the priestly town itself?"

Windbourne smoothed his new tunic—linen, not silk. "By next spring, we should have steam-gardens in one farm or the other." He glanced at Frostflower with an apologetic smile. "We'll also try techniques with some of our soft curds in the dairy houses. If we find some way to make firm cheese without . . . cow's stomach, I promise you will know of it as soon as possible."

Coyclaws rubbed against Eleva's leg.

"Cows' breath!" said Thorn on receiving the sheath. "Frost, I don't have any gift for you!"

"This is no gift, Thorn. It's payment. For all you've done for me."

"Unh. Friends don't pay each other."

"Why not? If payment could never be given to friends, then folk would either need to nurture enmity or cease trade."

Thorn grunted, grinned, and slid her knife into its new sheath. "All right. But this is full pay for the rest of the summer. Well, where now?"

Frostflower fingered Ennealdis' token. "I would like to stay here in Center for a hatching or two, Thorn. And read the secret scrolls. If you would not find it too boring."

The warrior chuckled. "There should be a priest somewhere in this town willing to listen to a few new ideas about how to win back his land. And sanctuary only extends for three days' walk from the outskirts of town. Yes, I think I can find some pretty good work for a hatching or two. But don't be in too big a hurry to convert to our gods when you read those scrolls, Frost. I may need you to patch me up before we head north again."

Dowl padded over to them and turned on his back with his legs up.

"Fleabitten dog!" Thorn remarked, rubbing his underside with a gentle foot. "And maybe I'll get another grub in my belly for you to sorcer out when we get back up to your mountains. I owe myself some pleasure. Spiked tails! I was almost ready to ask that blasted Windbourne if he didn't think I deserved first go at him."

"Even if I were to become convinced of the truth of your priestly creed," Frostflower said slowly, "could I really give up the practice of my skills? For I know they are true also, Thorn. However I have them, they are perhaps the only truth I can be sure of." And yet Windbourne seemed content to have exchanged them for Eleva and the priestly creed . . .

For now, however, the sun was warm, the breeze cool, and Lady Ena's garden fragrant. Frostflower had gained access to the priests' forbidden scrolls, and if she had not yet soothed her conscience far enough to permit herself the taste of cheese again, she was beginning to think this an odd scruple beside her delving into priestly secrets and handling parchment scrolls. She smiled. "And as for your pleasure, Thorn, another babe would be a welcome playmate for Starwind."